For Jackie

Nettlegrabbers

❋

CHRISTOPHER McKEOGH

TRAFFORD
• Canada • UK • Ireland • USA •

Cover design by Helen McKeogh, howgreathouart@blueyonder.co.uk

© Copyright 2006 Christopher McKeogh.
All rights reserved. No part of this publication may be reproduced, stored in a retrieval system, or transmitted, in any form or by any means, electronic, mechanical, photocopying, recording, or otherwise, without the written prior permission of the author.
All characters in this publication are fictitious and any resemblance to real persons, living or dead is purely coincidental.
Note for Librarians: A cataloguing record for this book is available from Library and Archives Canada at www.collectionscanada.ca/amicus/index-e.html
ISBN 1-4120-8965-4

Printed in Victoria, BC, Canada. Printed on paper with minimum 30% recycled fibre. Trafford's print shop runs on "green energy" from solar, wind and other environmentally-friendly power sources.

TRAFFORD
PUBLISHING

Offices in Canada, USA, Ireland and UK
This book was published *on-demand* in cooperation with Trafford Publishing. On-demand publishing is a unique process and service of making a book available for retail sale to the public taking advantage of on-demand manufacturing and Internet marketing. On-demand publishing includes promotions, retail sales, manufacturing, order fulfilment, accounting and collecting royalties on behalf of the author.

Book sales for North America and international:
Trafford Publishing, 6E–2333 Government St.,
Victoria, BC v8t 4p4 CANADA
phone 250 383 6864 (toll-free 1 888 232 4444)
fax 250 383 6804; email to orders@trafford.com

Book sales in Europe:
Trafford Publishing (UK) Limited, 9 Park End Street, 2nd Floor
Oxford, UK ox1 1hh UNITED KINGDOM
phone 44 (0)1865 722 113 (local rate 0845 230 9601)
facsimile 44 (0)1865 722 868; info.uk@trafford.com

Order online at:
trafford.com/06-0721

10 9 8 7 6 5 4 3 2

TABLE OF CONTENTS

I	Headhunt	1
II	Four Green Fields	24
III	A New IRA	46
IV	Eire	69
V	Seven Deadly Sins	82
VI	Chris the Hat	100
VII	The Making of a Monster	113
VIII	One-eye Jack	124
IX	Leprechauns & Banshees	161
X	The Brotherhood Sign	185
XI	Sympathy	193
XII	The Bordello Spy	200
XIII	A Loyalist Plot	222
XIV	Harry the Chat	227
XV	The Junta	242
XVI	Keystone	250
XVII	The Code	258
XVIII	IRA by Any Name	263

XIX	IRA English Department	274
XX	Ball of Twine	282
XXI	Big Tom	303
XXII	Two Birds with one Stone	321
XXIII	The Coventry Bomb	325
XXIV	The Sound of Silence	331
XXV	Plan B	342
XXVI	The Empty Safe	347
XXVII	The Duke of Lancaster	350
XXVIII	Mrs Goody	358
XXIX	Mr Heart	364
XXX	Post Trial Party	368

I

※

Headhunt

THE 9 A.M. EUSTON train was pulling out of Rugby station as Detective Inspector John Bayliss ran onto the platform. It was a big day in his police career and the sight of the moving train told him that things were not going to plan. If he failed to board the train he would be late for his interview. Lateness at this level was not recognised as a factor in the equation. If it were it would be tantamount to acknowledging that a mere mortal possessed the ability to interfere with the running of a Home Office selection panel.

In the past year Detective Inspector John Bayliss came to accept that he now moved in a world of funny handshakes, raised eyebrows and peculiar nods. Nothing was straightforward and it was necessary to decrypt clues in order to reveal hidden messages and pointers.

In most situations being late would be visited by a need

to furnish an explanation or perhaps an apology. But that was not the way here because one was not, strictly speaking, keeping an appointment with members of the panel. Instead one was told to make oneself available at a certain venue at a certain time. If one were there when one's name was called then one would be taken in front of the interview panel and processed. If one were not there the next name on the list would be called and the likelihood of successive candidates being absent was too small to contemplate.

A candidate who failed to answer when called would not be recalled. John Bayliss knew this and the sight of the moving train sent alarm signals to his mind, which in turn sent urgent signals to his legs. He knew the moving train represented his last chance, he had to be present when his name was called.

The venue was an office off Queen Ann's Gate, London. That gave a clue that the Home Office was running things and that the meeting was extraordinary. The head of anti-terrorism, New Scotland Yard would be in attendance as well as top brass from MI5 and the Home Office.

These were important people with the power to halt or advance John's career. They would not ask why the officer from the West Midlands Police was late. It was irrelevant to their purpose and John knew that if he were not present when his name was called his personal file would be endorsed and placed amongst the rejects. That would kill his prospects of becoming a spy.

The fact that the IRA had attempted to blow up Coventry Telephone Exchange the previous week would cut no ice in London. Nor would the consequential strain put on resources of the West Midlands Police M division. The rule was simple. If one wants the job one will get to the interview on time.

Earlier as John drove from Coventry to Rugby he was shocked when it dawned on him that something big had happened in Birmingham. Every radio station was focused on an atrocity committed by the IRA. Several young people had been killed or maimed by bombs set off in public houses. He recalled that his telephone had been disconnected and knew that he would have been called out to the incident. He also knew that he should divert to Lloyd House, the HQ of the West Midlands Police, but he continued to Rugby.

***

He was still running to catch the train when he heard a female voice; 'Come on sir you'll make it.' He looked up and grasped the extended hand of Jane Hogan.

'Jane it's you!' he exclaimed. 'What a surprise you're that last person I expected to see. Tell me I'm going to make it?'

'Yes sir I'm sure you'll make it.'

'That's great Jane. I thought I'd done myself a mischief running after the train. But never mind you've saved me. I owe you one.'

'You're fine sir, just take it easy.'

'You're right Jane. I need to sit down. I'll tell you what let me stand you breakfast. I'll buy you the best breakfast on the train, but you must stop calling me Sir. Have we a deal?'

It had been a hectic week for John Bayliss sparked off by the IRA's attempt to blow up Coventry Telephone Exchange, an attempt which ended in the death of the would-be-bomber. Tension was in the air and the police were busy ensuring that the removal of the remains of Jamie McDade to Belfast was not marked by major public disorder.

The situation had been tense on Thursday 21st November 1974. It was the day McDade's remains were taken from Coventry to Elmdon Airport to be flown to Belfast for burial the following day.

The Birmingham Battalion of the IRA had arranged a hero's farewell for their fallen comrade. Throngs of IRA sympathisers assembled at various places between Coventry and Elmdon to honour a fallen IRA soldier. To them he had died on active service in the fight for liberation against the English suppressor. It seems that the organisers had overlooked the fact that the people against whom McDade's bomb was aimed did not perceive him as a hero. To them he was a cowardly murderer whose intention to slaughter innocent people could not be justified. They rejoiced at the news that he had killed himself instead and were in no mood to permit others of his ilk to honour his passing.

John Bayliss was one of the many police officers allocated to keep the lid on the tinderbox. He followed the cortège out of Coventry along the A45 until it turned into Elmdon Airport. The situation was under control and John signed off duty. He went home and unplugged his telephone before going to bed. He needed a good night's sleep to clear his head for his big day.

The busy week had taken its toll and he felt exhausted as he sat opposite Jane on the train. He was a little puzzled as to why she was on the train. He studied her and felt suspicion drain from his mind. Jane was his friend and was one of the few people he could still trust.

***

Recent events had undermined his confidence and he was no longer sure about things. It was having flashbacks to incidents in his police career that bothered him. Silly little things like the time he failed to report causing minor damage to his police car. Things he knew could never come back to haunt him. But there they were flashing into his mind without warning and causing him unnecessary anxiety. Now his decision to continue to London instead of going to police HQ worried him.

If he had he would have found that police HQ was a hive of activity. The world press was causing havoc outside Lloyd House and the situation inside was chaotic. The focus of attention was on Detective Chief Superintendent Robinson, former head of Birmingham City Police CID and now head of the new West Midlands Police CID.

He had returned to his office from a difficult meeting with the chief constable and his aides. The subject of the meeting was the same as that on the minds of every person in Birmingham. It was the disaster of the previous evening and whether the police were going to be criticised.

Detective Chief Superintendent Robinson was known affectionately as Harry the Chat. This morning he looked pale and drawn. His laid-back style was nowhere to be seen as he removed files from a filing cabinet in his office. His mind was reaching overload as he sat down at his desk and looked at Detective Superintendent Malcolm Smith, 'If this goes wrong Malcolm we're in deep trouble,' he said handing Malcolm a thick file. 'There should be enough here to persuade the DPP to prosecute.'

'I'm not sure this is in the DPP's domain sir,' Malcolm said looking at the file. 'It may require the Attorney General's fiat.'

A flash of anger crossed Harry's face. It was like Malcolm to focus on a pedantic legal technicality. He had an irritating habit of missing the salient point. The point on this occasion was to gather evidence and present it to whomsoever had the responsibility of deciding its merits. It mattered not to Harry whom that was, provided the evidence was enough to secure a conviction. 'Malcolm I want you to concentrate on evidence,' Harry said impatiently. 'I think the file I have given you will point you in the right direction.'

Malcolm glanced at the file and recognised some of the names, 'Are we sure these men did it sir?'

Harry banged his closed fist hard on the desk, 'Look superintendent I'm surprised that a man with your apparent depth of legal knowledge should ask such a question,' he said engaging Malcolm's eyes. 'It's a question that is not relevant in the English Legal System. The question is whether we can prove beyond reasonable doubt that these men are responsible. Am I making myself clear?'

'Yes of course sir,' Malcolm said meekly. Harry had correctly stated the standard of the burden of proof on the prosecution in a criminal trial. 'I'll get Bill onto it straight away.'

'I don't want Bill to handle this one Malcolm,' Harry said picking up another folder. 'Remember that not only must justice be done it must be seen to be done. Bill's too close to show impartiality. What's needed here is a man unprejudiced by previous knowledge of the suspects. Use the detective superintendent from Wolverhampton.'

'George Reid, sir. Is he up to it?'

'I want you to make sure he is. You are to give him your full support and guidance. Am I making myself clear?'

'Yes sir,' Malcolm said. 'I'll get onto it straight away.'

***

Michael Lynch sat in his Dublin luxury apartment watching the morning news. That'll make them think twice he smirked as he watched several West Midland's Police officers recount the bombings of the previous night. He was startled by the telephone, and when he picked it up was speaking to the head of IRA in Dublin.

'What went wrong with the warning?' The unmistakable voice demanded.

'As far as I know a warning was given sir,' Lynch lied.

'You know what they're like, they're not going to give us any credit are they?'

'Suppose not,' the voice said flatly. 'Who are these men they've arrested in Heysham?'

'Not ours sir.'

'Ah well, I suppose that's something to be thankful for,' the voice said and the line went dead.

***

Major Maynard went to a locked safe in his MI5 Whitehall office. He looked at three box files marked, "Most Secret, Operation Nettle Grabber." He removed them and placed them in front of Larry, permanent secretary to the head of MI5.

'An interesting title don't you think old boy,' the major said for no apparent reason.

'Yes quite, I must say you chaps like your metaphors. Always contain a clue do they?'

'If I'm correct it compares the operation to a bed of nettles and suggests that one must be very careful if one is to avoid getting stung. Do you follow my drift Larry?'

'Not quite old boy. I'm a city chap, you know. Nettles, dock-leaves and dandelions, they're all the same to me.'

'I'm told that if one grabs a nettle tightly it looses its ability to sting the grabber.'

'That's very interesting.'

'Hence the metaphor encapsulates the notion that to survive one must master the art of identifying and grabbing the nettle which is about to sting one.'

'Of course, very good, very good indeed.' The secretary said appending his initials on several sheets of paper. 'Yes, I like it old chap, Nettle Grabber.'

'That's it Larry,' the major said placing a box on top of the two Larry was holding.

'Thank you major, before I go perhaps you could tell me how to differentiate between the nettles and the nettle grabbers?'

'That's a good question,' the major said thoughtfully. 'It depends on which side one's on.'

'These Australian chaps are they nettles or nettle grabbers?'

'I'm not sure Larry.'

***

John Bayliss was unaware that he featured in Operation Nettle Grabber. He almost believed that he was going to London to be promoted, but not quite. The one thing he was sure about was that his association with Detective Chief Inspector Seamus Ballivor would be on the agenda.

John now knew that Ballivor was a mole; a sleeper recently roused from his slumber and recalled to active IRA service. His disappearance shook the corridors of power at police headquarters. It drove home the fact that the IRA had infiltrated the force to such an extent that it knew every move the police were going to make. Ballivor was tipped off and made good his escape before the Serious Crime Squad had time to nail him.

John knew he was lucky not to be included in that dawn

raid. He would now be languishing on remand in Winston Green Prison if the detective chief superintendent had not intervened. Harry the Chat had been true to his word and saved John the inevitable fate that would befall him at the hands of criminals in prison. Instead he was on his way to London to claim the promotion Harry had promised.

John knew he had skeletons in his cupboard even though they were not of his making. Ballivor had worked him and made him vulnerable. As Harry explained, there was enough to prosecute John for aiding and abetting Ballivor.

John had not applied to join the anti-terrorist squad; he was being headhunted. He found out after he realised that strangers were following him and taking an inordinate interest in his activities. He asked what was going on and was told that he was being "sounded out" by MI5. That was the way the secret services went about their business. One is headhunted, but the hunters do not reveal themselves until they are sure they have their man.

When his commander sent for him, John put two and two together and worked out that he must have passed the sounding out stage. They now wanted him to go to London where he would be offered a position in the covert world of espionage and counter-espionage. Another promotion was as good as in the bag. All he had to do was impress the selection board.

The commander gave him an envelope containing train tickets; 'I've been instructed to tell you that you are to report to the head of anti-terrorism at the address shown.'

'Yes sir,' John said. 'Is there anything else I should know?'

'I believe you'll be told more in London,' the commander said picking up a document from his in-tray. 'Good luck.'

***

John's lifelong ambition was to become a policeman, an ambition he had not found easy to realise. He failed the entrance examination of Birmingham City Police three times and was advised to apply to join the Airport Police. He succeeded and was posted to Elmdon Airport, near Birmingham, where he served as a constable for two years. In that capacity he befriended a businessman called George Goody. And in return for favours rendered, Goody used his influence to assist John to become a member of the new Warwickshire and Coventry Constabulary.

Now as John looked at Jane sitting opposite him on the train she reminded him of the sequence of events that led to his meeting Detective Chief Inspector Ballivor. Had he missed something? Jane and Ballivor, they came as a pair. There was something odd about their relationship, something that John could not put his finger on. He looked at her from her pleasing face to her long slim legs and marked the elegant way she sat in front of him, approachable but not accessible.

Her innocent countenance might not be as harmless as it looked. Once again she had turned up at an opportune moment as though their meeting was a coincidence. Perhaps this was one coincidence too many, John thought, perhaps it's not a coincidence at all. On this occasion he would not be so eager to take at face value everything she said. After all Jane Hogan had been the live-in lover of an IRA infiltrator. In his new role John would have to view such people with great suspicion. What would Ballivor advise? John knew that Ballivor would tell him to keep his friends close, and his enemies closer.

***

When he first met her John was a seasoned tutor constable stationed at Coventry. He was not a high-flyer. Nobody, including himself, thought that he would become a detective inspector within three years. He had help passing the police entrance examination and had no plans to sit promotion examinations. Written tests were hurdles he knew he could not surmount and the Police College, Bramshill, was beyond his wildest dreams. But his association with Ballivor changed all that and now the fact was that he had been promoted twice and did attend Bramshill.

Jane was a beautiful naïve young probationary constable not tarnished by the trials and tribulations of police work. John was selected to be her tutor constable, charged with guiding her until she had enough experience to work alone. He could not believe it when his inspector told him that he had been chosen to look after the beautiful WPC recently graduated from the Police Training Centre at Ryton-on-Dunsmore.

Every male officer at the police station noticed Jane Hogan when she arrived at Little Park Street, Coventry. She looked fresh, accessible and a little lost when she was introduced to her new colleagues. It was not a question of whether; as more who would be the first to get inside her panties.

John had a reputation amongst his colleagues of being a "ladies' man " and he did not expect that the shift inspector would trust him with this attractive young policewoman. Perhaps the inspector was curious as to whether John's reputation was justified or thought that Jane was not going to fall for his charms. Whatever the reason, John did not question it and jumped at the chance of teaching Jane the ways of the police world.

At that time he did not know that Jane was involved romantically with Ballivor. That would come to light later after John made his move and it was too late. He did not blame himself because he felt that no one would have guessed that the new policewoman and the DCI were romantically involved. DCIs and probationary policewomen did not move in the same circles let alone live together.

Ballivor had come to Coventry on promotion from a different force a few months earlier. Little was known about him apart from the rumour that he was a high-flyer. Someone with friends in high places on his way to the top.

***

John saw an opportunity one Sunday morning shortly after Jane joined the shift. His mind was not focused on police work. Instead he was planning to seduce the young policewoman sitting next to him in his patrol car. It was a quiet Sunday morning; the only movement was the odd person going to church. John's plan required him to drive south out of the City along the Kenilworth Road towards the Memorial Park.

'This is where we hide to catch motorists,' John said casually as he turned into a spot known to experienced officers as the Seduction Post.

It was Jane's first time and John wanted to familiarise her with the location. His scheme was to ensure that she did not become suspicious when he took her there on night duty. The location was concealed and she might become alarmed if she saw it for the first time in the darkness. He did not want her to guess that the purpose of their visit was nothing to do with police work.

He switched off the engine and lay back in the seat. Jane gave the impression that she was relaxed. John was studying her body language. He watched the easy way she placed her hands at the back of her head, and closed her eyes as though she were asleep.

There was something luring about her poise. He felt that she might be giving him a message as he fixed his eyes on the provocative way her skirt had moved above her knees. Not only that her knees were slightly parted permitting him to see her thighs.

There was something about her demeanour that mesmerised him and made him suspect that she was teasing him. She was pushing on her feet causing her pelvic mound to protrude slightly. It was an invitation and John felt an overwhelming urge to answer it by placing his hand between her legs.

Be careful, he thought, as he checked to ensure they were not being watched.

He suspected that she knew what she was doing; her knees were slightly apart and the provocative protrusion was not accidental. She knows exactly what she's doing, he thought, as he slowly placed his right hand between her legs. The touch of her thigh sent sensational pulses through him. He became a slave to his lust; his mind was fogged with desire as his hand moved towards its goal.

Her legs parted just enough to permit him to go further. He could feel her straining harder on her feet as she pushed her pelvis towards him. He was dizzy anticipating the moment that his hand would touch her. He knew she wanted him by the way her body was reacting. Her barely audible gasp as his hand reached its destination left him in no doubt that she was consumed with desire. He advanced his hand and felt the warmth emitting through the silk bridle of her panties. He knew he had her under his spell and he was going to make his move here and now. Slowly does it, he chastened himself, don't frighten her show her that it's more than lust.

He had gone further than he intended on this their first visit to the Seduction Post. But it was too late; she offered no resistance as his finger passed beneath the silky material. He knew he could take her and that she wanted it as much as he did.

Then her legs relaxed, encouraging him to caress her. He

heard her short gasp as he went further. As he unbuckled his belt he moved to kiss her. As their lips met she opened her eyes. He could see her need; Jane Hogan had fallen for his magnetism like so many before her. The moment was here and he knew that he was going to take her in broad daylight in a police car.

'No we mustn't,' she said, turning her head away. 'Not here like this in a police car.'

'But you want it as much as I do,' he pleaded, 'we can't stop now.'

'It's too risky John,' she said, gently pushing him back onto his seat.

'I'm sorry,' he said, 'of course you're right.'

'Don't apologise,' she said, placing her hand on his erect penis, 'I shouldn't have let things go this far.'

She looked into his eyes as she caressed the outline of his penis through his trousers. 'Oh Jesus, I'm going to come,' he gasped. 'Stop it! Oh Jesus it's too late ... I'm firing in my trousers like a fucking kid.'

The spell was broken by their police radios. 'Patrol 23 receiving, over?'

'23 receiving, over,' Jane said calmly into her radio.

'23, go to Paradise Street, and make contact with a Mr Knight re a disturbance, over.'

'Willco, 23 over and out.'

***

Now on the train John wondered whether she still remembered. He was tempted to ask but knew subsequent events that Sunday morning had probably erased from her mind the memory of their brief romance. She had never mentioned the incident again and by the time they reached Paradise Street she was behaving as though nothing out of the ordinary had happened. 'Seems pretty quiet to me.' Jane said looking along the deserted street. 'Are you sure we're in the right place?'

That's when John saw the man walking towards them. 'Good afternoon officer,' the man said in a posh voice. 'I'm not quite sure whether you can assist me.'

'Perhaps if you tell us your problem sir?' John said.

'My wife suffers from depression and we had words earlier, after which I walked out in a bit of a huff. When I got back I attempted to open the door but I was unable. There's no reply from my wife.'

The three of them went to the man's house and after several loud knocks Jane resorted to calling through the letterbox, 'It's the police Mrs Knight, please open the door.'

There was no reply. Jane noticed that a ground floor window was open. Mr Knight climbed through and presently appeared at the front door. Inside the hallway the stairs began near the front door on the left. There was an eerie silence apart from the echo of Jane's voice as she spoke to Mr Knight. They were in the kitchen and John was standing at the front door near the bottom of the stairs. He looked up and found himself studying the banisters. They comprised the typical style of the period with spindles supporting a handrail.

John was not normally interested in the design of stairs

and shook his head when he realised what he was doing. Then it dawned on him that his mind was refusing to process what his eyes were looking at. It wanted to avoid confronting the real object of his curiosity, which was the body of a woman suspended from the upper rail.

John forced himself to look but his mind refused to register that the scene was real. Instead it locked onto her shoes which seemed somehow unnecessary on the feet of the hanging woman. Did she know when she bought them that she would wear them to meet her maker? Surely not, John thought, the soles were worn and she could not have known. Why wear shoes if you're going to hang yourself?

John's thoughts were broken by the sound of Jane's voice, 'If you have any other problems, Mr Knight, please don't hesitate to contact us, I think we've done all we can for the moment.'

'Yes, of course, thank you officer.'

Jane walked towards the front door where John's eyes were fixed on the corpse. She followed his gaze and saw the body. They both stood staring in shock. Mr Knight joined them and looked up at the body, 'There you are Mary,' he said calmly. 'Why didn't you answer the door?'

'I'm sorry sir, but I think you're wife's dead,' John said, 'I'm sorry.'

'Yes, yes, she must be … that's right,' Mr Knight said, 'I expect she put the children to bed.'

'Children! What children?' Jane gasped.

'Our children officer. They're asleep upstairs.'

'Mr Knight, we mustn't allow your children to see their mother like this,' John said. 'We'll go to them.'

'Fine, yes we should … yes, that's a splendid idea.'

As Mr Knight went up stairs he looked at his wife, 'I'll help you down in a minute Mary,' he said. 'You're a silly girl frightening the children like this.'

John followed observing the dead woman as she got progressively closer. Her unseeing eyes were open and she was staring straight ahead. There was a showing of white froth on her lips. He expected to find her hands gripping the ligature to relieve the strain on her neck but they hung aimlessly by her side.

He followed Mr Knight into a tastefully decorated child's bedroom. It was a pink room obviously belonging to the little girl he could see asleep in the bed. She was a pretty angelic child of about four years of age with pure blonde hair. Only her ivory face was visible above the bedclothes. In her peaceful sleep she was oblivious to the horror that surrounded her.

Mr Knight knelt by the bed, placed his hand beneath the bedclothes and took the little girl's hand. He stroked it and spoke softly to the child. It was as though he was sharing a secret with her, 'Daddy and mommy love you angel, don't be afraid everything's all right…'

The child was still asleep, not responding to her father's words. John looked at her and then he saw it, the insignificant showing of white froth on her lips. The child had been suffocated. 'Is there another child in the house Mr Knight?' John said.

'Yes Jonathan, He's asleep in his room.'

'Perhaps we should make sure he's alright?' John said.

Mr Knight looked at his daughter and gently placed his hand on her forehead. He kept his eyes fixed on her as he stood up, 'Wait there baby, daddy won't be long. I'm going to fetch Jona and then we'll all play our favourite game.'

When they got to the boy's room Mr Knight went to the bed. 'Daddy's home Jona,' he said, 'it's time to get up.'

John looked at the boy's blonde hair and could see the resemblance between the two children. The telltale showing of white froth between his lips made John realise that the boy would not respond to his father. Jane entered the room and stood silently looking at Mr Knight talking to his dead son. There were tears in her eyes and she looked vulnerable as she stood there not knowing what to do. John wanted to take her by the hand and walk with her down the stairs away from the eerie scene. The simultaneous sound of their police radios jolted them, 'Patrol 23 receiving, over?'

'Yes, go ahead, over.' John shouted.

John could not remember what exactly he said to the controller but he must have asked for assistance. Presently two CID officers arrived at the front door where Jane and John met them. It was the first time John met Detective Chief Inspector Ballivor.

***

There was another detective with Ballivor. But there was no doubt who was in charge. 'Hello, John isn't it?'

'Yes sir.'

'My name is Seamus and this is Stephen,' Ballivor said in a no nonsense manner. 'How can we help?'

'There's three dead people in there.' John blurted.

Jane still had traces of tears in her eyes and Ballivor went to her, 'It's okay, we'll look after things now,' he said reassuringly, 'Remain here with Stephen and only permit scene of crime officers to enter.'

'Of course,' Jane said.

'Will you come with me John?'

John led the way to Mrs Knight. Ballivor put his hand on her forehead to ascertain whether she was still alive. Then he went to the children's rooms and checked that each child was beyond help. 'Do we know how long the doctor's going to be John?'

The question broke John's chain of thought. He had been watching the professional way Ballivor went about his job. He checked the three bodies for signs of life, examined the scene like someone who knew exactly what to do and went about doing it.

In comparison John had failed to carry out the rudimentary checks drilled into every recruit at training school. "Your first job is to save life if at all possible, your second is to ask your controller to send professional medical and specialist help and your third is to preserve the scene. John had failed all three, 'The doctor! I've no idea sir,' John said uneasily.'

'That's all right, confirm with the controller that he has called out the necessary people.'

'Yes I'll do that straight away sir.' John said.

'I was given to understand that the husband's here John. Do you know where he is?'

'Mr Knight. Yes he was here. Where did he go?'

'Did someone call?' Mr Knight said walking from the kitchen.

'Mr Knight! We thought we'd lost you,' Ballivor said looking at him from head to toe. 'I'm Detective Ballivor and you've met my colleague. I understand you reside here with you wife and children?'

'Yes, my wife and two children.' Knight said proudly apparently oblivious to what had taken place.

'When did you last see them alive Mr Knight?'

To John's surprise Mr Knight did not flinch, 'It's like I explained to the two officers,' he said calmly. 'My wife suffers from depression and we had words this morning. I went out for a walk to cool off and when I got back I could not get into the house. The two officers kindly assisted me.'

'Are you saying you're wife and children were alive when you left the house to cool off?'

'Yes, yes, of course.'

'What time did you leave?'

'I'm not sure of the exact time.'

'An approximation will do for now.'

'It would have been about an hour before I called the station.'

'That would've been about 11.30 a.m. is that right?'

John was about to point out that the call was logged at 12 .10 p.m. and the DCI's arithmetic was wrong. Before he could do so Mr Knight said 'No not 11.30 a.m. it was nearer to 11 o'clock,' Knight said. 'Yes, I'm sure it was 11 o'clock.'

'How can you be sure?' Ballivor asked.

'My wife mentioned it before I left the house.'

'Your wife told you the time before you left to cool off?'

'Yes … that's it, she told me the time as I was leaving.'

Ballivor took John to one side and explained that he wanted to interview Mr Knight at the police station, 'You were first on the scene and if you wish I'm happy for you to make the arrest.'

'Arrest? What can I arrest him for?'

'On suspicion of murder John, these bodies have been dead for at least three, perhaps four hours. If you don't want to arrest him I'll do it.'

John was not about to forego the chance of making an arrest for murder. Ballivor was one of the few, if not the only CID officer that would have given him the opportunity.

'I'll make the arrest sir, if that's all right with you?'

John and Ballivor accompanied Knight to the police station where he was later disposed of under the Mental Health Act. John did not have to revisit the scene and Ballivor took charge of the case paperwork. Days later Ballivor ran into John in the police station, 'You did a good job last Sunday John. I'm surprised you've never applied for a secondment to CID. If you ever fancy one let me know.'

II

Four Green Fields

DENISE WARD-RILEY, HER BROTHER James and her fiancé Patrick O'Connell grew up together in Australia. Their great grandparents were numbered amongst Irish subjects transported by the British in the 19th century.

In 1968 the minds of the three were not concerned with the plight of their forefathers. James and Patrick were members of the Australian SAS fighting alongside the Americans in Vietnam. In early 1968 they were stationed in a forest on the outskirts of Nui Dat. Recently promoted Major James Ward-Riley was the officer commanding a platoon tasked with blowing up enemy supply lines. His second in command, Lieutenant Patrick O'Connell, had an aptitude for designing sophisticated explosive devices and was busy trying to solve a problem.

His reputation as a boffin in the field of explosives was known throughout the Australian SAS and beyond. On this occasion the problem was to do with small farm carts setting off explosives that had been placed to destroy VC supply vehicles. It had confounded the minds of top engineers at divisional level. Patrick saw that the answer lay in the difference in weight between the vehicles used by farmers and those of the enemy Vietcong. He designed a circuit, which relied on two metallic plates making contact. The plates were separated by non-conductive plastic coated springs designed to withstand sufficient weight to permit farmer's carts to pass over them without causing the metallic plates to touch.

In the centre of the springs he placed a pin that could be adjusted to accommodate different weights. The longer the pin the lighter the vehicle needed to complete the circuit. O'Connell's plan worked enabling farmer's carts to proceed safely. Heavier VC vehicles caused the pin to make contact completing the circuit and triggering the detonator.

***

Nearing the end of O'Connell's engagement, his fiancée Denise disappeared in Europe. It was beginning to look as though Patrick's reputation had reached the ears of IRA sub-recruiters. If the conjecture were correct it would explain her disappearance and would mean that history was about to repeat itself.

The name Ward-Riley came about when James' father and mother got married. That was nearly 30 years ago and the union brought together two of the richest Irish Australian families in the neighbourhood. On the Ward side,

Grandpa Ward was a successful sheep farmer and acquired the freehold of thousands of acres of land during his lifetime.

On the Riley side, Grandpa Riley had two callings. He was a prosperous wool merchant during normal working hours and 'A' commander of the New South Wales Circle of the Irish Republican Brotherhood (IRB) all of the time. In the latter capacity he was entitled to vote on decisions emanating from the Fenian Senate in America. In keeping with the declared objectives of the Fenian movement, Riley was totally committed to bringing about a United Ireland.

The Senate was agreed that the proclamation read by Padraig Pearse on the steps of the GPO, Dublin, during the Easter Rising of 1916, encapsulated the aims and aspirations of Irish nationalism. They had not reached consensus on the methods of achieving it.

The Senate was almost equally divided between doves and hawks. There were five doves and four hawks. Grandpa Riley was one of the former and was grateful that the movement's obsession with the number nine was the thing that tilted the vote in the dove's favour.

He had, for as long as he could remember, argued that the policy of pursuing violent means to achieve a united Ireland was self-defeating. He argued that it produced the opposite effect to that desired because it gave the Unionists what they wanted, a legitimate reason to maintain the status quo.

By the mid-1960s the doves' policies were being put into effect on the ground and Nationalists were pursuing a Civil

Rights campaign in Northern Ireland. Its effectiveness was one of the things used to underpin the contention that political persuasion could achieve more than the bomb and the bullet. The other was the passage of a Bill through the British Parliament. Riley saw it as an opportunity to bring at least two members of the Senate on side. That would give the doves a safe majority and prevent the hawks getting their way in the foreseeable future.

'Gentlemen I'm pleased to inform you that the Race Relations Bill is making unstoppable progress through the British Parliament,' he announced. 'As soon as it receives the Royal Assent it will give us a legal platform from which we can challenge discrimination against Ulster Catholics.'

The question before the Senate was whether to instruct Dublin to release a press statement to the effect that the Official IRA was changing its status from permanent ceasefire to dissolution. The senate had heard arguments from Sean MacStoinfoin, vehemently opposing the motion and from Cathal Goulding supporting it.

Both had travelled from Dublin to address the Senate, and on balance MacStoinfoin's address was more appealing in that it questioned the wisdom of making a promise that might prove impossible to keep. He concluded by reminding the Senate that the British Parliament was long on promises and short on delivery. That Parnell's Home Rule Bill was defeated despite the fact that it did not contain provisions to sever Ireland from Great Britain, 'I would ask you to keep your powder dry gentlemen,' he said as he sat down.

Goulding's address lacked impact. He was unable to cite events in Irish history to support his contention that a United Ireland would not be achieved through the bomb and the bullet. The mainstay of his argument called into question the wisdom of Irish heroes who had died fighting the British. He did not say so in so many words, but it was implicit in his argument that non-violence would succeed where violence had failed. 'I would ask the Senate not to permit sentimentality to cloud its judgement,' he said. 'The thing to remember is that without violence, the Unionists cannot continue to deny Catholics the same voting rights as Protestants.'

As the senior member present Grandpa Riley had the last word on the matter before it went to the vote. He was convinced that the Race Relations Bill would swing wavers behind Goulding. 'The Bill will become the law of Great Britain gentlemen. I want you to think about that. Not a law forced on it by a foreign country. No, a law passed by the British themselves, which makes amongst other things discrimination on the grounds of religion a crime.'

'Think about that before you vote. The British courts will be bound to uphold the provisions of a statute passed by Parliament. Within the year Catholics will have equal voting rights, equal opportunities and equal treatment with their Protestant neighbours. I think that a signal from this Senate that we are fully committed to the democratic process of government will stand us in good stead in the long run.'

Grandpa Riley got his way and the vote was carried by

six votes to three. It was his last visit to America and he died within six months still believing that the Race Relations Act 1967 would ensure a lasting peace in the land he loved. When the Act was passed it expressly excluded Northern Ireland from its provisions.

MacStoinfoin then approached the Senate to declare that the vote disbanding the IRA was null and void because it was passed on a false premise. The Senate declined explaining that despite the drawback, the Civil Rights movement was making good progress.

***

Grandpa Riley's son was christened Patrick Joseph, but for as long as anyone could remember he was called PJ. When he married Maureen Ward he was obliged to change his surname on the insistence of her father. The reason was that Maureen had no brothers to carry on the family name.

It was rumoured that when Grandpa Ward married, aged fifty years, to a twenty-five-year old woman of Irish descent he did so for the purpose of begetting a son and heir. He wanted a son to carry on the Ward dynasty. The first born to the union was a daughter and she was christened Maureen after his mother. Three stillborn children were laid to rest in the local churchyard over the ensuing three years. At the age of twenty-nine Grandma Ward was buried with her forth-stillborn child.

Maureen grew up devoted to her father and when it was proposed that she should marry PJ Riley on her sixteenth birthday she consented. The agreement was that they would live with Maureen's father on the Ward estate. The arrangement included a proviso that the name Ward would be retained and that the newly weds be called Ward-Riley. James was born a year later, followed by Denise a year after that. Maureen gave birth to stillborn twins the following year and was advised not to attempt a further pregnancy.

***

Patrick O'Connell met James Ward-Riley at junior school. They became friends and before long Patrick was regarded as part of the Ward-Riley family. Denise was eight years of age at the time and even at that early age she knew that one-day she would marry Patrick. The three played, studied and grew up together in happy surroundings and there was never any doubt that their futures were entwined.

After Grandpa Ward passed away Grandpa Riley was invited to take his place in the Ward-Riley home. He was well read, good humoured and strong minded. His presence helped fill the void left by Grandpa Ward's passing. He helped in other ways and like Grandpa Ward, assumed control of the administration of the estate, including financial matters.

The arrangement suited PJ whose main interests were horseracing and gambling. As far as Denise and James were concerned, the family finances were sound and they had an awareness that one day they would inherit the family estate. Meanwhile they continued their education and lived happily in the knowledge that they were lucky to be part of the richest family in the neighbourhood.

By the age of fourteen Denise had grown into a beautiful young woman. Boys in the neighbourhood envied Patrick, and he regarded himself as the luckiest man in Australia. Denise never doubted her earlier commitment to Patrick and on her sixteenth birthday they became unofficially engaged. Both Patrick and Denise loved James who by the age of seventeen had emerged as the natural leader.

The landscape against which they painted a picture of their future portrayed blue skies. What they did not suspect was that there were clouds forming in the distance. The signs were there if they had looked for them. Grandpa Riley lost his sense of humour and for the first time spoke of a need to curb spending. The Mercedes sports car promised to James for his eighteenth birthday did not materialise and Denise's university education was put on hold.

There were other signs and no doubt Grandpa Riley would have eventually been called to account but the opportunity never arose. One morning at breakfast James said to his mother. 'Grandpa hasn't come down for his breakfast yet.'

'I know James,' she said with a tinge of concern. 'It's not like him to miss breakfast. Maybe you should see if he's all right?'

***

James found Grandpa Riley apparently fast asleep. But when he tried to waken him he realised that the old man had died in his sleep aged 80 years and three months. He was laid to rest beside his wife three days later. His coffin was carried from the hearse and lowered into the grave by six men dressed in military style uniforms wearing black balaclavas. After lowering the coffin they stepped back and the priest officiating conducted the service. When he had finished a spade was passed around each member of the family who in turn used it to place soil into the grave.

After that, the soldiers performed drill movements in response to commands shouted by one of their number. They encircled the grave, halted and stood to attention. One of them gave the command to present arms whereupon the squad produced weapons and aimed them into the air. Several mourners were shocked at what was taking place.

The spectacle of a paramilitary guard of honour standing perfectly still aiming pistols at the sky told its own story. A spontaneous silence fell on the mourners as they gaped in disbelief wondering what was going to happen next.

The guard of honour maintained its stance for one minute after which the silence was ranted by the command "Fire!" echoing throughout the graveyard. The report of several pistols was heard after which the guard of honour about turned and dispersed.

PJ was more than a little embarrassed at the display that took place at his father's graveside. He knew that his father was involved in Irish nationalism, but he did not know to what extent. The subject was seldom discussed after PJ married Maureen. There was an understanding between father and son that neither James nor Denise would be told that their grandpa was an 'A' commander in the Irish Republican Brotherhood. Both PJ and his wife were agreed that such matters were not germane to the proper upbringing of their children.

***

Shortly after grandpa took up residence in the Ward-Riley home Maureen noticed strangers coming and going. Grandpa received a throng of serious looking men and women late at night. Several had strong Irish accents and it did not take much to work out that they were engaged in subversive discussions to do with Ireland.

Both PJ and Maureen were concerned that their home was being used as a meeting place. They found comfort in the fact that there was no sign of strife in Ireland at the time. On the contrary there was harmony in Northern Ireland and there were more immediate problems to worry about. The Australia army was fighting alongside the Americans in Vietnam and both James and Patrick were talking about joining the SAS. The upshot was that grandpa's ramblings about the state of play in Ireland went unheeded.

After his death Maureen regretted that she did not pay more attention to what the old man was saying. She knew that he would have told her more if she were receptive. But she found it hard going to maintain interest because she was worried about her son going to Vietnam. Her regret was more to do with the fact that she did not know what her father-in-law had done with his money. She knew he was well off but after he died she found just over one thousand Australian dollars in his account.

That was the extent of his life's savings as far as she

could find out. He had not made a will and nobody knew what he had done with the money from the sale of his estate. After his death, PJ and Maureen spent long hours trying to fathom out what had happened to his fortune. They felt it was their own fault that they did not know because he often gave hints. He implied that he had sufficient investments to make them all rich in the future. If their memory served them right the money was tied up in Irish investments. He often gave the impression that he was going to explain outright what he had done with his money, but he never did.

The problem was that he would not talk about money with his son. He chose Maureen, but he would broach the subject in a roundabout way. It was his way to talk about Ireland and then move onto the subject of investments. He took wide sweeps and by the time he reached the subject Maureen's mind would be elsewhere. When he got the wrong signal he would withdraw into himself. It was impossible to work out what it was that he wanted to say without going through the full charade.

That involved listening to a long drawn out lecture about his role in managing to persuade the Senate to pursue a peaceful and political solution. He would explain that Britain and Ireland would eventually have to join the new Common Market and when that happened borders would come down. He would also speak about the Race Relations Bill going through the British Parliament. It was all too heavy for Maureen. The political and economic developments in Great Britain and Ireland were subjects that Maureen found boring.

He could read her body language and would withdraw into himself. Then he would erect an invisible barrier between them. There was also the fact that the old man's ties with Irish nationalism embarrassed both PJ and Maureen. Many of their friends had strong British connections and would be offended if they knew about grandpa's links with the IRB.

The situation made communication with Grandpa difficult. It was as though he felt that if he could not air his views on the Irish question he would impose similar restrictions to every topic. It later became something of a game in the family to work out the teasers or cryptic clues emanating from grandpa's conversations.

Since his death the game had become more serious. Maureen's mind continued to search for the clues she knew were there. She recalled the time he acquired an Irish record called Four Green Fields. He played it loud and often and his antics reminded Maureen of a naughty child.

At meals he would often adopt the role of a great orator addressing an assembly, "What did I have, said the proud old woman? What did I have the proud old woman did say? I have four green fields. But one of them's in bondage."

The children would encourage him and he would continue, "My sons have sons as brave as were their fathers," he would proclaim like a Shakespearean actor pointing at PJ.

"And my four green fields will bloom once again said she…"

The children would clap and Patrick O'Connell would laugh. Even PJ found it amusing.

***

One day Maureen found herself singing the song as she prepared dinner. Grandpa came into the kitchen and was there for some time before she realised. When she became aware of his presence she immediately stopped.

'Go on, you've a good singing voice,' he said smiling and encouraging her to continue. 'Your father would have loved to hear you.'

'I'm too embarrassed to sing in front of people. I didn't know you were there.' Maureen said looking at the potato she was peeling.

'Well, you shouldn't be, you've a great voice,' he said. 'Do you understand what the song's about?'

'I've never thought about it dad; I like the tune I suppose.'

'Yes but do you understand the words?'

'Not really. I suppose you're going to tell me it's one of those banned rebel songs?' She said light-heartedly.

'No, at least it's not banned,' he said sitting down at the table. 'Basically the song is referring to the four provinces of Ireland, Ulster, Munster, Leinster and Connacht. They're the four green fields, and the one in bondage is Ulster. Do you follow?'

'Yes I think I understand dad,' Maureen said attempting to portray a deeper understanding than she felt. 'Ulster, that's Northern Ireland isn't it?'

If grandpa felt he was dropping pearl to swine he did not show it. He had an audience and he was not about to discourage her by pointing out that even a kangaroo should know that Ulster is in Northern Ireland.

'Yes, you're right dear,' he said looking down at the table. 'The old woman is Ireland and the field in bondage is Ulster.'

That was the prelude to a conversation, in which he mentioned that he had investments in the Fenian movement, 'It's a good investment and in a few years I'll cash it in,' he said turning to leave the kitchen. 'Don't worry about money dear.'

It was the last time he spoke about his investments. Shortly after that he began to fail. He was worried about James and Patrick joining the army, 'You know where they'll end up?' he would say to PJ. 'Vietnam that's where they'll send them two young lads.'

'If they don't join they'll be called up anyway dad,' PJ would reason. 'If they volunteer they have a good chance of getting a commission.'

He died six months after returning from America and a week before the boys were due to report for military training. The extent of the financial problems came to light shortly after his death. The bank statement showed that the balance was in the red and was accompanied by a curt notice that the bank had cancelled all facilities on the account.

PJ was dumbfounded when he had to liquidate assets including his beloved horses to remain solvent.

Maureen was sure there must be some mix up. She knew that Grandpa Riley had left money to his family in his will. The problem was that neither the will nor the money could be found. Nevertheless in the back of her mind Maureen could not rid herself of the feeling that Grandpa Riley had investments.

PJ was not so sure and went through a phase of questioning the wisdom of allowing the old man unsupervised control of the families' finances. He suspected that his father had subscribed more money than they could afford to the Fenians.

PJ recalled that shortly after his father's death two men came unannounced and demanded access to his room. They said they were looking for "sensitive papers". They were allowed to search the old man's room unsupervised and after an hour left carrying several boxes.

***

Within a few years the Ward-Riley estate was on the brink of insolvency. The date of James and Patrick's discharge from the army was on the horizon. They would be leaving the killing fields of Cambodia and Vietnam and returning to the safety of Australia.

Denise and Patrick had arranged to marry as soon as he was safely home from Vietnam. Meanwhile Denise found employment in a local solicitor's office. It helped the financial situation and kept her from worrying about James and Patrick.

The impact of the loss of the family fortune was offset by the threat of a much greater loss. The news from Vietnam was far from reassuring; every telephone call, every knock on the door and every letter gave rise to pangs of fear.

The Ward-Riley household, like thousands of others, was on constant alert. There were mixed feelings about the post. Whilst the post van was eagerly awaited the possibility that it could be the harbinger of bad news was never far from the minds of recipients.

PJ was more worried about James being in Vietnam than he cared to admit. He did not have to articulate his feelings because they were obvious from his actions. He watched for the post every day and perhaps it was not surprising that when there was a break in the routine he panicked.

It happened one day when the post-lady rang the doorbell. PJ watched the post-van and was waiting to collect the mail as it came through the letterbox. He did not expect the sound of the doorbell and when it rang it shocked him. The promptness with which he opened the door startled the post-lady and PJ mistook her fright for sombreness, 'Good morning PJ, I have a registered letter for you,' she said, trying to regain her composure. 'Will you sign here please?'

PJ noticed that his hand was shaking when he signed. He did not speak when the post-lady handed him the envelope he just looked at it. It's from the army, he thought, as he turned and walked into the hallway. 'Maureen! There's a registered letter from the army. It's James; something's happened to him...' he called and then fainted.

Maureen rushed into the hall and picked up the unopened envelope. She was oblivious of her husband prostrate on the floor as she examined the envelope. She felt her legs getting weak and sat on the stairs. "AFPO 32 Registered Mail." The postmark jumped up at her. She was familiar with normal Australian Forces Post Office mail but this letter was registered. A grip of fear overtook her and she sat spellbound staring at the envelope.

How long both husband and wife were mesmerised is unknown. When PJ recovered he immediately telephoned Denise. 'Come home at once I think the worst has happened.'

***

Denise looked pale; 'What's happened, dad?' She said as soon as she entered the house and saw both her parents sitting in silence in the hall. 'Oh God! Has something happened to James or Patrick?' Denise asked kneeling down in front of her mother.

Maureen gave her the envelope without speaking. 'What does it say mom?' she said before realising that the envelope was still intact. 'It hasn't been opened! You haven't read it!' She exclaimed turning the envelope over and over in her hand. 'Maybe it's not as bad as we think. It's not a telegram. Nobody from army welfare came,' she said as she ripped open the envelope.

She saw the letter in James' handwriting and a sealed envelope, 'It's a letter from James! He's all right.'

'Thank you sweet Jesus,' Maureen said. 'Read it to us dear, tell us what he has to say?'

'Dad, did you hear me?' Denise said. 'I'm going to read the letter.'

PJ nodded.

> *"Hello Mom, Dad & Denise,*
>
> *Just a quick note to explain that the enclosed envelope was left for me by one of our officers. I believe it's a letter from Grandpa Riley that was inadvertently removed with papers collected by his friends. Fancy it turning up in Vietnam! I'm sure he would have been amused. I hope it's what you've been looking for. I can't wait to hear what's in it.*
>
> *Much love to you all,*
> *James."*

***

Later that day PJ and Maureen retired to the sitting room to read grandpa's letter again. It was in effect his will and explained that there was no money from the sale of his land because he gave it back to the Aborigines from whom, he thought, it had been stolen.

"Perhaps as things have turned out you may not be able to find it in you heart to understand why I did this. But, as you know I spent my life preaching that Irish land should be returned

to its rightful owners. I think the Aborigines are like the Irish in that respect and it would be hypocritical of me to keep their land."

'Put that way I suppose he was right,' PJ said. 'What do you think dear?'

'Yes I agree darling. It's like that song you know the one Four Green Fields?'

'These Irish Republican Bonds, did he ever mention them to you?'

'Not in so many words you know what your father was like.'

'Well they have me stumped,' PJ said pacing the floor. 'I never knew such things existed.'

'How many bonds did he leave us?'

'Twenty-thousand with a face value of $5 each, that makes $100'000 American dollars, plus interest of six percent per annum since 1865,' PJ said. 'Jesus if I'm right they're worth a fortune.'

'Good on him, you see your dad didn't let us down,' Maureen said. 'Where did he hide them?'

'In a bank in Panama for some reason.'

***

The Australian army did not want to lose two experienced commissioned officers. 'Think about it fellas,' the colonel said. 'If you change your minds I guarantee you both promotion if you re-enlist.'

'My sister is still missing, sir.' James said. 'We're going to spend some time finding out what's happened to her.'

'Yes of course I understand James. I wish you all the best in that regard and my offer will remain open for the foreseeable future.'

The Australian army was not the only party interested in recruiting ex-SAS officers. Sub-recruiters of the Irish Republican Brotherhood were coming out of the woodwork in keeping with heightening tension in Northern Ireland.

The sub-recruitment of Irish descendants was practised by the Fenian Brotherhood for centuries. British, American, Australian and French Foreign Legion armies were combed by activists in search of suitable candidates. Trained officers and soldiers were highly prized to assist in the struggle for Irish independence. James had heard that such recruiters were not above creating circumstances to encourage volunteers.

He had learned much about Irish nationalism since he received the letter from his mother informing him that Denise had gone to Panama to collect grandpa's Fenian bonds. Although his mother did not say so in as many words he could read between the lines that something was wrong.

"Denise went to Panama to get the bonds I told you about. She telephoned to say that she arrived safely and explained that she had to go to Ireland to redeem them. She phoned us from Amsterdam and promised to call us again when she reached Birmingham. From there she was going on to Dublin. We have not heard from her since and I expect she will get in touch soon."

That was three weeks ago. In mother's latest letter she did not mention Denise nor had she written to James or

Patrick. These omissions led to one conclusion. She was still missing.

'Staff Sergeant Duffy,' James said to Patrick, 'he'll find out if anyone can about these Fenian bonds.'

'I'll talk to him as soon as he gets back from patrol.'

The next day Duffy stood to attention in James' office. 'Take a seat Staff, you know what I want to see you about.'

Duffy explained that Fenian Bonds were issued in America in 1865 to raise funds for "The Cause." He believed that the bonds were honoured when Ireland was granted independence in the 1920s. As far he knew there had been no re-issue. He went on to explain that the bonds had the stamp of treason. They were not things in which an Australian officer should get involved.

'Yes I see Peter. As an Australian officer I owe my allegiance to the Queen of England.'

'That's about it, 'Duffy said. 'The declared objectives of the Fenians is the overthrow of British authority in Ireland.'

'Yes, but if they were issued to help ordinary Irish people that would fall outside your definition, wouldn't it?'

'Yes, if that was the case, but the declared objectives of the bonds were "*for the purchase of arms and munitions of war for the Irish Republican Army.*"

'An open and shut case of treason members of the jury,' James said with an air of despondency.

***

Denise did not know these things when she decided

to go to Panama to collect grandpa's bonds. No doubt she acted on impulse thinking she was going to enhance the family purse. Grandpa Riley's letter was an unexpected gift from heaven. It would never occur to her that there was any danger in going to collect the bequest.

James could now see the undercurrent and regretted that he had not opened grandpa's letter before sending it home. He should have realised that something was amiss when he found it on his pillow along with the unsigned typed note. *"Attached envelope was inadvertently taken from your grandfather's home after he died."*

James regretted that he had disposed of the note after reading it. He should have known better. Grandpa's letter turning up in Vietnam was suspicious in itself. There had been too many slips and there would be no more, he vowed.

III

✸

A New IRA

DENISE LANDED IN AMSTERDAM on 27th January 1973 the day Dr Kissinger and Le Duc Tho signed a cease-fire agreement in Paris. The Vietnam War was drawing to a close and Nixon's tactic of "bombing them to the negotiation table" was in tatters. James had predicted that Saigon would be under Communist rule within the year.

Three weeks later James and Patrick boarded the military flight from Saigon to Durban. They looked down at Vietnam as the plane headed for the Golden Triangle and home, 'We've made it James,' Patrick said. 'I often thought we'd never leave Vietnam alive.'

'And what about you Peter?' James said turning to the man sitting on his left. 'Will you miss the army?'

'We had some good times sir, but on the whole I don't think I'm going to miss being shot at.'

'You don't have to call me sir anymore Peter, 'James said light heartily. 'Where we're going all men are equal.'

Peter Duffy leaned forward and looked at Patrick seated at the other side of James, 'And what do I call you sir?' he asked.

'Whatever you like staff,' Patrick said mockingly. 'But I'd prefer not to be called it too early in the morning.'

The plane touched down on Australian soil and the three men walked together in silence. As they made their way into the arrivals hall they saw Maureen standing alone waiting for them. She must have noticed the look of disappointment on their faces. The excitement of the reunion was overshadowed by Denise's absence.

James and Patrick hugged Maureen and there were tears in her eyes when James said, 'This is our friend Peter Duffy, he's going to stay with us for a while.'

On the way home James and Patrick were listening to every word Maureen spoke hoping to hear that Denise was too busy preparing things to come to the airport. They both new it was wishful thinking, for if Denise were in Australia she would not have missed their homecoming. Maureen could not bring herself to say what she was thinking. Instead she skirted around the subject by saying things from which one could deduce what was on her mind.

'Your father wanted to come but decided to wait by the telephone in case Denise rang.'

It was not bad news in itself and an impartial bystander would have pointed out that Maureen was merely apologising for the fact that her husband had not accompanied her.

The reason was that he expected an important telephone call from Denise.

But James knew that the time had come to face up to reality. Looking at his mother's body language and reading between the lines the message that she wanted to convey was that Denise was still missing and that PJ was too worried to leave the telephone unattended.

***

A month later Denise was still missing. The lack of information surrounding her disappearance was a cause of concern. If she were the victim of a "normal" mishap there would have been feedback from hospitals, police stations, European embassies or one of the several enquiries made since her disappearance. All that was known was that she left Panama en-route to Amsterdam. There was no record of her boarding a flight from Amsterdam to Birmingham on the date she telephoned. And the Irish authorities had no record of her landing at Dublin Airport.

The Australian circle of the IRB confirmed that Fenian bonds were issued in 1865. They were called in and honoured by Eamonn De Valera when the Irish Republic was formed. The bonds could no longer be redeemed and their only value was as collectibles. The Fenian Society had no current interest in them.

'There may be something James, but you know the rules of our society. We cannot discuss brotherhood intelligence with non-members,' the IRB official said solemnly to James.

James gave the man a knowing look. 'Okay that's fair enough I suppose. How does one join your society?'

'It's not you we want James. Now if you can persuade your mates to join I think we might do something in return.'

'Might, is not a word that would persuade me to part with my two friends, I prefer the word will.'

'I think I can say that James.'

'Look we'll be playing this game all day if you don't stop using half-negatives. "I might," "I think," are not good enough. The question is simple and a plain yes or no will suffice. Now can you help me find my sister or not?'

'Yes.'

***

By the end of 1970 British Intelligence was aware that the military wing of Sinn Fein was active. It also knew that there was a split in the Irish republican camp because it had played a part in bringing it about.

The Marxist Official IRA led by Goulding announced a cease-fire in 1963 to permit its political wing to pursue a civil rights and socialisation campaign. The campaign focused, amongst other things, on the non-democratic voting rights of Northern Irish Catholics.

As the cradle of democracy, Britain was embarrassed at the democratic defect in its own back garden. Paradoxically many English MPs were agreed that Northern Irish Catholics had a grievance, and that the gerrymandered electoral system put in place to maintain power in the hands of Ulster Protestants could not be defended in a democracy.

But the problem throughout history was that whenever the subject was raised in the House of Commons it was overshadowed by the activities of Irish terrorists. Britain had international backing in its declared stance of not negotiating with terrorists. Hence right-minded people could see that if terrorism were taken out of the equation Britain would not be able to use it as an excuse for not confronting the Irish problem. It seemed that Irish republicans by their own activities were bent on scuppering their declared objectives.

***

By the mid 1960s it was beginning to seem as though the nationalists finally accepted that the way forward was to argue their case in the British Parliament. The non-violent approach was working and the plight of Catholics was being discussed in the British House of Commons.

In the absence of the sounds of bombs and bullets, anti-Ulster MP's message was being heard in the House of Commons. It was enough to shock Ulster Unionists into realising that their worst nightmare was about to become reality.

The voting system was the keystone upon which their domination stood. If Catholics were given anything approaching proportional representation they would flood the Province with their Southern brethren. Before long the balance of power would tilt in their favour and they would drag the North into a United Ireland. What was needed was the old remedy. The sound of a bomb never failed to remind "Progressive" English MPs which side their bread was buttered.

Then a new nationalist group calling itself the Provisional IRA under Sean MacStiafoin emerged to answer the prayers of Unionists. He propounded that the only way around the partition problem was to bomb the English out of Ireland. MacStiafoin and his followers moved into the old paramilitary infrastructure vacated by Goulding. Sinn Fein became their political wing and within a comparatively short time the patriot game was up and running again.

MacStiafoin's coup d'etat was easy. There was little Goulding could do because most of his hard line paramilitary men had joined the new Provos. To the outside world it looked as though nothing had changed. The IRA was still in the game; the only difference was that instead of calling itself the Official IRA it was now the Provisional IRA or the Provos. It was easy to sell the new threat as the old enemy up to its old tricks. Factionalism within the IRA was nothing new. All it meant was that the quest for a united Ireland was off the political agenda.

***

The Provisional IRA was content to be seen by the world in that light. In fact it was what it wanted. Britain could be relied upon to provide the paint for the picture the Provos wanted to portray to the Irish masses. It was a picture of Irish freedom fighters pitted against the might of the British Empire. A glaring mismatch, that portrayed Catholic Ireland as the downtrodden victim of the mighty Imperialist. The bully was Britain and the bullied was little Ireland. On that canvas the IRA were assured the sympathy and support of Catholics throughout Ireland and beyond.

The IRB was not happy. Goulding was its man pursuing a political agenda based on the treatment of Catholics in Northern Ireland. Until 1969 the policy was working better than expected and it was beginning to look as though a United Ireland could be achieved under the banner of Civil Rights for Catholics.

A united socialist Ireland would emerge governed by old Fenians, if Sinn Fein and the Provisional IRA had not come to the rescue of the Orange Order in Ulster.

When the bombs started exploding and the guns started firing it was no longer politically correct or logically supportable to suggest that a peaceful transition to a United Ireland could be achieved. British politicians found that the ground had crumbled under their feet. The argument that Protestant and Catholics had at last come to a meeting of minds could not be sustained in the face of tit-for-tat killings.

***

The shakers and movers that brought about a resurgence of violence in Ulster worked to a well-planned schedule. The idea was hatched in Ulster Orange Lodges to encourage militant young Catholics to rise up against the British establishment. Putting the plan into effect was easy; all that was needed was to give them the wherewithal and time to organise.

Security and law enforcement in Ulster is influenced by Orange Lodges. The lodges are affiliated with Orange, and, to a lesser extent, Masonic Lodges in Scotland and England. They are old hands at the power game and by 1970 had nationalists dancing to the sound of Orange flutes disguised to sound like nationalist's harps.

***

Peter Duffy was born in London in 1944 the illegitimate son of an Irish mother and an American soldier. His father absconded leaving Peter and his mother to fend for themselves in post-war London. She was a despised Irish foreigner subjected to deplorable racial discrimination. Worst still, she bore the shame of being an unmarried mother, a status that made her an outcast in the eyes of the Catholic Church.

Anne Duffy did not blame her son for the situation she found herself in. She loved him and worked her fingers to the bones in order to sustain them above the poverty line. Peter was the only ray of sunlight in her otherwise gloomy world. Together they learned to ignore gibes and rebuffs and got on with the business of surviving. Their home was the garret of a four-story house in Harlesden High Street, NW10.

Anne Duffy found work wherever she could and by the time he was six Peter was accustomed to being alone for long periods. As he grew up he began to realise that he was treated different than other children at school and in the local Catholic community. He would later learn that his illegitimate status was the reason.

From an early age he was disturbed by the way people treated his mother. He realised that she walked with her head down presumably to make herself less noticeable. Other women shunned her and discouraged their children from associating with him or his mother.

He learned to read their body language. By the age of ten he could look at persons in the street and tell whether they were friends or foe. It was a talent that would later stand him in good stead. Years later whilst serving in Vietnam his ability to spot a VC soldier dissimulating amongst ordinary villagers could mean the difference between life and death. His comrades learned to rely on his instincts without question.

One day whilst on patrol he and six comrades happened upon a village. They were greeted by smiling villagers bowing in a friendly gesture with their hands joined. Peter walked forward returning their greeting. As he got close he fired three shots killing three men. It was later ascertained that they were VC soldiers waiting to ambush the patrol.

To understand Duffy's persona one must return to his youth in London. On his twelfth birthday he studied his reflection in a mirror. He could not wait to grow up because he wanted to take the burden of making a living off his mother. She would tell him not to worry that he was her big man. But he found growing up a slow process and wondered if the day would ever come when he would be big enough to put right all the wrongs she had suffered.

Perhaps it was his obsession with making his mother's life more bearable that caused him to act out of character. When the store detective grabbed him he knew that it had been a mistake to take the risk.

'I'm a store detective and I've observed you removing items from the store for which you haven't paid.' The man said as he placed his hand on Peter's shoulder.

The items were articles of clothing, which Peter had removed from the ladies department of a Marks & Spencer. It was not out of character for Peter to purloin gifts for his mother. What was out of character was that he did not take the necessary precautions to avoid being caught. It was a mistake he thought he would never make and now one he vowed never to repeat.

His pleadings that it had all been a terrible mistake fell on deaf ears.

'Please give me a chance, I promise I'll never do it again,' he begged but the store detective was unmoved.

The police were called and the store detective related what had taken place to the two officers.

'Duffy, that's an Irish name, ain't it?' The mocking policeman asked.

'Yes sir,'

'A little bog-trotter,' the policeman said sardonically, 'and a little thieving one at that.'

'Well now Mr P Duffy,' he said in the same tone. 'You say that the P stands for Peter are you sure it ain't for Paddy?'

'No sir, Peter'

To the sound of laughter the officer continued, 'I know most of you Irish can't read son and that you're all called Paddy. So are you sure that's not your name?'

'Yes sir, I'm sure my name's Peter.'

'Very good my son,' the officer said slapping Peter on the head. 'Let's go down the nick and see what else you've been up to.'

At Harlesden Police Station, the officer's hostility was never far from the surface. When he learned that Peter's father was unknown he said, 'So you're a real Irish bastard Duffy.'

'I'm only half-Irish,' Peter said hoping that would enhance his standing in the eyes of the policeman. 'My dad was American.'

The door opened and the other officer entered. The first officer stood up and walked to the door. Before leaving he turned round and said to his colleague, 'if he gives you any trouble just call me and I'll come back and teach him manners.'

This officer was friendlier than his colleague and had no obvious animosity. Peter felt more at ease.

'You're in quite a bit of trouble son,' he said in an avuncular tone. 'I'm sure your old mom will be very disappointed in you.'

'Do you have to tell my mother sir?'

'I'm afraid she'll have to know, I've no alternative.'

'Please don't tell her sir.' Peter pleaded.

'It's difficult son, but let's clear up everything you've

done,' the constable said. 'If you're helpful we'll see what we can do about keeping your mom out of the picture. Do you follow me son?'

'I'll tell you everything sir, I just don't want my mother worried that's all.'

'That's the way lad, you help me and I'll help you. Start by telling me everything you know; clean your slate. It'll make life easier all round, you'll see,' the officer said sincerely. 'This isn't the first time you've got presents for your old mom. Is it son?'

Kindness and understanding were things Peter was not used to and he fought hard to prevent tears welling up in his eyes. He looked at the officer's face and was convinced that he had found someone he could trust. He felt he could confide in the officer that there had been previous occasions when he stole things to give to his mother.

The officer listened sympathetically and when Peter had finished looked at the rather short list.

'I don't think there's enough here to persuade my gaffer that you've told us everything son. No, this won't do. It looks like we'll have to get your mom after all.'

'But you promised me sir.'

'Yes son and I'm a man of my word.' The officer said in the same sincere voice. 'Look lad we need more than this, you must have done other things which have slipped your mind. No one will believe that's all you've done, you're a bright lad, look at it from our point of view. A few petty shopliftings won't get you any favours. You must have done other things that you can't remember?'

'But that's everything.' Peter said scratching his head, not wanting to alienate the friendly officer. 'That's all I can remember, I swear sir.'

'There's a way we can get round this son. I want to help you to remember,' the officer said. 'Can I trust you?'

'You can sir! I'll do anything so long as you don't tell her,' Peter said enthusiastically.

'I know that son. I'd do the same in your shoes. All that worry and for what?' the officer said. 'All right then I'll take a chance but it's more than my job's worth if you let me down lad.'

'I wont sir. I promise on my mother's life.'

'Good lad, I believe you. I have to get someone to sit in whilst I take a statement from you,' the constable said standing up. 'You must understand that if you disagree with anything I put in your statement all bets are off. I'll have to get your mother.'

Two hours later Peter signed a statement to the effect that he had committed numerous thefts from shops and broken into five houses.

The next morning he was taken before a juvenile court charged under the Larceny Act 1916 with six counts of larceny and five of entering dwellings with intent. The police officer asked the court to remand Peter to secure accommodation on the grounds that he was out of parental control.

'The boy's father is unknown,' he told the court. 'He resides in a rented room with his mother, your worships. And we have reason to believe that he is in moral danger because his mother is an Irish common prostitute.'

'My mother's not a prostitute, you fucking liar!' Peter shouted. 'You never told me that you were going to tell lies about her when you got me to sign that statement.'

'Be quiet boy,' the presiding magistrate said sternly. 'You're obviously out of control. I've never heard such foul language from a boy of your age. I've heard enough to grant the officer's application. You are remanded to a suitable institution for seven days.'

***

Three months later as Peter was escorted on board the ship bound for Australia he looked over his shoulder hoping to catch a glance of his mother. But he knew that she could not get to Southampton and wondered if he would ever see her again. He was now a ward of court off to a new life with other British children in the New World.

Peter had a tough time adapting to the demands of his new life. At first he reacted violently to being institutionalised and found it difficult to settle. He missed his mother and he vowed that one day he would return to London to find her.

In time he learned to conceal his hate for those who held him captive. He studied them and began to imitate their ways. He learned to pretend, to cajole, to lie and hide his true feelings. He realised they expected him to show gratitude, to thank them and be eternally grateful that they had come to his rescue. They had saved him from his loving mother and baptised him with the waters of cold charity.

For that he would always remember them but not with affection.

By the time Peter joined the Australian army at the age of eighteenth he knew about IRA sub-recruiters and the Irish struggle. He was determined to do whatever it took to get to Ireland and from there to his mother in London. He became adept in the art of diplomatic deception a phrase he learned from his old Irish friend. The one who told him what he had to do in order to be accepted as a member of the IRA.

He was accepted into the SAS and trained hard. He pushed himself until he knew he would graduate amongst the top three in his squad. He volunteered to be posted to Vietnam with his regiment.

His officers and comrades came to regard him as a first class soldier. Even the enemy VC learned to fear the platoon headed by Duffy. Its members became known as the Phantoms because of their ability to appear without warning, inflict maximum damage and disappear.

Peter felt that he was part of a family. His fellow soldiers respected him and he was no longer an outcast. He attributed the change in his fortunes to the patience and guidance given to him by Major J Ward-Riley and Lieutenant P O'Connell.

***

James Ward-Riley wasted no time in coming up with a plan to find out what had happened to his sister. He analysed and reanalysed the blueprint before presenting it to

Patrick and Peter. The plan did not offer a quick solution to the problem but what it lacked in speed it compensated for in thoroughness.

The logistics were easy to comprehend and in short involved Patrick O'Connell and Peter Duffy going to Ireland and joining the IRA, whilst James went to England to work with MI5. Getting the two boys into the IRA presented no difficulty given that the IRA probably snatched Denise with that objective in mind. The trick was to bear in mind that probabilities were not certainties and the only thing that was certain was that the IRB had told James that they were interested in recruiting Peter and Patrick.

Getting a toehold into MI5 was proving much more difficult. In the not too distant past James would have found it easy to sell his plan to the Brits. But nowadays things were different. The USSR was winning the Cold War and Eastern Bloc spies were running rings around the Western Alliance.

Echoes of the Cambridge spy ring could still be heard in the corridors of Whitehall. The Profumo Affair was the latest embarrassment and a reminder that gifts that looked too good to be true invariably turn out to be just that. The deal James brought to the table looked too good to be true and in the current political climate that was a disadvantage.

British intelligence was navigating stormy seas whilst attempting to re-establish its credibility. It could not afford another scandal but in the murky world of espionage scandal is never far from the surface. The officer appointed to conduct a "feasibility assessment" of James' proposal was warned to proceed with extreme caution. The Northern Ireland security scene was strewn with many pitfalls at the best of times but in the current climate it was almost too sensitive to touch.

James Ward-Riley had strayed into an area in which were concealed many embarrassing secrets. There were surreptitious deals that would be difficult to explain if exposed to public scrutiny. Nothing was straightforward in Northern Ireland. That which pleased one side offended the other and vice-versa. Security forces were given the impossible task of appeasing both sides in a conflict out of which no winner could emerge.

***

James was not concerned with the finer points of Irish Nationalism. He had made it his business to bring himself up to speed on the basics of the conflict. His quick mind soon absorbed the salient points and he came to the conclusion that his only interest in the Irish "Troubles" was the welfare of his sister.

He would be loyal to whichever side offered him the better chance of saving Denise. His offer to work for British Intelligence was his way of improving that chance. It ensured that he had a foot in each camp. It was not beyond the realms of possibility that the Brits had played a part in Denise's disappearance. James had long since learned that in the world of politics and spies nothing could be taken for granted. He had played the game himself in Vietnam where he soon realised that people were expendable.

The Brits were nobody's fool and by now would have a thick file on the likes and dislikes of Major (retired) James Ward-Riley, ex Australian SAS. That was not surprising given Grandpa Riley's antecedents, an element that James had not overlooked. He believed he turned it to his advantage by highlighting it as a reason he would be trusted by Irish republicans. The good news was that the Brits had responded and wanted to meet him.

The meeting was today and had been arranged in the typical cloak and dagger fashion amateur spies go about their business. The venue was kept secret until the last possible moment and turned out to be a remote two-star hotel, which James had never heard before the telephone call. 'Go to the restaurant of the Transport Hotel in Wellington Avenue and order lunch for three.'

At the restaurant after James placed the order two men came to his table. One was Major Wakefield from the British Embassy who was James' "handler," and was accompanied by a man unknown to James.

'That looks disgusting old man,' Major Wakefield said sitting down. 'Take a seat Tom, this is Major Ward-Riley who is going to solve all our problems in Ireland.'

Tom gave a frosty nod in James' direction and sat down. Wakefield broke the silence, 'Any news about your sister's whereabouts James?'

'No. I was hoping you might know something?'

'Afraid not old man … it's a bit of a mystery. Can't find out a thing. Are you still pursuing your Irish theory?'

'Yes, that's one line I'm pursuing.'

'Yes I see, of course you suspect we may have her?'
'Do you?'
'That's what I like about you Australians,' the major said light-heartily, 'straight to the point.'

That was an encouraging sign. At previous meetings Major Wakefield was stiff and very "British" but today he was relaxed. James knew that they were leading up to the sixty-four thousand-dollar question and wondered if this was a good moment for him to ask it.

Perhaps not he decided to wait for the major. He was taking his time and spending an inordinate amount of it on busy trivialities. Then the major became more business like and turned to Tom.

'Colonel Tom Smite here is a senior field officer with MI5. He has come from England to see you James. If we decide to move he'll be your handler. Over to you sir.'

'Right, thank you Brian,' Tom said turning to James. 'I'll get straight to the point, our people have looked at your proposition and want me to go into it further with you. You know the type of thing, risk, feasibility, cost and political implications if things go wrong. In other words if you can sell it to me they feel I can sell it to them. Are you with me so far?'

James knew that the plan he had put forward would raise eyebrows in London. But the presence of Colonel Smite in Australia meant London was interested. James' research had paid off and he could see that the British had made the same mistake in Ireland that the Americans did in Vietnam.

They had assumed that the side they were backing was using the same rulebook as themselves. That in time the population of Ulster, regardless of their religious persuasions, would see sense. The formula for peaceful co-existence was simple. Equal opportunities and treatment of citizens coupled with a higher standard of living than was on offer elsewhere.

James could find no fault in that provided all the players were aiming for the same thing. His analysis of the situation led him to the contrary view. The thing that struck him was that the Irish terrorists had stolen a march. They had succeeded beyond the expectations of military analysts. The similarity between the way the Vietcong had held the might of American forces and their allies at bay was striking. The question was whether there was a similarity in the way it was achieved.

The indigenous South Vietnamese warlords hoodwinked the Americans by pretending that they shared their values and commitment to democracy. Instead, they were in cahoots with the enemy, up to their necks in corruption and brinkmanship. James could draw an analogy with the relationship between the British and the Orange Order in Northern Ireland. Britain was prepared to recognise its obligation to protect Ulster Protestants but the price was equal treatment of Northern Irish Catholics. On the world stage Britain could not be seen to support an administration that blatantly practised discrimination between its citizens.

To that end Britain had committed itself to making fundamental changes in the voting system in Northern Ireland.

That was the bone of contention from which most other grievances sprung. The Catholics were getting what they wanted and on the face of it there should not be an Irish problem.

But there was an Irish problem and James' sister Denise was caught somewhere in its web. James suspected that British intelligence knew the answer. After all there were at least ten security personnel to every terrorist, a statistic that did not favour the terrorists. So why were they having so much success? That was the question on James' mind as he looked at Colonel Smite.

'Yes I believe I see where you're coming from sir.' James said.

'Good. Now what I want to know is how your plan is going? Have you got your men in yet?'

Patrick and Peter were currently in Ireland being checked out by the IRA and James was ready to go to England with or without the assistance of British Intelligence. But he was too well versed in protocol to spurt out every detail without knowing what was on offer. He knew that the British were unhappy with Peter Duffy's track record and felt he was too volatile for the job. As an ex-commissioned officer Patrick O'Connell was more in keeping with what they wanted. But that was not how James saw it, and he had taken the decision to deliver Duffy to the IRA as requested.

'Yes the plan is going well Colonel. We are in the process of infiltrating the IRA as we speak.'

'I wont beat about the bush James; I'm sure you have

considered the danger and feel that the risk is worth it,' the colonel said. 'It's the one area of your plan that concerns me. Can you imagine the propaganda advantage to the IRA if this goes arse up and we are found to be involved?'

'Yes sir, I realise that,' James said. 'But we intend to find out what's happened to my sister and we'll move with or without your help.'

'Steady on old man,' Major Wakefield said, 'hear the colonel out.'

James sat back in his chair with his arms folded assuming the listening position, 'Please go ahead sir.'

'We are prepared to help but not in the direct way you suggested.' The colonel said pausing to gauge James' reaction. 'What we have come up with is a plan that will put clear water between us. But the important thing is that it will put you in the area you want to be.'

'Is that Birmingham, England sir?'

'Yes in fact it is, and I've gone out on a limb to get our people to go along with what I'm going to propose. It's not in the bag yet, but I'm confident I can persuade the wavers if we reach an accommodation here. Do you follow?'

'Yes sir, please fill me in on the details,' James said.

'Please excuse me gentlemen.' Major Wakefield said as he stood up to leave the table. 'I just have to pop to the gents. It's the wine I think.'

'Yes certainly, carry on old chap,' the colonel said and as soon as the major was out of earshot, 'We must adhere to strict need-to-know policy on this one James. Do you follow?'

'Yes of course sir, I forgot about the major, I'm sorry it was foolish of me.' James said with more sincerity than he felt. He knew that the two Brits would have discussed every detail of the plan before meeting James. This was their way of telling him who was in control.

'Good man, point made, now to answer your question. Your application to join British Intelligence is denied in the formal sense. That is to say that you will not be taken into the service directly and for all outward appearances will have nothing whatsoever to do with us. However, we are prepared to have a special liaison with you through the police. What do you think so far?'

'Sounds very good sir.'

'Yes it is good. It's going to involve a lot of work for you old man. There's the question of your accent and introducing you to the force without arousing too much suspicion. Do you think you can handle it?'

'I'll do whatever's necessary sir.'

'That's the ticket. You can leave that side of things to us. All you have to do is play your part and deliver on your promises.'

'Of course sir. That goes without saying.'

IV

✺

Eire

PATRICK O'CONNELL AND PETER Duffy spent their first week in Ireland in Dublin public houses. Perhaps it was understandable why nobody turned up at Dublin Airport to greet them with the "hundred thousand welcomes" promised to visitors landing on Irish shores.

After all, their status was precarious and they had been warned. The state of Eire existed on conflicting levels. The Fenians perceive Eire as encompassing the whole island of Ireland. That is an abstract notion that refuses to accept the government of the Irish Republic or the British administration in Northern Ireland.

It represents the State existing in the minds of those that opposed and oppose the Anglo-Irish Treaty of 1921. The treaty divided Ireland into two separate states, Northern Ireland and the Irish Republic. It thus failed to achieve the aspiration of the instigators of the Easter Rising of 1916. The proclamation made on the steps of Dublin GPO by the leaders of the Rising spoke of an Irish Republic that comprised thirty-two counties.

'It's important that you understand the significance of the Easter Rising in the minds of the people you will be amongst;' James said to both Patrick and Peter shortly before they set off for Ireland. 'When they speak of Eire they are referring to the whole island of Ireland.'

'I always thought Eire was the Irish Republic and Ulster was the six counties under British rule,' Patrick said.

'That's how people have come to see it, but it's not how the people you are going to be with perceive it.' James said. 'What you have done is confused the abstract State with reality. The people you are going to join live in a thirty-two county United Ireland. The British presence in Ulster is seen as a force of occupation and the government of the Irish Republic is not recognised.'

Peter scratched his head as he paced around the room, 'Let me see if I've got this right,' he said more to himself than to James or Patrick. 'The movement we are about to join does not recognise the authority of the Irish government in the Republic nor the British presence in Ulster.' He held his hand up to indicate that he did not want his train of thought interrupted. 'Okay, that's up to them, but from a strategic point of view it leaves them with no hiding place if I'm right?'

'Well, yes and no,' James said, smiling at the logic of his words. 'The key is to understand that the abstract State exists in most Irish minds. The evidence of historic skulduggery is staring them in the face every day. They look at the geographical composition of Ireland and see no natural dividing line between the North and the rest of the island. What I mean is that if a Martian landed on Ireland he would assume that it was one country under one government.'

Both Patrick and Peter looked at James in bewilderment. It was obvious that the thrust of James' argument had failed to make its mark.

'Okay, fine,' James continued with good humour. 'Let's forget Martians and look at it from a different prospective. If I say that the one thing about which everyone, except the Loyalists agree, is that Ireland should be united. Does that explain matters better?'

'I think I understand,' Patrick said. 'What you mean is that because of the concept you expostulated we should be able to extrapolate the existence of an imaginary State with a real army calling itself the IRA.

'I think our Martian is here,' Peter said pointing at Patrick. 'I hope he brought his interpreter.'

Patrick joined in the humour. 'I thought he was getting a bit carried away,' he said looking at James. 'Maybe we should hear what the other ranks think? Come on Staff Sergeant Duffy let's have your synopsis of the Irish situation?'

Peter performed an about turn and brought himself to attention in front of James. 'Sir!' he exclaimed maintaining his military stance. 'How many flying-saucers have we at our disposal?'

'All right, I give up, you win,' James said holding his

hands up. 'Just remember that in Ireland things are not what they seem.'

They all laughed and for a moment the serious side of their involvement in Irish republicanism was forgotten.

***

Patrick O'Connell and Peter Duffy landed at Dublin Airport three days later from where they made a telephone call which led to their being met by a "sympathiser." The expression provides a buffer between the authorities and IRA members. It's not a crime to be a sympathiser, but membership of the IRA is proscribed in both the Irish Republic and Britain. 'Come with me,' the man said after eyeing them up suspiciously.

He took them to a street of terraced houses somewhere in the backwaters of Dublin. 'Yous are to stay there until yous are contacted again,' the man said pointing to a squalid dwelling with a green door. 'Just knock twice and tell the woman that Brendan sent yous.'

The woman who answered the door seemed disinterested in her guests. Peter mentioned Brendan and that was enough. She immediately showed them an under furnished but clean upstairs bedroom. 'I hope this'll do ye,' she said and added, 'It's the best I can do anyway.'

Peter and Patrick went to bed and slept soundly. The next day the woman went about her business as though she were alone. Peter reckoned that she had been instructed not to ask questions and to deny all knowledge of her two visitors if asked. It was as though she believed that if she pretended they were not there she would be able to do likewise under interrogation.

'Do we have to remain indoors, ma'am?' Peter asked as evening approached. 'We haven't been given any instructions.'

'It's up to yourselves what ye do,' the woman said noncommittally. 'There's Kelly's pub at the bottom of the street.'

It was Patrick's job to assess the situation and he studied his landlady with interest. He guessed she was a victim of circumstances and being tested by the IRA for more serious work. The Provos were taking advantage of the opportunity to kill two birds with one stone. They would test the reliability of the safe house and at the same time check out the two Australians. The woman had been instructed to direct them to Kelly's.

They went to the pub daily. By day four they were beginning to break ice with Kelly's "regulars." The whispering and nudging that greeted them initially was being replaced by the occasional nod of acknowledgement. Patrick was hard pushed to read the situation. He ascribed the atmosphere to the likelihood that Kelly's patrons suspected that the two strangers were involved with the IRA.

On one visit to the pub Peter picked out an unlikely candidate that entered the bar near the end of the session. He was a small oily man with black hair dressed in a scruffy combat jacket. He acknowledged one or two men in the bar before ordering a drink. He drank alone and there was nothing about him that led Patrick to support Peter's hunch. After consuming his drink the man left.

'If he's not waiting for us outside I don't think he's our man.' Patrick said. The man was not waiting and another night passed without contact.

The next night they returned to Kelly's and things seemed much the same. Peter was uneasy with the lack of progress, 'Look Patrick we're being jerked about here. If nothing happens by tomorrow night I'm off to London to look for my mother.'

Patrick was also getting fed up with the situation and considered it very bad form that nobody had made contact. He was about to comment on Peter's statement when he felt him tug his sleeve.

'I think we're on mate, we have contact,' Peter said, using an expression they both knew from Vietnam. 'The two men at the end of the bar are causing a bit of worry to the locals.'

Patrick glanced at the two men and thought that on this occasion Peter's instincts were correct. An hour elapsed but still there was no sign that an approach was going to happen. Both men were still showing more than a passing interest in Peter and Patrick but that was it. They seemed more interested in consuming vast quantities of Guinness than getting down to business.

The pub landlord was flapping and fussing around them and made sure he was there to answer their every beck and call. Near-empty glasses were replenished in quick time and if further evidence of their influence was needed it was provided by the fact that money was not demanded or offered for the service.

There was whispering between the landlord and the two men followed by furtive glances towards Patrick and Peter. 'They're asking him about us,' Peter whispered. 'Why don't we just go over to them over and introduce ourselves?'

'No … if they're our contact they'll come to us,' Patrick said looking down to avoid making eye contact. He felt that Peter had already exceeded the bounds of normal curiosity and was staring too much at the men. 'We can't be sure they're who we think they are.'

One of the men had obviously clocked that Peter was throwing an inordinate amount of glances in their direction. The man, the bigger of the two, was seated on a tall barstool half facing the bar and found it necessary to glance over his left shoulder in order to see Patrick and Peter. He whispered something to his friend, stood up and walked towards their table. He stretched to his full height and projected an air of sang-froid as he swaggered across the room. Patrick felt apprehensive.

'Can I help you lads?' The big man said looking at Patrick.

'I'm sorry.' Patrick said, 'for a moment I thought I recognised you.'

'And do you?' The man said bending down so that his face was aligned with Patrick's. 'Here, take a good look.'

'No, I've made a mistake,' Patrick said humbly. 'I'm sorry I didn't mean any offence.'

'That's all right sweetie,' the man said pinching Patrick's

cheek. 'I thought for a minute that you fancied me, but now I see that you've got your girlfriend with you. And what's your name miss?' He said turning to Peter.

'Mary from the Mountain Glen who mustn't speak to ugly men.' Peter retorted sardonically.

The man leaned towards Peter and gave him a solid slap across the face. 'Don't be cheeky lady or I'll…'

Patrick watched as the big man's head jerked backwards and all sixteen-stone of him was lifted off the floor. He never finished his sentence as he landed unconscious about a metre from where he had been standing. Patrick was the only other person aware of what had happened and was standing beside the second man in seconds.

The realisation that something was wrong with his comrade slowly dawned on the face of the second man. One could tell that they had played this game before and were accustomed to winning. The patronising sneer froze and was being replaced by a look of bewilderment. This never happened before; nobody was capable of flooring big Pat the second man thought as he turned to go to the aid of his friend. He never saw Patrick standing beside him or the karate chop delivered with uncanny precision just below his right ear.

The action was over in seconds and the only sign of trouble was the two men unconscious on the floor. Customers were mumbling to each other in an attempt to fathom out what had happened. The landlord was the first to read the situation. 'Jesus Christ Almighty!' Do yous realise who you've just marbleised?' He asked nobody in particular as he walked around the two men scratching his head.

'Yous better come with me,' a small oily man whispered to James pulling at his sleeve. 'Hurry up and bring your mate.'

Outside the man fumbled with car keys. 'I'm who yous are waiting for … They're two cops yous are after marbleising.' The man said nervously attempting to find the right key. 'Are your things at Mrs Doyle's house? I suppose they are. Let's get them and get to fuck out of here.'

***

That was three weeks ago and in the meantime Patrick and Peter had spent their time being indoctrinated in the ways of the IRA. They were housed in basic makeshift billets in a remote farm somewhere in Kerry. The billeting and equipment was far inferior to that which they were accustomed to in the Australian army. They received no pay and were not allowed to leave the training camp. The incident at Kelly's was used to justify the restriction but Patrick and Peter suspected that there was a different reason.

Jim Doran looked much older than his twenty-five years. His jet-black hair and dark complexion gave a clue that one of his ancestors had landed on Irish shores with the Spanish Armada. In every other respect Jim was a paradigm Irishman whose devil-may-care attitude was a mask for what was really going on inside his head. He did not fool Peter Duffy who had him marked as a killer from the first time he saw him.

Doran had a great deal of nervous energy which he expended doing the bidding of his commander. He was Michael Lynch stationed in Dublin and as yet unknown to Peter or Patrick. Lynch was suspicious about the two men who arrived from Australia on tickets provided by the IRB. He was not convinced that their cover story held water. Someone was fooling somebody and Lynch instructed Jim Doran to find out who it was.

When Jim happened upon Patrick and Peter in Kelly's bar it was not a chance meeting. The two men left prostrate on the bar floor were members of the Garda Siochana Special Branch. The speed with which they were dispatched had not been anticipated but it produced the desired result. It created a situation in which Jim could come to the rescue and take the two strangers to a suitable place for their induction or assassination.

The pub scene had not unfolded as anticipated. Jim Doran had been caught on the hop and as he transported the two Australians out of Dublin he was acting on his own initiative. The original plan was that the two police officers would take them in for questioning on suspicion of being members of a proscribed organisation.

They would have been interrogated and subjected to rough treatment to test their resolve and commitment. Afterwards their fate would depend on how they checked out, but the plan had misfired. The police had underestimated what they were up against and Doran had to move in to save the situation going from bad to worse.

***

Michael Lynch was one of the top IRA men in Dublin and was very interested in the two Australians. He knew that sub-recruiters had been instructed by the IRB to recruit O'Connell because of his expertise in bomb making. But that was before they decided to call a cease-fire and disband the Official IRA. Duffy had not been "requisitioned" and his presence could mean several things, amongst which was the possibility that the whole charade was being run by the IRB or the Brits.

The IRB were to the Official IRA what Sinn Fein was to the Provos. They were not happy with Sinn Fein or its military wing. They were opposed to the current campaign, all of which meant that volunteers arriving from their stable would be viewed with great suspicion. Weighed against this was the fact that the two men were precisely what was needed in the current climate.

Lynch knew about Grandpa Riley's Fenian bonds and remembered seeing Denise cavorting with a Loyalist pimp in Panama. From what he saw he did not get the impression that she was being held against her will or that she belonged to Patrick O'Connell. But he would not be the first man to be fooled by a woman. The set up appealed to Lynch, there was a puzzle and he liked solving mysteries.

Jim Doran was put in charge of looking after the two Australians. He was a good man with a strong survival instinct, which Lynch had come to trust. 'Its up to you Jim whether they live or die.'

Jim Doran volunteered when he was fifteen and had ten years service under his belt. He was one of the Provos top snipers. The fact that he had been selected to decide the fate of the two Australians was enough to signify that it may be necessary to assassinate them.

Doran did not kill for the thrill and liked to justify every execution in his mind. He was sick the first time he shot a young British soldier who had been lured into a "honey-trap." Girls were used to pickup soldiers in bars and clubs and lead them into an ambush. Doran felt sorry for the young soldier pleading for his life. Anyone would feel the same, he thought, as he saw the fear overtake the soldier when it dawned on him that he was in a trap. 'Please don't kill me,' he begged. 'My parents are Irish. I'm just doing my job.'

'Yeah, you're in the killing business like us,' someone said as the shot rang out.

'God help me, I'm going to die,' the soldier cried when he felt the sting of the first bullet. Then each member of the Active Service Unit (ASU) fired a shot into the body of the young soldier and he lay motionless on the ground.

Afterwards members of the ASU went to a safe house where they washed after burning their clothing. Some were rejoicing and saying stupid things like 'That's one less Brit. to worry about.' But Jim Doran felt no elation or sense of achievement. He kept asking himself whether it had been worth it? What did we achieve? Why are we killing young British soldiers instead of Protestant paramilitaries?

From Doran's perspective "The Struggle" was not merely a question of removing British Imperialism from Irish shores. The Irish Republic as constituted in the 1920s was also his enemy. The notion that the Irish Free State acted as a model for a United Ireland did not appeal to him. He disliked the way that Ireland had been carved up in the 1920s to accommodate the insular policies of Eamonn de Valera on one hand and the Ulster Loyalist Protestants on the other.

He perceived it as a ploy designed to appease two extremes leaving the majority of Irish people in the lurch. De Valera's Catholic Irish Republic and the King's Protestant Ulster were both deficient. They left the silent majority out in the cold to fend for themselves.

Doran resented the fact that the British aristocracy had killed Parnell's "Home Rule" in the 19th century. It would have been a success. Ireland with 85 members of parliament in the British House of Commons would have real power. It was too much to ask intelligent people to believe that the opportunity was lost because Parnell was having an affair with a married woman.

No, the truth was concealed somewhere in the political skulduggery to remove Lloyd George from power. The old British establishment could not stomach a Welshman and an Irishman deciding the fate of the empire.

Perhaps Doran had an over simplistic view of what derailed the Irish Home Rule Bill. All he knew was that it would have been a better deal for Ireland than the hotchpotch that was served up in the 1920s. No matter how one attempted to explain it the bottom line was that there was less on the table for ordinary Irish families after the Irish Republic came into being.

V

Seven Deadly Sins

EAMONN DE VALERA AND his cronies got more than their fair share of the new Irish Republic. In 1932 they moved into the institutions vacated by the British and when Southern Ireland became a republic in 1949 went about sharing the spoils. Ordinary families were fed a diet of Catholic doctrine with great emphasis on the sins of gluttony, envy and sloth.

The sin of gluttony was used as a tool to browbeat those who had the temerity to ask for more. It was reinforced by the sin of envy, the tool used to browbeat those who dared question why their share was less than that of the chosen few. The deadly sin of sloth was preached from altars to frighten those that failed or refused to expend the sweat of their brow on servile work. The remaining four of the seven deadly sins served to tighten the Church's total control over its flock.

NETTLEGRABBERS

Jim Doran did not always see the Catholic Church in league with the State as an instrument of suppression. As a young boy he joined the elite classes when he became an altar boy. There were no altar girls and he did not see any harm in the discrimination. In truth he never thought that it was peculiar that girls were excluded. It was the way things were, girls were treated differently. They did not serve Mass, they did not go into public houses and they did not have babies unless they were married.

Jim Doran came to realise that he was living in a poor country. Poverty was the price of the liberty "yearned" for by republicans. The only industry thriving was that dedicated to transporting millions of emigrants to every corner of the world.

The lucky ones were those who could scrape together their fare by whatever means. Doran could hear Rose Brennan singing "Goodbye mother dear." The tune was pleasant enough but the lyrics for Doran said it all. "Write a letter now and then and send her all you can!"

Although only ten years of age at the time Doran found the words depressing. The proud mothers of Ireland reduced to accepting that their children had to emigrate was bad, but not as bad as having to rely on their children's hand-outs to survive.

The Catholic Church's answer to living below the poverty line was to encourage parents to have more children. Sex was a dirty word; in fact it was a word seldom used. "There are more souls burning in Hell because of sins of the flesh than for all other sins put together," the priest warned in his sermons.

Sins of the flesh were many and varied. Impure thoughts were as bad as masturbation in the eyes of the Church. Women were presumed not to have any sexual propensities except those necessary for procreation, and only then if they had received the sacrament of matrimony.

Those unfortunates who rebutted that presumption were bound to regret it. It was acknowledged that men were prone to temptation. Mortal sins ranging from impure thoughts to physical deeds were pitfalls awaiting men who did not have the grace to resist temptation.

As a pious altar boy, Jim Doran at the age of twelve knew he had the grace to resist temptation. He also knew that his favourite sister Brigitte then aged fifteen would not succumb to temptation. He was not sure about his older sister Mary, because he had seen her kissing a boy behind a haystack.

Jim was thirteen when the family crisis occurred. The sound of crying and whaling erupted around 4 a.m. It was enough to awaken the dead and it sent a cold shiver through him. Jim fathomed out that something was wrong with Brigitte. She was screaming and then he heard his mother's distress, 'No, not this. Holy Mother of God, tell me I'm having a nightmare!'

But it was not a nightmare. Jim could hear Brigitte making awful sounds as he jumped out of bed. He noticed his two young brothers huddled against each other crying.

'What's happening, Jim? What's happening to Brigitte?' One asked.

'Shush, keep quiet,' Jim said as he gingerly edged nearer the source of the commotion.

He got as far as the bedroom door when he heard the sound of a baby crying. But he knew there was no baby and in his confusion he went into his sister's bedroom. Brigitte was lying contorted on her bed and there was blood everywhere. The sound was coming from a slimy ugly looking creature lying between her legs. Jim heard his mother shouting at him to get out and that was the last thing he heard before he fainted.

When he awoke the next morning he was in his bed. He looked around his drab bedroom and noticed that the bed where his two brothers slept was empty. The image of his sister Brigitte screaming in pain came into his mind like a thunderbolt. It must have been a nightmare I had, he thought, bolting upright in his bed.

The images recurred in his mind with such clarity that he reassessed his belief that he had a nightmare. The images were too realistic, but on the other hand if there had been an emergency why was everything so quiet?

Then he began to listen and realised that everything was not normal. He could hear people talking like they do when there is a dead body in the room. It was his mother and father talking and he had heard them converse in similar half-whispers in the past. It was when his grandmother had died in her sleep and they were in shock. Like then Jim could not make out the words but somehow he knew that they were talking about his nightmare.

He heard his father's footsteps on the stairs and knew that he was coming to speak to him. The door to Jim's bedroom did not have sufficient height to permit his father to walk through without stooping. It opened and his father's head appeared.

Paddy Doran was a man of few words. Jim found him fair but there was awkwardness between them that made communication difficult. 'Are you all right?' his father asked from the bedroom door.

'Yes I'm all right. Is there something wrong daddy?'

'Things aren't too great Jim,' his father said averting his gaze. 'We've all had a terrible shock.'

There was an awkward silence during which Jim was desperately trying to think of something to say. He thought he caught the sight of tears in his father's eyes and looked away to avoid embarrassment. He realised that his father had lost his air of invincibility. He seemed vulnerable and it frightened Jim. His father broke the silence, 'Never breathe a word of what happened here last night. Will you promise me never to mention it to anyone son?'

'Yes, daddy I'll never mention it.'

'Good man', his father said turning and walking down the stairs.

***

Six months passed and Jim was finding the promise he made to his father hard to keep. There were many questions that he wanted to ask. Where is Brigitte? Why is her name never mentioned? Why are people whispering about us? Why has the priest told me that I can't serve as an altar boy anymore?

Jim suspected that the priest knew what happened to Brigitte. Since her disappearance his sermon every Sunday was about sins of the flesh. About the responsibility of parents to ensure that their daughters were not disgracing the parish by flaunting themselves and luring men into temptation. "They're doing the Devil's work and their sins will bring plague and tempest upon their parents, brothers and sisters."

The congregation knew who he was talking about and many could not resist gawking at whichever member of the Doran family happened to be within visible range.

By the time he was fourteen Jim felt anger inside him. He was angry at the sneers and jeers of his neighbours and the effect they were having on his parents. His mother had become a nervous wreck ashamed to go outside her home. His father was similarly cowed except when he found Dutch courage in the bottle. Then he would rant and rave about the hypocrisy and injustices that forced him to renounce his daughter and grandchild.

'We're nobody's,' he would say as the effects of the liquor loosened his tongue. 'I'll show them that my daughter's as good as that bastard. If she were a rich farmer's daughter he wouldn't have sent her away.'

Jim listened but never asked any questions. The story was unfolding and Jim was beginning to piece together bits of the jigsaw. The picture showed a poor Irish girl giving birth to a child outside wedlock. That was the easy bit, what was more difficult to ascertain was what had happened to the mothers and children? Why had her family been forced to send her away? Who made them do it?

At the age of fifteen Jim had made up his mind to join the IRA. If things had been different he would have joined the thousands of young emigrants departing Irish shores to make a living in some foreign land. Ireland was defunct and held no hope for the lower classes. The institutions were wrapped up in packages addressed to the lucky few that were foxy enough to grab all round them when the going was good. Nepotism was the flavour of the day and if one's father did not have influence there was nothing on offer.

The art of class discrimination was practised in the new republic from the outset. In order to get a job worthy of the name it was necessary to be adept in the Gaelic language. It was a tall order in a country where the majority of the population spoke English as their first language, and could not afford the education necessary to reach the standard required for a job in the public sector.

Application forms in Gaelic were as easy to comprehend by Jim and thousands like him as the hieroglyphics on the tombs of Egyptian Pharaohs. Someone had pulled a clever trick and one that achieved its purpose. It ensured that the proletariat either had to emigrate or starve. It was known that most would opt for the first option and that they would be a source of much needed foreign currency.

Jim hated "them" and by that he meant the ruling classes in the new Irish Republic.

***

When he joined the IRA he did so in the belief that he was joining an altruistic organisation not shackled to the corrupt institutions of the Irish Free State, the Catholic Church or Britain. The State promised by Sinn Fein was sufficiently aligned with Marxism to satisfy Jim's ideology.

The new State envisaged was the country promised by the Fenians the name of which was an anagram of the Great Lakes of America. The true Eire comprised thirty-two counties of Ireland united under one flag, not the hotchpotch served up in 1922.

Implicit in its constitution was a just society where the national cake would be divided equally. A society bound by a common desire to share the trials and tribulations of life equally. Governed by the people for the people to provide a country where favouritism took second place to meritocracy.

It was goodbye to nepotism, cronyism and all things that led to an unfair society. Kennedy was right, "Don't ask what your country can do for you, ask what you can do for your country?"

The existing infrastructures and institutions of Northern Ireland and the Irish Free State were capable of carrying the new order. When merged and honed they would provide the framework to support the three pillars of the new State, the executive, administration, and judiciary. That was what

Jim heard at Sinn Fein meetings and although many of the constitutional issues went over his head he had a good feeling about the way things were going to be.

In this mindset Jim did not see the IRA as an illegal organisation; to him it was the legitimate army of the new State. Its role and objectives were clear and distinguishable. The former was to protect and defend, and the latter to use whatever force was necessary to defeat enemies of the State. There were two enemies, the first of which was British occupation of the North and the second was the Irish Free State.

From a strategic viewpoint it was obvious that British occupation was the immediate problem and had to be solved before turning to the Free State. In fact it was generally believed that once the British withdrew, the Irish Free State would no longer exist in its present form. The birth of Eire would follow automatically and the electorate would reward those who delivered it.

What was on the table, as far as Jim could see, was the opportunity to join the army that would deliver the Irish people from the clutches of a corrupt and insular government in the Irish Free State. And bring the North, the missing link, back to its rightful place as an integral part of a United Ireland.

Such were the declared objectives of Sinn Fein whose leaders propounded that when the British were out of Ireland the rest would fall into place. It was a noble calling, and not only that, it was the only calling available to the lower classes of the Free State and Northern Catholics. The facts and figures were there for anyone who cared to look at them. The Irish government politely ignored the working classes in the Free State while Britain connived at the treatment of Catholics in the Six Counties as second class citizens.

That was the equation from which Sinn Fein had extrapolated its winning formula. In order to mount a successful campaign it was necessary to have the support or at least the silent acquiescence of a substantial proportion of the population. That was essential and could only be guaranteed in a society where a significant number of the population were sufficiently dissatisfied with government to cooperate with or at the very least not move against those active in bringing about change.

Such a situation existed in Ireland and it was a fundamental flaw which could be exploited. It existed because the vast majority of the population of the Irish Free State was sympathetic to a united Ireland, and Northern Catholics were discontented. The rudimentary ingredients were in place and all that remained was for Sinn Fein and the IRA to keep sufficient numbers of sympathisers on side.

Before Jim's mother died, she went through a tormented phase of rambling and raving in a confused state. Although only forty-five years of age, she looked much older and one did not have to be a doctor to realise that the source of her complaint was the loss of her daughter and grandchild. In her rambling she frequently referred to a horrible place where her child was being held. 'They made me do it, the priest made me do it,' were her last words. Jim heard those words and vowed that he would find his sister and save her from the "horrible place."

***

The priest was arrogant. He spoke as though it was none of Jim's business what had happened to his sister. She was evil, a non-person who brought shame on her people. 'Now get out of here before I call the guards and have you arrested,' the priest said looking down his nose at Jim. 'How dare you come in here and cross-examine me.'

The priest had regained his confidence after the mild shock of finding Jim in his office. The interview unfolded much as Jim had anticipated. He had gained entry to the Parochial House earlier through an open window and was sitting in the parish priest's office examining records when he returned. The priest was shocked, but when he recognised Jim he quickly regained his composure. 'It's you!' he said, 'what do you want?'

'I want to know where my sister Brigitte is?' Jim said without looking up from the document he was reading. 'My mother told me before she died that you arranged things.'

In Jim's eyes the parish priest represented much of what was wrong with the Irish Free State. He displayed a smug sense of superiority coupled with a peppering of intellectual arrogance. The humility and love of mankind he demanded in his sermons were nowhere to be seen now as he looked with disdain at Jim.

The priest had the same look when he was officiating at Jim's mother's funeral. It was the look of someone who had been called upon to perform a task he thought was beneath him. Not only that, the priest failed to ask the congregation to offer up prayers for the repose of the soul of the late Mrs Doran. It was a dreadful insult and implied that her soul was beyond redemption.

'You want to know about your sister?' The priest said moving to pick up the telephone. 'Very well if that's all you want I'll see what I can do,' he said dialling a number. 'I have a Mister James Doran here and he demands to know the whereabouts of his sister,' the priest said into the telephone. 'Yes that's the one, Brigitte.'

Jim remained seated waiting for the priest to conclude his call. After a short exchange the priest said, 'It would be better if you tell him yourself, I'm sure he'll wait.' He hung up the telephone, walked over to a drinks cabinet and poured himself a whisky from a decanter, 'The person I've spoken to will be here shortly to discuss your sister with you.'

In less than five minutes two policemen rushed into the room where Jim was seated on the priest's chair. 'Well if it isn't Mister Doran himself,' the sergeant said. 'We thought you'd be in The North blowing up innocent Protestants. Instead of that here you are breaking into the Parochial House pretending you're looking for your dear sister. Stand up when I speak to you! Don't they teach you any discipline in the IRA?'

Jim remained seated and to his surprise he was not frightened. He would later realise that the reason he was not afraid was that he had noticed a look of fear cross the priest's face when he heard the sergeant mention the IRA. The sergeant was renowned for his lack of discretion. He was a big awkward man whose manner was more germane to that of a loud farmer than his actual occupation. He was an advocate of summary justice and one could tell that on this occasion he was on the verge of delivering his sentence.

His fist was closed and he was looking for a suitable opening to batter Jim. But he stopped in his tracks and it seemed that he was having second thoughts. It was as though the message of his own words rebounded from the priest and the shock of being confronted by a member of the IRA dawned on him.

Jim broke the pregnant silence, 'The priest tells me you know where my sister is sergeant,' Jim heard himself say with an air of authority. 'If you would be kind enough to tell me I'll be on my way?'

'Yes I told him you could help,' the priest said walking between the sergeant and Jim. 'I never mentioned anything about the IRA. I didn't know mister Doran was a member.'

The sergeant seemed confused but eventually the implications of what the priest was saying found its mark. In recent times it had become prudent to avoid mentioning that one knew a member of the IRA and this extended to the Garda. The sergeant fumbled to say something but when nothing came out his comrade said, 'Your sister was committed to the asylum in Kerry. Fr O'Brien here can tell you more if he wants to.'

'Well father?' Jim asked.

'Now mister Doran it's not right to say she's in the asylum. No, that's not the way it is. The Sisters of Mercy are looking after your sister very well. Do you follow?'

'Can I see her?'

'Well there are procedures, but as your parish priest I'm not without influence. I think I can arrange something. Of course I'll need about a week to sort things out. Will that be agreeable to you?'

Jim spent some time considering this. He was not accustomed to being treated with this degree of civility by either members of the Garda Siochana or the Irish priesthood. The incident reinforced his belief that membership of the IRA brought with it a kudos not previously available to him. Not only that for the first time in his life he felt that he had acquired a little power in the community. He liked it, and he knew that if he were going to retain it he would have to handle it with care.

The three men before him were merely temporarily indisposed and if pushed too far would retaliate, 'That's very nice of you father,' Jim said in his most respectful tone. 'I'll get in touch next week.'

Ten years had elapsed since then and Jim never saw his sister. They told him she had committed suicide whilst the balance of her mind was disturbed. The nuns buried her in the convent graveyard and a suitable Catholic family in America adopted her son. Jim suspected that he had never been told the truth.

***

The arrival of the two Australians revived memories of Brigitte in Jim's mind. There were old scores to settle and he began to see that O'Connell and Duffy might be the answer. Duffy was illegitimate and had received harsh treatment at the hands of British institutions. He was bitter, perhaps more so than he cared to admit. Was his visit to Ireland really motivated by a desire to assist O'Connell to trace his fiancée? Or was he taking advantage of a situation to even old scores of his own?

Now Jim looked at his boss and realised that he was waiting for an answer, 'Sorry Michael I lost my train of thought, what did you say?'

'The two Australians, what do you think?'

'I don't think they're serious players in the patriot game but we can use them for the time being.'

'Jim for fuck sakes can't you answer a straight question? All I want to know for now is whether we can trust them?'

'One is never sure about anything in this day and age Michael, but on this occasion I'm almost sure we can.'

'Jesus, that's a very good reference coming from you Jim. What are we going to do with them?'

'I'll use them to help me for the time being if you have no objections, Michael?'

'On your head be it.'

***

Jim saw that the combined talents of the two men could be the answer to a problem he had identified a year earlier. That was when he was twenty-four years of age and was beginning to see flaws in the ideology of his youth. It was a process that happened gradually and its cause was difficult to pinpoint.

If asked to attribute his disillusionment to a particular event he would have explained that it was the realisation that the new order was as corrupt as the old. Eire was not going to provide the panacea he believed it would when he joined the IRA. There was too much internal bickering and jockeying for positions of power.

He had not given sufficient thought to the effects of factor X in the equation. The human imperative that is best described as the pecking order innate in the makeup of mankind. The quest for a United Ireland was proving expensive in terms of human life and sacrificial lambs were paying the price. The blood of innocent bystanders detracted from the nobility of the cause.

Jim disagreed with sectarian killings that involved tit-for-tat murders. An innocent Protestant's life for that of an innocent Catholic, that was the way things were turning out. Although he followed orders and pulled the trigger, he did so with a heavy heart. 'What good is it doing?' He would ask.

'It's not for us to ask why,' he was told, 'our job is to carry out orders.'

But Jim Doran did ask, and was given no logical explanation. It began to occur to him that the war was a charade. An excuse for gangsters to partake in criminal activities; Loyalist paramilitaries seldom confronted the IRA and vice-versa.

It was as though an understanding existed between Nationalist and Loyalist terrorist groups that they would not shoot each other. Instead they would use innocent members of the opposing community as an indirect way of inflicting pain on each other.

At first the explanation expounded for this strategy had perverse logic. The paradox was that instead of harming the standing of paramilitary organisations in their respective communities, it enhanced it. Ordinary people seldom looked further than the organisation that carried out the atrocity.

Protestants blamed the IRA and Catholics blamed the Loyalists. Nobody asked why the opposing paramilitaries were not shooting at each other. If the question had been asked people might come to realise that their supposed protectors were exploiting them. Of course that was not going to happen because the irony of sectarian killings is that victims turned to paramilitaries for protection.

From an IRA perspective the killing of Protestants had two advantages. First it made it seem that the IRA was avenging the killing of Catholics, and second, it gave Catholics the impression that the IRA could be trusted more than the Royal Ulster Constabulary to protect them.

Jim Doran saw himself as an executioner in the sense that he executed people sentenced to death by his bosses. Instructions came from above and were passed down the chain of command. The command structure was designed to ensure that the executioner would not know from whence the death order originated.

As Jim Doran matured he started to question whether he was his own man or merely a tool being exploited by someone he'd never met. He read the papers and kept abreast of movers and shakers in the Patriot Game. Cracks began to appear in the ideological shield that he had envisaged when he first took up arms.

The most disturbing thing was the realisation that not all of the people selected for execution were enemies of the republic. Some were selected because they were merely in the way or would not bend to the demands of Sinn Fein. There was also a lucrative demand for the services of an executioner and there was no doubt in Jim's mind that his bosses had been well paid for many of the assassinations he carried out.

Mercedes cars complimented recently acquired opulent homes of people Jim knew to be high up in the Patriot Game. They were the same people that could not afford a decent standard of living a few years before. It was obvious that money was being diverted and the high ideals preached by Sinn Fein were written in sand. Jim Doran could see history repeating itself in the event of a United Ireland.

VI

Chris the Hat

AFTER BALLIVOR'S COMMENT TO John he began to think about joining the CID. He now had a murder arrest under his belt and had moved up in the popularity polls with his sergeant and inspector. More importantly, the detective chief inspector had as good as told him that a secondment was his for the asking.

If John had any lingering doubts they were put to rest by the intervention of fate one night whilst he was on duty. He was alone at 3 a.m. parked in his patrol car. The streets were deserted and he was about to leave his observation point when he noticed a lone man walking towards the City Centre. He was wearing a pork-pie hat and John kept him under observation until he disappeared under a bridge called The Railway Arches.

The man did not seem to be taking any notice as he sauntered along the pavement with his head down. The police car was not fully concealed but neither was it exposed. John was surprised when the man walked up to him and said pointing to his hat, 'They call me Chris the Hat because I always wear this.'

John passed the time with the man and listened dutifully as he rambled on about nothing in particular. After a time John realised that the topic had taken on a more serious tone.

'Ya can tell that half-Irish bastard that I'll shoot him the fist chance I get if ya like.' Chris announced as he walked off into the night.

Police experience had taught John that words could be taken at their natural and grammatical face value regardless of their intended meaning. The literal meaning of the words used was enough to give him a chance to test Ballivor's sincerity. If he was serious about my joining the CID this will do the trick, John thought, when he submitted a report to Ballivor.

The following night John was summoned to Ballivor's office. He was reading John's report and asked for explanations and expansions of certain details. When he had finished reading the report he placed it on his desk. He looked at John whilst maintaining attention on the report by tapping it with his index finger. 'Have you discussed the contents of this with anyone, John?' He asked still tapping the report.

'No, sir.'

'Does that include WPC Hogan?'

John was shocked by the impertinent question. He had

since learned that Jane Hogan and Ballivor lived together as man and wife. He must know something about what happened at the Seduction Post, John thought. 'No sir, I haven't discussed it with anyone.'

To John's relief Ballivor changed the subject, 'I'm very grateful to you for coming directly to me with your suspicion John.'

John relaxed and could see an opportunity to discuss his joining the CID. 'I'm glad you're pleased sir. Would this be a good time to talk about me doing a spell in CI D?

'Of course, have you thought about joining us?'

'Yes, it's what I want to do sir,' John said. 'If you still think I'm suitable?'

'I've been thinking about that John,' Ballivor said leaning back in his chair. 'But I want to be sure I'm backing a winner. There's something bothering me.'

He wants to know what happened at the Seduction Post, John thought. That's why he pretended he wanted me in the CID. I should have known all he wanted was a chance to cross-examine me. 'Bothering you sir?'

'It's a little embarrassing John, but I suppose we should clear it up if you have no objections?'

What am I going to say, John thought, I'll deny everything, obviously Jane hasn't told him or he wouldn't be asking me. 'I've no objections sir, ask me anything you like?'

Ballivor was relaxed and there was no indication that he was going to break into a jealous fit. John was anticipating what he would say and knew he had to be careful. Ballivor was not going to be fobbed off with platitudes but neither was John going to submit to a browbeating. The bottom line was that he had not screwed Jane and no doubt that is what Ballivor wanted confirming.

'Did you piss yourself when you saw Mrs Knight?' Ballivor asked as though it was the most natural thing in the world.

John never saw it coming. He recoiled as the implications of the question hit him. It was as though Ballivor had struck him a physical blow. If I say I pissed myself it'll kill any chance I have of getting into the CID, John thought, if I tell the truth it's tantamount to admitting that I screwed his woman. The first commandment of survival in the police is to deny everything to the death, but Ballivor saw what he saw and was not playing fair. 'Why do you think that sir?' John fudged.'

'There were wet stains around your crotch when I saw you and I am curious as to how they got there.'

John resented being reminded of the embarrassment of ejaculating in his trousers. He summoned as much dignity as he could muster, 'No sir, I didn't urinate in my trousers.'

'In that case you must have ejaculated either shortly before you arrived at the scene or when you saw the dead body?'

Ballivor had put it in such a way that one was glad to tell the truth. The alternative was tantamount to admitting to suffering from some sort of necrophilia. Fuck you! John thought, if you want to know I nearly screwed your woman that's up to you. 'It was shortly before I arrived at the scene sir … It was my fault sir…I want to apologise…'

'Thank you John, I've got the picture,' Ballivor interrupted. 'When do you finish your tour of nights?'

John looked up relieved but bewildered. What next, he thought, where's the next low ball going to come from? 'Sunday is my last night sir.'

'Fine,' Ballivor said as though they had just concluded a game of chess. 'I want you to check how often Chris uses that route and the precise time he emerges from under the Railway Arches. Please let me have the information by Monday afternoon.'

***

At 2.45 a.m. the following Tuesday John found himself off duty in uniform with Ballivor. They parked in the same spot where John had first seen Chris and John's job was to walk up to Chris and engage him in conversation until Ballivor took over.

'That's him sir.' John said when he saw Chris in the distance.

'Don't call me Sir all the time John. The reason I wear civilian clothing is to make it less obvious that I'm a policeman. If you insist on calling me Sir I may as well wear a blue light on my forehead!'

'Sorry Seamus.'

'As soon as our man comes out of the dark I want you to hit him as hard as you can in the stomach.'

John thought he had misheard. It was against police

procedures and a criminal offence to batter someone. 'I'm sorry Seamus what did you say?'

'You heard.' Ballivor said flatly. 'Are you up for it?'

'How do you know you can trust me?' John asked.

'I don't,' Ballivor said. 'Of course, if you think about it, you're the one who should ask whether you can trust me.'

'Of course, sorry I asked.' John said getting out of the car. When he saw the outline of Chris walking towards him John began his patrol. He adjusted his pace in order to arrive at the mouth of the Arch at the same time as the target. But Chris took longer than John anticipated and he was beginning to doubt whether he would emerge.

Then he heard footsteps and a Scots accent, 'Good night officer.'

The element of surprise was supposed to be the other way round and was lost to John. It was not going to be easy to administer a sucker punch, but he knew what he had to do and delivered a short jab that made feeble contact with Chris.

'What the fuck are ya doing!' Chris exclaimed landing a left hook on John's jaw followed by a painful kick to the groin. John reeled back expecting further pain but it did not happen. Ballivor had rendered Chris helpless in a hammerlock and bar.

'Steady on old man,' Ballivor said forcing Chris's arm up his back.

'Donna break ma fucking arm ya Irish cunt.'

'Is that a proper way to greet someone you have sent a message to?'

'Ya know me, Seamus I was just a shouting ma big mouth off,' Chris said, struggling to free himself. 'Jesus Christ man you're breaking ma fucking arm.'

'Handcuff, and search him,' Ballivor said to John.

Ballivor walked under the Arch. After what seemed like eternity he emerged brandishing a Browning semi-automatic pistol. He showed it to Chris. 'Is this loaded?'

'I donna know what you're talking about,' Chris said turning his gaze away from the pistol.

'There's one way of finding out,' Ballivor said pointing the gun at Chris's private parts.

'Far fuck sake man donna it's loaded.'

John saw Ballivor engage the gun and thought he was about to fire. 'Don't do it sir, he's not worth it.'

'Did someone call me Sir?' Ballivor asked looking at John.

'I'm sorry.' John said. 'I thought you were going to shoot him.'

'Maybe you're right,' Ballivor said removing the magazine from the pistol butt and handing it to John. 'Are there any rounds in this?'

John checked the magazine and counted eight 9mm rounds. He reloaded and handed it to Ballivor. He replaced the magazine in the pistol and pointed it at Chris.

'Look Seamus donna do anything silly, I'm no a killer.'

There was a short silence after which Ballivor said, 'Remove his handcuffs John please?'

After John did so Ballivor tossed the loaded gun to Chris, 'Here's your gun mate.'

Chris caught it and looked around him. John realised that the situation had changed. Chris was no longer cowed and seemed to have regained his cocky stance as he looked at the pistol in his hand. John knew what was going through Chris' mind and before he could put it into action John stunned him with a blow that landed just under his left ear.

Later the three men sat in the police car waiting for Chris to come round. John sat in the front passenger seat in silence. He was bewildered at the course of events and realised that it was not over. Ballivor sat behind the steering wheel studying the pistol. Chris, still dazed managed to sit up in the rear seat and was holding his hands to his face.

John knew that Chris could be arrested for being in possession of a section one firearm and ammunition. That was the least that could happen to him, not to mention threatening to kill a police officer and assaulting a police officer in the execution of his duty. Perhaps things were going better than they looked and if they were he had Ballivor to thank for it. 'Who gave you the gun Chris?' Ballivor said after a long silence.

There was no reply and John could feel a knot in his stomach as he anticipated what was going to happen next. Why don't you answer him you silly bastard? He thought looking at Chris.

'What gun?' Chris said, 'I have no gun.'

'This one, it has your grubby fingerprints all over it. If you've forgotten John here can confirm that when he turned out your lights you were holding it. Isn't that right John?'

'Yes, that's right.' John said realising for the first time why Ballivor gave Chris the gun. What was not so clear was why he had also made sure John's fingerprints were on the magazine.

'Okay Seamus you've got me over a barrel.' Chris said with an air of despondency. 'They'll kill me if I grass them and you'll fit me up if I don't.'

'I don't know about them Chris but you're right about me.'

'What exactly do you want me to do?'

'Name the person who gave you this and we can be on our way.' Ballivor said brandishing the pistol.

'All right I'll tell you; it's one of your own. Detective Sergeant Priest gave me the gun.' Chris said looking at Ballivor. 'Now can I go?'

Ballivor thought for a moment. 'I'm sorry old man I should have made it clear at the beginning that there are two parts to the question. You have answered part A. Part B is not as difficult but it's just as important.'

'I should have known,' Chris said, 'Never trust a fucking copper.'

'You trusted Priest so now all we want to know is whether you are prepared to change your allegiance to us?'

'You're asking me to work for you?'

'There you are Chris, you've unpacked question B straight away.'

'I'll work for you Seamus but I'll only deal with this man here.' Chris said touching John's arm. 'You know where to find me if I'm no dead.'

NETTLEGRABBERS

***

John submitted his application and within a week was informed that he had been granted a secondment to CID as a trainee detective constable. It was his last night in uniform and after the shift briefing he walked out of the police station to his patrol car. He was making an entry in the logbook when he noticed Ballivor. 'I'm glad I've caught up with you John. I want you to do something for me around midnight if you don't mind?'

John was keen to help his new boss and did not question the reason he wanted someone breathalysed. Ballivor explained that he and the target would walk out of the Irish Club at 11.55 p.m. and go their separate ways. When the target drove onto the public road John was to follow him for a short distance before commencing the breathalyser procedure.

The target's car would have a defective rear light, which was a moving traffic offence and enough to give John legal reason to breathalyse the driver. Ballivor had thought of everything and John saw no problem in obliging his future boss.

At the appointed time he kept observations and saw Ballivor walk out of the club with the target. They went to their respective car's and John waited until the target drove out of the club car park. He saw that the rear light was defective and after a short distance he activated his sirens and blue lights. The target came to a halt and waited for John. 'Good evening sir, are you aware that your rear light's inoperative?'

'No officer.' The man said calmly.

'You're committing a moving traffic offence and I'm therefore empowered to require you to provide a breath specimen. If you fail or refuse you will be guilty of an offence. Do you understand?'

'Of course I understand I'm a detective sergeant on police business.' The driver said in an authoritative tone, '...this is a police car so you'll also have to prosecute the Chief Constable for permitting its use!'

This is not as straightforward as I was led to believe, John thought. In fact it's a crock of shit, another Ballivor special. He should have warned me that I was going to be confronted with a police officer on duty. 'May I see your warrant card please sergeant?'

'You may, and then I want to get on with my work if that's all right with you constable.' The sergeant said holding up his warrant card for John to read.

"Detective Sergeant Priest!" The name leaped out at John. That was the person Chris the Hat said gave him the gun to shoot Ballivor. This is too much, John thought; I've a good mind not to go through with it. Ballivor should have told me the score. But on second thoughts perhaps he's testing me before he allows me to handle Chris? If I mess up, he'll know that I'm not up to it. That's it; he wants to see how I react under pressure.

John could smell the alcohol on Priest's breath and decided to go ahead with Ballivor's instructions. 'I'm sorry sergeant, I can smell alcohol on your breath and I suspect that your are driving with over the prescribed amount of alcohol in your blood. I require you to provide me with a specimen of your breath. If you fail or refuse I shall arrest you.' John said, reaching into Priest's car and removing the ignition keys.

'Get fucked, you stupid bastard,' Priest said in a flash of anger. 'If you don't give me back those keys I'll arrest you.'

'Please don't use obscene language sergeant you're only making things worse for yourself.'

'I'll do more than that if you don't give me my keys back!' Priest threatened getting out of his car and moving towards John menacingly.

John radioed his controller for assistance. The significance of this was not lost on Priest and he changed tactics. He apologised and pleaded with John to forget the whole thing. 'I've only had a few but you know I won't pass the breathalyser. Let me go and I'll owe you a favour.'

John's assistance call brought several police cars with their lights flashing and within minutes the area looked like a major crime scene. The duty inspector arrived and instructed John to arrest Priest.

***

Later Priest refused to speak except to demand his right to make a telephone call. He used it to speak in private to the head of Birmingham Serious Crime Squad. Later a senior detective from Birmingham City Police arrived in Coventry and took possession of £2000 in various envelopes that Priest was carrying when arrested. The senior detective's explanation that the money belonged to the police informer's fund lacked credibility.

After speaking to the Birmingham detective John's inspector distanced himself from the instruction he earlier gave John to arrest Priest. There is little doubt that if it could have been done safely they would have permitted Priest to walk free. But it was too late, the system was in motion and it would be more dangerous to reverse it than to permit it to run its course.

John could see that his inspector wanted to put as much clear water between himself and the decision to breathalyse Priest as possible. The inspector went over every detail of the arrest looking for any excuse to refuse the charge. There was no flaw in the procedure and the exercise only served to remind John that he could not rely on the inspector's support in this matter.

John realised that Ballivor had exposed him to the wrath of Priest's powerful friends. They would not let this rest and would create their chance to get even. That was how the game was played. The Dirty Tricks Brigade with long arms and wide brushes worked their magic through the Complaints Department. A specious investigation was all that was needed to gain access to the public and private lives of wayward police officers. It was doubtful that even the famous Ballivor could withstand the might of the police internal disciplinary machine.

VII

✷

The Making of a Monster

SIR EDWARD BROWN-COX HEAD of MI5 was schooled at Eaton, read history at Oxford and from there to the Officer Training Academy, Sandhurst. There he underwent basic officer training before turning his attention to the study of military intelligence.

Implicit, but not expressed in the Sandhurst curriculum there is a collateral subject that runs from day one to graduation. Trainee commissioned officers are schooled in the art of maintaining a dignified aloofness over commoners. The lesson is delivered through a subtle reliance on reverse psychology on the Drill Square and Assault Course.

Non-commissioned officers are in charge of both and are encouraged to give trainee commissioned officers "hell" whilst under their span of control. "Get those fucking arms up sir/madam," is one of the milder rebukes often heard echoing off the surrounding walls. Sir Edward understood the significance of the lesson.

It was a reminder of what would happen if the balance of power in the British constitution shifted in favour of the majority. "Deliver the coup de grace gracefully gentlemen. Always remember that officers are gentlemen and sergeant majors are bastards. If one has to deal with commoners the better part of valour is to humour them. The pecking order in nature will do the rest."

***

Sir Edward spent most of his army service in military intelligence apart from a period of three years when he was the Assistant Provost Marshall in Northern Ireland. He held the rank of colonel when he was appointed head of MI5 at the age of 50. He was an English aristocrat, a gentleman with a sense of fair play iced with positive charm and grace.

His other attributes included a brilliant tactical mind capable of analysing complex problems. In his ten years as head of MI5 he never faltered. He maintained the delicate balance necessary to keep government ministers at bay and his aristocratic obligations fulfilled.

Sir Edward came to the helm at a time when MI5 and MI6 were still reeling from the effects of several scandals. Whitehall mandarins had carefully selected him because he was clean. His public persona was untarnished and he could be relied upon to "do the right thing." The latter expression meant that he could be relied upon to safeguard the interests of the Crown and the Aristocracy.

To Sir Edward there was no conflict of interest in his paying homage to his ancestral roots. Britain was a two-tier constitution in which the House of Commons looked after the interests of non-aristocrats. That was the way it had been for centuries. There are checks and balances in the British Constitution, which provide fairness for all.

The demarcation lines had been blurred somewhat in recent times. A resurgence of The Rule of Law was partly to blame. Sir Edward knew the origins of the Rule from the writings of Aristotle and its plagiarism by Dicey, an English legal clerk. It means that everyone except the monarch is subject to the law and its effect in theory at least is that public and private individuals can be prosecuted if they act outside the law.

In practice the rule of law does not deliver the high ideals it implies. On the contrary, it encourages State institutions to employ surreptitious means to frustrate it. High and low officials soon learn that there is a limit to idealistic restriction on power. If the right circumstances exist, abuse of power will be tolerated and even encouraged by the masses. National security is high on the list and those involved in its administration are well versed in creating the right circumstances.

On the other hand one could not take for granted that the might of the English Legal System would not be invoked if it were expedient to do so. The British people expected as much and the key to avoiding such an event was to ensure that one's secret activities were kept secret. Sir Edward was a realist and worked on the assumption that one could be called to account.

***

By the early 1970s Sir Edward came to recognise that he had a problem in Northern Ireland. He was not happy with the situation or the methods employed to hoodwink him. The problem was that he had been a party to creating a monster in Northern Ireland. He connived with the Orange Order and the Royal Ulster Constabulary in permitting the Provisional IRA to come into being.

The Provisional IRA represented the seminal seed from which the proliferation of paramilitary organisations had grown. Things were out of hand and Sir Edward suspected that was what was envisaged from the outset. The more he studied and reviewed the situation the more he came to the conclusion that bad people had used him to do bad things.

The proposal was first mooted by representatives of Ulster Orange Lodges in the exclusive Athenaeum Club, London in 1967. It was founded on the belief that the Fenians were planning something big. The Orange Order did not accept that the civil rights campaign in Ulster was what it seemed. They would not believe that for the first time since Irish independence, Irish nationalists were pursuing a non-violent political campaign and they produced evidence to that effect.

Sir Edward now knew that the evidence provided to bring him on side was convincing and contrived.

NETTLEGRABBERS

***

On the surface nationalists abandoned objections to their politicians sitting as members of the British Parliament. Nationalist MPs had taken their place in the House of Commons for the first time since the partition.

Maiden speeches demanding equal voting rights for Catholics were making waves in the "cradle of democracy". They were being greeted by standing ovations and were bound to lead to a change in the Northern Irish voting system. Hitherto the sound of IRA bombs could be relied upon to drown the effect of nationalist speeches. But that was no longer the case and the Official IRA had woken up to the fact that its bombs merely served to defeat its purpose.

The Unionists could see a United Ireland on the horizon and went about preventing it. That was their right and to many their duty. The problem was that in the absence of IRA activity it was almost impossible to justify refusing to share power with nationalists. It was obvious that something must be done.

The something to be done could be left to the Unionists. They knew their enemy and that if the right conditions were created it would not be long before the IRA would show its ugly head. The Royal Ulster Constabulary could be relied upon to flush out potential terrorists in the Nationalist Bogside of Derry. The favour required from MI5 was to turn a blind eye whilst Orange double agents penetrated the Nationalists population in their back yard.

It was agreed, and by 1970 the Provisional IRA was up and running. It had delivered as expected and it was safe to resume normal services. But something had changed and MI5 found it impossible to put the genie back in its bottle. The intelligence service was being frustrated at every attempt and Sir Edward began to see through the Orange rouse. The excuse that the Provisional IRA was better prepared than originally thought flew in the face of intelligence reports on Sir Edward's desk.

He realised that he had been hoodwinked and that he had made a mistake. If it ever came to light that the British Secret Service had played a part in bringing about the current Ulster situation it would cause great damage to the service. The only saving grace was that the new Provisional IRA was perceived as the old enemy under a new name. Nobody stood back and asked why?

Sir Edward did not ponder that question because there were more immediate questions that could cause great embarrassment. Heads would roll in high places if the truth ever emerged. The "Rule of Law" would be used against those who had permitted the use of brothels to raise funds for Ulster Loyalist terrorists. The scheme was well established before word of it reached the ears of MI5 spymasters. It mattered little now because of the overwhelming evidence that MI5 had been involved in the scheme.

***

Sir Edward had a quick eye for similarities in situations that in the normal course of events would be different. It was spotted by his boss way back when Edward was a young army intelligence officer. He would call Edward into

NETTLEGRABBERS

his office and order him to employ his "unusual talent" to spot the flaw in some report or other. After a time the term was used by whomsoever required Edward's assistance and it stuck with him thereafter.

Over the years Edward himself refined it so that in modern usage it conveyed a special meaning. It communicated to those close to him that something was not quite right with the matter at hand. Operation Nettle Grabbers owed its existence to two things. First, reports emanating from field officers about the Birmingham Serious Crime Squad, and second James Ward-Riley's application to join MI5 or MI6.

***

Problems in Birmingham City Police were known to MI5 for several years. There were numerous reports about the activities of its Serious Crime Squad from various sources. The Home Office, ordinary police officers and members of the public were on record expressing misgivings. The official line was that the matter would be rectified when Birmingham Police became part of the proposed new West Midlands Police in the near future.

The Home Office was on tenterhooks and constantly applied pressure on Sir Edward to ensure that the situation in Birmingham was contained. But in typical Home Office style that was as far as it was prepared to go. There were countless objections to the proposed boundary changes in the area and it was not politically expedient to officially acknowledge that there was a problem in the police. Sir Edward was given a free hand provided he did not show it.

The amalgamation of police forces ranging from Coventry to Wolverhampton took place and it was believed that the "Birmingham Mafia" as the Serious Crime Squad was now known would drown in the new force. Sir Edward had his doubts and his unusual talent had warned him on several occasions that the problem would not be so easily resolved.

***

James Ward-Riley's proposal had traversed the diplomatic circuit before it landed on Sir Edward's desk. There was great debate as to whether it should be handled by the Australian Embassy in England or the British Embassy in Australia. There were no precedence or standing orders to guide the Civil Service, a situation that caused great confusion in an environment where strict adherence to one or the other is deemed essential.

If a procedure had been in place it is unlikely that James' proposal would have reached the head of MI5. But it did and Sir Edward saw in it the possible answer to an ongoing problem with the police in Birmingham. It looked almost too good to be true and would have been rejected for that reason but for Sir Edward's unusual talent for spotting analogies.

The mention of Fenian Bonds, the disappearance of an Australian girl and the suggestion of IRA involvement at Birmingham Airport could all be connected to current intelligence. The Fenian Bond drug scam was common knowledge. Ulster Loyalist terrorists bragged openly about the way they embarrassed the IRA in the Irish Republic. James Ward-Riley's proposal added a new dimension. His suggestion that the bonds were smuggled through Birmingham Airport, if accurate, was a significant breakthrough.

That coupled with references to his sister going missing at Birmingham Airport highlighted a different problem. It was not the first document in which it was suggested that girls were taken from the English Midlands to Belfast for the purpose of prostitution. That would not normally concern MI5, but there was a clandestine purpose behind the brothels. The purpose was a potential nightmare for MI5 and it was in danger of leaking into the public domain.

***

Aristocrats from birth are taught the importance of maintaining social cohesion amongst themselves. Sir Edward was well versed in the art and his conscience would not permit him to violate the rules of "cricket" when interacting with members of his own class. A gentleman's word is his bond, but only when given to a fellow gentleman.

When dealing with commoners the rule was not binding if it conflicted with the interests of the State as perceived by the ruling classes. The ruling class is confined to aristocrats and does not embrace members of parliament, nouveau-riche or bourgeoisie. In such cases a gentleman is not bound by his word and this subtle distinction was foremost in Sir Edward's mind when he gave certain undertakings to James-Ward Riley.

In practice it made little difference because James Ward-Riley was not aware of the special bond between aristocrats. Like most other people he had heard the expression that a gentleman's word is his bond. And on that basis he understood correctly that Sir Edward would do all he could to keep his word and that was enough. Sir Edward omitted to mention MI5's involvement in Ulster brothels to James and that was the difference. If James had been a member of the club he would have been told everything.

***

This morning Sir Edward was concerned at the loss of life and maiming of innocent people by IRA bombs in Birmingham the previous evening. He refused to permit his mind to dwell on the possibility that the Orange Order were in some way responsible. He knew they would not be directly involved. They were merely facilitators, a role they had played on previous occasions.

But on this occasion things might not pan out as they planned. There was a weakness in their chain and it came in the form of a West Midlands Police Officer. 'This fellow Bayliss, is he on the move?'

'Yes Sir Edward,' his secretary said, 'Everything's in hand, our people have reported that things are going to plan.'

'Any further developments regarding the bombing of Birmingham?'

'Yes. The West Midlands Police claim to have the men responsible in custody Sir Edward.'

'Really, how odd. Have we been watching the wrong people?'

VIII

❋

One-eye Jack

MICHAEL LYNCH, CHIEF OF IRA Intelligence, Head of Sinn Fein Justice Department and Liaison Officer IRA English Department, had acquired great power within his sphere of influence. This was his 40th birthday and the morning after the Birmingham Bombings.

The bombings coincided with other things that were happening in his life. In the recent past he had come to look forward to the time when his efforts in the English Midlands would come to a head. He found himself thinking that once the project was over he should retire to a sunny Caribbean island. But he knew that he would not be happy because the woman he loved was indisposed. She was currently detained at Her Majesty's pleasure in Holloway prison.

Michael Lynch knew that he had been lucky. He had walked many tight ropes in his life. Diverting funds from

IRA coffers was not a healthy occupation anymore than involvement in the mayhem in Birmingham. The first carried an outright death sentence and the latter was nearly worse because it involved a slow lingering death in an English prison. Uncle Pat was right; 'If you keep at it long enough you're sure to be caught.'

Michael Lynch was adept at keeping one step ahead of the authorities. And he had something else, he was lucky. For example today the West Midlands Police were providing him with an alibi. It could only happen to me, he thought, watching the police news conference on TV.

"The police have announced a significant breakthrough in their investigation into last night's bombings in Birmingham. A police spokesman has confirmed that an unspecified number of men were detained in Heysham attempting to board the Duke of Lancaster ferry to Belfast. Detectives from the West Midlands Police Bomb Squad and the Regional Crime Squad are believed to have been sent to Heysham to assist the local police."

***

Lynch did not fit the picture portrayed in the media of the paradigm Irish terrorist. If one met him on the street he would give the impression of being a middle aged, well-to-do businessman. Perhaps a solicitor or doctor going about his business and not very much concerned with the hustle and bustle taking place around him. His pleasant countenance and polite manner would encourage one to approach him if one wanted to know the time. And in such an event one would receive the information requested and any additional help Mr Lynch felt was needed.

That was the side of his personality Lynch spontaneously rather than deliberately showed to the world. To his face people called him Jack Heart, but behind his back they called him One-Eyed-Jack. The nickname referred to the Jack of Hearts in a pack of playing cards. Card players know that the Jack of Hearts is one of the knaves whose head is shown side on. Many people presume that the reason is that the hidden side is too ugly to be shown.

Those who had seen the other side of Michael Lynch's personality could testify to the appropriateness of his nickname. It was not always so, because in his youth Lynch was a pleasant boy. His mother had earmarked him for the priesthood but as things turned out that was not to be.

That episode of his life had long been relegated to the remote recesses of his mind. It was unimportant, irrelevant and a little embarrassing. There were more important things to think about. Decisions to be made and as Uncle Pat would say, "Worlds to be conquered." Uncle Pat Doherty introduced Michael to the Patriot Game, an introduction Pat would live to regret.

***

Pat was a mild serious man who used to pop in and out of the Lynch household for as far back as Michael could remember. He would arrive unannounced in his big American car, stay the night, and leave early the following morning. The most memorable thing about his visits was that he always brought sweets for the children. His comings and goings were never to be discussed, just that he lived somewhere in Dublin, and that he was mother's brother.

The Lynch household gave no hint of its political affiliations. Michael's father was a well-off member of the local community who spent his time running his 200-acre farm. The Lynch's were rich by Irish standards and were reared in the knowledge that they were numbered amongst the upper classes. Mrs Mary Lynch, nee Doherty came from good stock and received a strict Catholic convent education. Whilst her husband looked after the farm she oversaw domestic matters. She went to inordinate lengths to ensure that her children maintained a well-polished aloofness from "ordinary folk" in the neighbourhood. Her speciality was the art of gentle persuasion and indirect indoctrination. By providing hypothetical examples of the gloom and doom that was the inevitable outcome of certain conduct, she was able to steer her children in the direction she wanted without actually addressing her remarks to anyone in particular.

Instead she relied on a process of eliminating various "types" through a litany of forbidden conduct. People who visited public houses and drank too much would come to a bad end. So would people who assembled at street corners, or did not go to Mass, or did not take the sacraments or did not honour their father and mother.

By the time her two daughter's reached their twenties they were married into families of similar standing. Her three sons received education at top institutions, Joe was well on his way to becoming the local senator, Patrick was the heir apparent and was at school at an agricultural institution in mainland Europe.

***

In recognition of the goodness of God, Mary Lynch harboured a desire that her remaining son would become a priest. Hence Michael was dispatched to read theology at Maynooth Seminary College in preparation for his ordination.

But Michael had more secular inclinations and soon succumbed to his penchant for Dublin nightlife. He found the road to Dublin discotheques more appealing than parodies about the Road to Damascus. To him parables about lame camels were more difficult to assimilate than hot gossip about the Dublin night scene. In less than six months at the seminary, Michael had spent all his savings and found that his allowance from his parents was insufficient to support his life style. He devised various ploys to elicit additional funds from the only source he knew, his parents.

He felt confident that he had achieved the impossible and that the extra allowance allocated was a permanent arrangement. But he underestimated his mother. To his surprise word of his activities reached her and he received a summons to go home.

Michael was surprised at the depth and accuracy of his mother's information about his activities. She countered every lie with a fact, the accuracy of which astounded him.

He believed that she must have had him followed, for she knew too much to be guessing.

Her rebuke was subtly garnished with an air of disappointment at the way she had been let down by her youngest son. She prognosticated that Hell and damnation were the inevitable outcome in the next life, but meanwhile certain changes would be made in this one. The sacrifice of the Mass would be offered to appease God for the betrayal committed by her son. The Virgin Mother would be implored to intercede on his behalf.

In addition Mary Lynch would make the ultimate sacrifice of bearing the pain of withdrawing her son from Maynooth. The shame of it was too great to contemplate. How could she face the indignity of having to live amongst people who would come to know her dark secret? People who were expecting to join her at the village chapel to hear her son say his first Mass. The same people who would extend the counterfeit hand of sorrow whilst secretly rejoicing at her humiliation. It was a terrible cross for a mother to bear. Michael felt bad; he had let his mother down and that was something he never wanted to do. She was a good woman whose only fault was that she had been brought up in a cocoon, shielded from the harsh realities of the world by a loving husband and fawning children. Yes, Michael would play the role of the prodigal son and provide his mother with a purpose. She was now bent on saving his soul and this would be achieved by sending him to Trinity College, Dublin, where he would study for a degree.

Her brother Patrick Doherty had agreed to be his guardian and to allow Michael to share his flat. It was settled, Michael found that he had been expertly manoeuvred into playing the alternative role mapped out for him by his mother.

***

Trinity College, Dublin, is Ireland's answer to Oxbridge. An educational institution established under British Rule to cater for the sons of high-ranking British officials. Today, the offspring of the Irish bourgeoisie are educated in this hallowed institution. It produces graduates who have been encouraged to carry themselves with a degree of aloofness. A showing of intellectual arrogance founded on the premise that they have been set apart from the proletariat.

A degree from Trinity is a key capable of opening many doors of opportunity in the new republic. Doors firmly closed to ordinary members of the Irish population. Uncle Pat was educated in the "British North". The education system there was better, and further education was available to everyone. The system in the Irish Free State excluded pupils whose parents could not afford to pay the hidden costs involved. Michael Lynch's parents could afford to pay and that was enough to secure him a place in the highest educational institution in the Free State.

At the age of nineteen, he took up residence in his uncle's flat and became an undergraduate. At the age of twenty-two, he graduated from Trinity armed with a degree in sociology.

Meanwhile he learned that his Uncle Pat was a B commander in the Irish Republican Brotherhood. He would never have guessed; the news came as a complete shock. Michael had in his mind a different picture of what members of the Irish Republican Brotherhood looked like. Uncle Pat did not fit that picture he was too nice, a quiet man not given to violence in word or deed.

To the normal Irish person the Irish Republican Brotherhood was an association seldom heard of. Sinn Fein and the Provisional Irish Republican Army were the order of the day. Few understood the subtle interplay between the different organisations.

Michael had much to learn but he already knew that there was a deep-rooted respect amongst the population of Ireland for members of subversive organisations. "Rebels," was the collective popular label used to identify those engaged in "The Cause."

The Cause was also a collective term, a broad definition that conjured up the notion of a United Ireland free from British influence. It was a vague notion inasmuch as it failed to provide a clear agenda of how its objectives would be achieved. To the average person in the street the why and wherefore of what was taking place in the name of achieving a United Ireland was something about which they had no say. Different factions had different opinions and methods that they kept to themselves. The only thing about which everyone was to some degree in accord was that Ireland belonged to the Irish. That somewhere in the distant past there was an "English" invasion that resulted in England taking control.

In 1922 Britain returned twenty-six counties, but retained control of the six counties of Ulster. The struggle today was to persuade England to return these six-counties. Uncle Pat did not see "The Cause" in such simple terms and explained that it did not tell the whole story, but it was the way Nationalists wanted ordinary people to see it. It was important because in order to mount a successful campaign it was necessary to have the sympathy of sufficient people. Otherwise the campaign would be doomed.

The notion of a United Ireland was close to the heart of all nationalists but to gain sympathy one had to have more. It was necessary to persuade people that they would be better off under a new constitution or at the very least that they would not be worse off. Michael listened to his uncle and believed he was a true patriot. A man dedicated to achieving something he believed in and thought was right. 'Unfortunately it's the only way,' he would say in an attempt to justify the killings associated with Nationalism. 'The Orange Order will never surrender their hold without a fight.'

He was prepared to die for his beliefs and this was his weakness. He mistakenly believed that all players in the "patriot game" were similarly committed. Michael had different ideas; he saw himself as a victim cheated at birth because he was born into a middle class family. Granted, they were well-off compared to the majority of Irish families, but not rich enough to be numbered amongst the big players in Irish political and social life. Michael expected better and knew that his rightful place was to be found in the higher echelons of society.

***

To Michael people like Uncle Pat were stupid. They risked their lives and their freedom because they had an unquenchable thirst for martyrdom. Deep down they harboured a desire to be killed by the enemy so that their names would enter into the annals of Irish folklore. Their deeds would be honoured "in song and in story" like those of former patriot men. It was a fanaticism in some people that manifested itself in different ways. If Uncle Pat had not found an outlet for his cravings in the patriot game he would have probably found it in religion.

Michael saw himself aligned with the majority of players who were in the game for personal advancement. There were rich pickings for those bright enough to find them. The other thing that appealed to Michael was that to be a known player was enough to cause heads to turn. The idea of a United Ireland was inherent in the Irish and those who espoused to achieve it attracted a sort of hero worship. They were perceived as fearless "harum-scarum men," not to be crossed.

When Michael found out that his uncle was a member of the IRB he was surprised. But it explained many things. The way people showed him respect and came to him with their problems. Even Michael's father, who was not known for his humility, gave the impression that he respected Pat. The heightening of tension in Ulster was accompanied by increased activity in Pat's flat. Michael became aware of serious men coming and going. It became obvious that Pat was a leading figure in what was going on. His visitors addressed him as sir, and there was a clandestine air in the way they went about their business. Michael did not get involved and knew that he was not expected to ask questions.

***

Michael's introduction to the patriot game came one afternoon when he was alone in his uncle's flat. A man arrived and asked for Mr Doherty. 'He's not in.' Michael said.

'When will he be back?'

'Don't know.'

'He's taught you well me boy,' the man said handing Michael two plastic bags. 'Give him these.'

'Thanks. I will.' Michael said taking the bags.

The man walked off and Michael looked at the bags; they were not sealed and his curiosity got the better of him. He peered inside one and saw it contained a great deal of money. He looked in the other and saw a pistol and several rounds of ammunition. He quickly folded them closed and his instincts told him to hide them. He placed them in a cupboard under the stairs.

He went to his room, but could not stop thinking about the two bags. He convinced himself that his eyes must have deceived him and he went back to the cupboard to check. As he sat on the floor he looked in the first bag that came to hand. Sure enough there it was, his eyes had not deceived him there was a handgun and ammunition. He opened the other bag and saw the money. Loose ten and twenty-pound notes and bundles of higher denomination.

Money! The root of all evil and just what's needed, Michael thought, would Uncle Pat miss a few notes out of this lot? He removed Ir£500 from the bag and placed it back in the cupboard. As he turned to stand up he became aware that Pat was standing behind him. Michael had not heard his uncle enter and had no idea how long he had been standing there. 'Someone left these for you Uncle Pat,' he said taking the bags from the cupboard. 'I was just hiding them…'

'Who was it?' Pat said in a normal voice.

'He never said,'

'Thanks Mike … I should have been here myself to meet him. Do you know what's in the bags?'

'Yes, Uncle Pat,' Michael said, uneasily thinking it was not like his uncle to probe him. 'I suppose I shouldn't have looked, I'm sorry.'

'Do you want to know why he left them here Mike?'

'No, it's none of my business.' Michel said standing up.

'I'm afraid it is Mike, you see you've been mistaken for someone else and now you know too much.'

'What do you mean, I know too much Uncle Pat? I know nothing and I don't want to know.'

'Don't get cross Mike, it's too late for that kind of talk. The man who gave you the packages thinks you work for me and if he finds out that he made a mistake he will want to correct it. That's the way things are in Ireland at the moment. You really must learn to listen and do what I say. Do you understand what I'm trying to tell you?'

'I think so … because I answered your door and took two bags from that fellow; I'm in some kind of danger. Is that it Uncle Pat?'

'More or less. I did tell you not to answer the door if I wasn't here.'

'Yes, but I forgot … Jesus Christ, what's this fucking country coming to when it's not safe to answer the door?'

'Mike, you know I don't like that sort of blasphemy and cursing. It's not right and your mother expects more of you.'

'Sorry Uncle Pat, can't you do something. You are in charge of these creatures aren't you? At least they seem to do what you tell them.'

'Mike, what's up with you? Don't ever say anything like that again. You must never discuss anything that takes place here. Not to anyone … even to me. Do you understand?'

That was the closest Michael ever saw his Uncle Pat come to anger. He normally carried himself with complete composure and projected a mild manner. Softly spoken, with the patience of a saint, that was how he was known; this loss of composure was out of character.

Michael could feel the money in his pocket and began to suspect that it was somehow connected with Pat's anger. He was looking at him with a disapproving look and there was something about it that caused Michael to feel uneasy. His uncle removed the pistol from the bag and loaded it. He did it with the ease of a man who had done the same thing many times before. The gun in his hand made him look different; it brought about an immediate transformation and the only thing Michael could think of was that he had grossly underestimated his uncle. 'Yes I understand, I'm very sorry.' Michael said looking down at the floor.

'Sorry for what Michael?' his uncle said looking at him straight in the eyes.

Christ! He's going to shoot me, he saw me take the money and he's going to kill me, Michael thought, pulling the money out of his pocket. 'Here Uncle Pat, I'm sorry I don't know what came over me.'

'Ingratitude that's what came over you Mike. You're an ungrateful cur and you've had this coming for a long time,' Pat said, and struck Michael causing him to fall backwards onto the floor.

The force of the blow was disproportionate to the size of its source, and Michael abandoned his instinct to answer the attack. He lay awkwardly on the floor where he fell and could feel the warm trickle of blood on his lip. He looked at his uncle and said in a feeble voice, 'You're right Uncle Pat. I've had it coming.'

'You're family Mike, I don't like inflicting pain on my own flesh and blood. You know I had to do that for your own good. It's not the money Mike. You know all you have to do is ask me for anything you want. Here you can have it. Money the root of all evil.' Pat said pushing the money back to Michael.

'No thanks Uncle Pat. I was wrong and I deserve to be punished for what I did. I'm sorry.'

'People are too fond of meaningless apologies nowadays Mike. Do you mean it?'

'Yes, I was wrong to take your money. I'm sorry for what I did…I'm really sorry.'

'Jesus Christ Mike you sound so … so insincere the way you say it. The money is nothing it's not the money and it's not just a question of saying you're sorry can't you see that?'

'I'm not sure I know what you mean?'

'It's trust Mike, no it's more than trust; it's loyalty, gratitude, appreciation and respect all rolled into one. If you steal from someone you bring all these questions into play and more. Now do you see what I'm getting at?'

'Yes, you're saying I should be ashamed and that you can't trust me. Well, I suppose that's a start.'

'If you give me another chance Uncle Pat I'll never let you down again? I swear you can trust me from this moment on.'

'Good, that's what I want to hear;' Pat said offering his hand to Michael. 'Come on get up, I'm sorry I hit you.'

Michael saw a smile appear on his uncle's face and the same hand that had moments earlier hit out in anger was now extended in friendship. Michael took it and could feel tears welling in his eyes. Uncle Pat saw the tears as both looked at each other in silence. What he did not see behind the tears was the well-concealed resentment in Michael's eyes. The only tinge of regret in his mind was traceable to the fact that he had been caught red-handed. That won't happen again, he thought, and Uncle Pat will pay dearly for having struck me.

The indignity of it, having to lie on the floor listening to a load of sanctimonious claptrap! Who the fuck is he to expound the Sermon on the Mountain? Bags of money, guns and ammunition delivered by unsavoury characters do not give the recipient licence to deliver sermons on propriety.

It certainly did not give uncle Pat leave or authority to attack someone going out of his way to ensure that the authorities did not find the said items. And what of the Ir£500.00 taken from the bag? Anyone else would either have taken the lot or at least a great deal more. Uncle Pat was mad because his little secret was out and he knew he would either have to kill his nephew or let him in on the act. If trust and respect is the price of joining this lucrative club you can have it dear uncle at least for the time being, Michael thought as he embraced his uncle.

***

With that in mind Michael went about the task of convincing his uncle that they were both as committed to Irish unity as each other. In less than a year he knew most of what was going on within Uncle Pat's circle. More importantly, Uncle Pat was happy with his nephew. In fact he was more than happy and had come to the point where he trusted Mike completely. He had matured and was showing great promise. He was intelligent, a good administrator and people liked him. The latter was extremely important to the movement because without the support of the public it was impossible to sustain an active circle.

Uncle Pat lost no opportunity to sing his protégé's praise at the highest level. 'A' was pleased and made it known that if Michael continued in the same vein he would be offered a commission in the Brotherhood.

Michael received the news with false modesty. 'Thank you Uncle Pat, its much more than I deserve.'

Michael's words did not carry his true feelings. What he really thought was that it was exactly what he deserved and planned for. He had his finger on the pulse of criminal activity, prostitution, drug dealing and protection not only inside his sector but also throughout Dublin City. But that was bread and butter stuff, and did not reveal his true talent. That lay in his ability to see the whole picture. To understand that people wanted something in return for their money.

***

Michael realised that his ace in the hole was that the Irish criminal fraternity had a grudging respect for the IRA, enough to make them think twice before questioning its franchise. There was a residual respect from the old days born out of the IRA's reputation to ruthlessly guard its status as cock-of-the-walk and with unfettered authority to operate in any part of the Irish Republic.

Tales of men, called the "Daddyhawkers," dressed in long dark coats abroad at night were part of Irish folklore. These fearsome men would find you out and wreak vengeance on those who had the temerity or misfortune of invoking their wrath. Storytellers in homes, pubs and clubs of Ireland passed down tales of the Daddyhawkers' dreadful deeds from generation to generation.

There was a ritual about the way such tales were narrated. The correct atmosphere was essential but it was not possible to create. It came about spontaneously when all the necessary ingredients were in place. Nobody knew for certain what ingredients were necessary or how to arrange them. All that can be said is that at some point in the proceedings an onlooker would be aware that there was a cluster of people focused on a central figure.

Perhaps the first sign that something big was happening would be in the form of a person calling for silence. Then there would be an increase in the flow of porter towards one person who if everything were going right would have established himself as the central figure. He would tell his story and keep his audience spellbound. "And that's a candid fact I'm telling yous and yous can laugh if yous like." The narrator would say, pointing an accusing finger at any person showing the least sign of incredulity or disrespect.

"I've seen many like you … and you … me boy lying dead. Let me tell you this me buck it was a horrible sight, by God it was awful. And I'll tell you another thing there was no grin on their faces. No what you could see was fear and shock written all over them even with their eyes closed.

It was like the devil himself had come to claim their souls, God rest them. It was the realisation that they didn't listen to good advice. The fear of death that's what it was I know it well and have often seen it. It's a terrible thing an unnatural thing and you smart young bucks would do well to wipe that grin off your face and pay heed to what I'm telling yous."

There would be nervous laughter but deep down everyone knew that the man was imparting sound advice. "The thing to remember is not to cross them in thought or deed. If you do they'll come for vengeance and the price is death."

The physiological advantage derived from such folklore was not lost on Michael. He insisted that his bully-boys carry out their activities in the manner of the "old brigade." To let it be known that the boys were back in business and long coats would be donned if necessary. It would encourage slackers to pay their dues, something that was very good for business.

***

To his bosses it demonstrated Michael's finesse in dealing with customers. He was able to achieve results by applying psychological pressure rather than resorting to the crude beatings relied on by other commanders. The boy had something special in the way he set out his stall. He was a careful planner not given to using physical force unless it was the last possible resort. Once that happened he showed no mercy and word soon spread that Michael Lynch was a man not to be crossed.

Lynch's talents did not end there. He put in place a database of people engaged in activities on which he felt they should pay a levy to the IRA. Researchers were dispatched to obtain details of persons appearing in court on drug and criminal charges. The system was extended to include prostitution and associated offences such as controlling prostitutes or brothels.

Players on the drug and criminal scene were given the option of paying a percentage of their turnover to the IRA or ceasing to trade. At first there was strong resistance from the Dublin criminal fraternity and Lynch had to demonstrate that he was in a position to enforce his will. A successful Dublin criminal called the General was contemptuous of the new IRA scheme and its author. He had run rings around Dublin police for several years and refused to bend to the will of an "upstart gobshite still wet behind the ears." After he was assassinated word spread and most criminals reached "an accommodation" with Mr Lynch.

***

A database was the rock upon which Michael Lynch founded his empire. He did not allow any opportunity to make money go unnoticed. He employed modern management techniques in his circle by putting his best people in charge of various departments. He adhered to the brotherhood's rank structure and placed 'Ds' in charge of a particular function. Hitherto it had been the policy to divide a circle into nine cells, each covering a given territory. Michael took a more abstract approach and replaced territory with functions.

This had the advantages of giving a wider distribution

base to cell managers whilst ensuring that they were more accountable. Functions were divided into manageable units, for example drugs were split into three categories, suppliers, dealers and street traffickers. Similarly prostitution was divided into two, brothels and streetwalkers.

Michael established a strong administration control centre from where he monitored operational activities. He utilised researchers to maintain a flow of information into his database. They comprised three accountants, two disbarred solicitors, a defrocked priest and three ex-police officers. Lynch knew how to get the best out of his "staff".

There were three women amongst the nine one of whom, an ex-solicitor, was a boffin in community affairs. She saw that there was a market to provide justice where the State had failed. She pointed out that over 50 per cent of not-guilty pleas led to acquittals and thus a large number of victims were denied justice. Also, many were dissatisfied with the sentences handed down by courts.

Michael liked the idea on the grounds that it was a public relations winner. He could envisage word spreading in the community that people had somewhere to turn in their hour of need. 'I like it Nancy,' he said enthusiastically. 'What do we have to do to get it up and running?'

An alcoholic solicitor was happy to rent part of his office-bloc in the centre of Blackrock, Dublin. The premises were ideal circle headquarters, and it had the added attraction of allowing throngs of people to come and go without raising suspicion. Within six weeks Michael Lynch, legal executive, had the perfect front. 'We'll call it The Department of Justice,' he announced.

At that time Michael was a C commander in the IRB. He wanted to move up a notch in the rank structure and in order to do that he had to impress 'A' whose identity he did not know. There is a four tier rank structure in the IRB. The first two letters of the alphabet are commissioned and as a C Michael was at the top of the non-commissioned rank structure. He had nine cells under his span of control but if he could convince the hierarchy that was insufficient manpower to do justice to the extent of his operation he would be promoted. On promotion he would have nine C's under his control each with nine D's.

The significance of the number nine in the IRB rank structure is traceable to its importance in Fenian mythology. To Michael its importance had a more realistic foundation and meant that if he were promoted, instead of controlling nine IRB personnel he would have an additional eighty-four. That was not counting the vast number of IRA volunteers that would be automatically brought under his wing on promotion. The majority of IRB personnel were high-ranking members of the IRA.

Michael suspected that his 'A' commander probably wore two hats or to be more precise a balaclava and a hat. There was an overlap between the military wing and the political wing of the movement and there was little doubt that 'A' had considerable influence in both areas. Sinn Fein, the political wing, was toying with the idea of creating a justice department. Michael was ahead of the game and saw his justice department as the prototype and the path to promotion.

***

On his thirtieth birthday Michael was accepted into the Irish Republican Brotherhood. It was the day he took the Fenian Oath and he was well prepared. He was mindful that he was under the watchful eye of those with power to influence his future and he uttered the sacred words by heart:

"I Michael Lynch solemnly pledge my sacred word of honour as a truthful an honest man that I will labour with earnest zeal for the liberation of Ireland from the yoke of England and for the establishment of a free and independent government on Irish soil."

The words echoed from the four-corners of the room and he made sure that all those present were aware that he did not refer to an aide-memoir. He projected an air of pride and confidence tinged with a degree of reverence. A true son of Erin that was how he wanted the influential spectators to perceive him.

It was important to conceal from them his real reason, which was that Michael Lynch wanted to get rich, to amass sufficient funds to enable him to live the good life on some far off shore. To leave behind the stink of death and corruption that was part of his everyday life in Ireland.

What he wanted to say was not contained in the ancient oath. He wanted to say thank you gentlemen for permitting me to join your band of gangsters and murderers. I look forward to reaping the benefits and intend to use your facilities to the full, but he suppressed that urge.

***

Secrecy within the brotherhood was its biggest enemy. It was not healthy to ask too many questions. The idea of circles or rings was to ensure that information was distributed on a strict need-to-know basis. To ask the wrong question was to invite suspicion and once that happened the onus was on the suspect to remove it.

The need for strong deterrents was necessary and easy to understand. Infiltration by British and Irish spies was the prime reason closely followed by members' revealing too much under interrogation or when bragging about their exploits. The organisation of the movement into circles was designed to minimise such risks. It made life difficult for Michael because it meant that he did not know the identity of his contemporaries nor that of 'A.'

The problem boiled down to one of perception. To advance his ambitions it was necessary for Michael to align his perception of his role within the Brotherhood with that of his senior officers. What did they expect of him? The popular notion that players in the patriot game were all singing from the same hymn sheet was sadly mistaken.

In fact it was impossible because of the lack of communication between top brass and operators in the field. There was no critical path nor was there a review of performance to ascertain whether one was achieving one's goals. Yet there existed a sort of invisible framework capable of exerting control. It manifested itself in the form of gentlemen called the enforcers.

Lesser mortals called communications staff officers were the only visible link with the hierarchy. Men trusted to make contact with circle commanders, to collect contributions and report anything amiss to the Enforcer. Michael made it his first priority to befriend his communications officer.

He also conducted secret enquiries into his habits and lifestyle, the object of which were to erect a safety net. It was considered prudent to have something up one's sleeve in case of an emergency. Communication officers had a reputation of throwing their weight about. They had unfettered power over circle commanders and like all men endowed with power were inclined to abuse it.

***

From the outset staff-officer Ron Keegan's attitude towards Michael fell squarely within the reputed mould. Although Ron looked over fifty-years of age he was in fact forty-five and a big overweight country-yokel with a chip on his shoulder. Ron Keegan was also a detective sergeant stationed at Dublin Castle. Thus in addition to the considerable power he wheeled within the Brotherhood, he had a reserve tank as a member of the all powerful garda schiconna. One might think that being a member of both organisations would present something of a conflict of interest but one would be mistaken.

Once a week Ron would meet Michael at one of three

locations specified by Ron. Michael would receive a telephone call and be given a number that indicated which location to attend.

Ron never arrived at the location first. Michael saw no harm in giving the impression that Ron was winning the little game of cat and mouse. On the contrary he used it as a source from which he could bestow a little flattery on Ron. Michael acted the part of the humble servant honoured to be in the presence of his omnipotent master.

There were routine weekly meetings when Ron would come to collect Michael's contributions. Ron would issue platitudes in exchange for a sum of money in the region of IR£190'000. That was the average weekly contribution to central funds made by Michael's circle.

It was the same routine every week except one day Michael got a call to attend a meeting at location three. That told him to go to the restaurant in the Spa Hotel, off the N4 West of Dublin. As Michael drove there he was attempting to fathom out what was wrong. It was a Friday afternoon and Ron was not due a contribution.

Michael drove into the car park, opened the glove compartment and felt around until he touched the pistol. He looked around to ensure that no one was watching and then he placed the pistol in the inside pocket of his jacket.

He scanned the car park to look for signs of an ambush; Parked vans, cars with one way vision and finally he looked at the buildings. There could be a sniper behind that chimney, he thought. Just in case I'll park closer to the wall to obstruct his line of fire. As he did so he caught sight of Ron waiting in his car pretending not to see Michael. He was alone which was a good sign.

Michael got out of his car, pretended he had not seen Ron and walked into the restaurant where the manager greeted him, 'Usual table Mr Lynch?'

'Yes please, that'll be grand.'

Michael sat with his back to the wall and looked at his watch. Five minutes later Ron came to the table. 'How do you do that Ron,' Michael said extending a friendly hand.

'Do what?' Ron asked sitting heavily on a chair.

'You know, always get here after me. I've tried everything but you never fail to outsmart me.'

'The old dog for the hard road Mick.' Ron said with a patronising smirk, '...you know the rest.'

'Indeed I do and a truer saying I've never heard Ron.'

'Having any problems on your patch Mick?' Ron said ignoring the flattery.

That's the first clue about what was on the agenda. Michael thought, still looking straight at Ron, 'None I can't handle up to now anyway Ron.'

'We're expecting a big contribution next week.'

'It's always big, don't you think Ron?' Michael said.

'We wondered whether you authorised that Building Society job on your patch the other night?'

'No, unfortunately we were not consulted. I'm looking into it though and I might want some advice later. Over a hundred grand according to the papers?'

'That's what they say Mick. A lot of money to be taken from under your nose?'

So that's it, Michael thought. 'Don't I know it, sounds like a professional job, firearms and all. I hope none of the others are poaching, have you heard anything yourself?'

'No, we were hoping you would be able to enlighten us, you being in charge and all?

Michael did not like the way things were going. Ron was being picky. He was an obnoxious prig at the best of times but today he was being insufferable. 'Yes, I can see that, and I'm doing something about it. I hope to have news for you at our next meeting.' Michael said hoping to end the subject.

'Good lad Mick, now there's something else; have you heard anything about the death of the priest in Corpus Christi vestry?'

Michael took time to think. Unusual again the death of a priest is normally outside our domain, 'Only what was in the papers, that Fr Murphy was found dead in the vestry. I thought he had a heart attack or something like that? '

'It's not that simple Mick there's suspicious circumstances. You say you've heard nothing?'

'Not really, of course people have mentioned it. Someone said he was a friend of yours.'

'Who said that?'

Michael noticed the urgency in Ron's voice and wanted time to think. 'You like a refill Ron?'

'No thanks. Who told you the priest was a friend of mine?'

I've hit a raw nerve, Michael thought, it's the murder of the priest. That's why he's here. Michael took a sip of his drink and noticed that Ron was waiting for an answer. 'Did you hear me Mick? I asked you who said I was a friend of Fr Murphy?'

'Jesus, I can't remember Ron, does it matter?'

'You know fucking well it matters!' Ron said striking the table, 'Why would anyone mention my friends to you? '

Good question Michael thought. A very good fucking question, I've slipped badly. Nobody is supposed to know that we know each other. 'Your right Ron, you've caught me out again. Jesus I should know better than to try and get one over you.' Michael said. 'All right, you win I was just guessing because you seem so concerned. I guessed there was something personal. Am I right?'

Ron relaxed slightly, sat back in his chair obviously considering whether to believe Michael. The implications of Michael discussing Ron with anyone were serious. To have reached a point where his associates and friends were discussed was dangerous. It was not like Michael to make such a rudimentary slip. 'Yes, it was a good guess. Remarkable in fact.' Ron said pointedly.

I'm not out of the woods yet, Michael thought. Another slip like that won't get passed him so easily. 'Well that's different. If he was a friend of yours I want to help. Is there anything I can do?'

'Yes, in fact there is. It was murder; the cold- blooded murder of a priest in his vestry. I want whoever did this arrested and charged. I want you to give this top priority. Is that understood Mick?'

'Of course Ron, anything you want,' Michael said.

The sincere look on his face was not in tandem with what he was thinking. Going through his mind was the possibility that Ron had flipped. It was as though Ron was performing a police briefing. 'Yes, I'll see to it straight away Ron. I'll get the justice department on to it straight away.'

'Yes, we like that Justice Department of yours. It was a good idea Mick it went down well with A. Do you think you'll get results?'

'I'll do my best, you know that Ron.'

'Your best is what's needed Mick. How long do you think it'll take?'

Michael was confused. How long do I think it'll take? That's nice coming from a cop. Christ, the tail is beginning to wag the dog! 'An arrest Ron, Jesus I was hoping you could tell me?'

'What does that mean?' Ron said sharply.

What does that mean, it means that you are the fucking arsehole sworn to uphold the law. Don't say that for Christ's sakes look at him, bags under his eyes, as nervous as a whore in church and apt to explode at any moment, 'I'm just saying that we haven't the same facilities as the garda. We're not trained investigators like you and your colleagues. It's going to take time.'

'I'm surprised to hear you say that Mick,' Ron interrupted. 'What about your Justice Department?'

'Yes, of course, I'll pull out all the stops but we're not geared up to handle a murder enquiry.'

'You misunderstand where I'm coming from Mick. We want this put to bed without too much fuss. It's the elections you know this sort of thing upsets the voters. It could affect our man's chances. We want him re-elected he's our man and we're not taking any chances. Do you follow?'

Maybe I've missed a few tricks along the way but I follow your drift, Michael thought. You're saying more than you've ever said about the way things work at the top. You've told me in a roundabout way that the present incumbent in Dail Eireann representing my constituency is a member of the Brotherhood. If my local knowledge is correct that senator is in government occupying the post of Director of Public Prosecutions. So yes, the electorate may feel disinclined to vote for him if a priest has been murdered in his constituency. That's what your saying but why are you saying it to me? 'Jesus I'm not sure that I do follow,' Michael said feigning bewilderment. 'It's very complicated Ron but I see that we'll have to do something to help our man. You know when I said earlier that I would ask for your help, to tell you the truth I think I need it now, have you any suggestions?'

'Get a volunteer Mick.'

In this context "volunteer," meant someone willing to admit to the murder to save the real culprit. But we only use volunteers to save someone very important within the Brotherhood. First, it is going to be very difficult to persuade someone to volunteer, and second, why should we. He's already answered the second question but the first will be problematic. 'It's that important is it Ron?'

'It is to you Mick.'

To me! Michael thought, what the fuck does he mean? 'To me?'

'I wasn't going to bring this up today Mick, but I think you should know that I might have to put your name forward to the auditor,' Ron said with the sly trappings of a blackmailer. 'It looks bad, they have the goods on you Mick. A Photostat of the contents of your briefcase was taken when you recently went through Dublin Airport. Do I need to go on Mick?'

The auditor! Photostat! Dublin Airport! As the words left Ron's mouth they had a visible impact on Michael. It was as though his mind was refusing to admit the words that had entered his ears. He was dumbfounded.

There was a smug look on Ron's face. It wasn't necessary for him to look at Michael in order to ascertain the effect of his words. He knew from experience that the mention of the Auditor was enough in itself to put the fear of Christ into those who collected Sinn Fein funds.

The additional information that there existed evidence in the form of documentation that the collector was embezzling, was tantamount to informing him that his death warrant had been signed. Michael Lynch was smart. Perhaps too smart for his own good, Ron thought.

The disappearance of his uncle, Pat Doherty, had never been explained. There were rumours that Michael had a hand in it, rumours to which Ron ascribed credence, but was unable to support with evidence. Let's see how he wriggles out of this, Ron thought, turning to look at Michael for a reply.

'A Photostat of the contents of my briefcase, that's what you said Ron?'

'Yes Mick, one taken when your hand luggage was checked at Dublin Airport a few months ago. I think it was when you were going to the Cayman Islands on holidays. Is that where you went?'

Fucking hell! The bastard was stringing me along all the time. Photostat of my briefcase full of money. It's enough to hang me. 'Thanks for the wink Ron. Do you know who's holding this document?' Michael asked pointedly.

'Yes, Mick I've got it but not on me. It's safe and you have my word that it will be handed to you in return for a volunteer. There are no copies. Have we a deal?'

You bet your arse we have a deal, Michael thought, I think I've underestimated you Ron, you're not as thick as you look. Yes, a crafty fucking cop to the end. 'Thank you again Ron. When do you want your volunteer?'

'Could we say forty-eight hours. He'll have to be good, have to know things only the murderer could know, I'll fill you in with the details. Here's something that'll help. It's the priest's wallet I took it out of his pocket.'

'Great, that's great Ron. Is there anything else?'

'No Mick. Would you mind walking with me back to my car?'

***

En route back to Blackrock Michael could not shake off the feeling that he had been outmanoeuvred. Ron's ace in the hole was the Auditor. It was played skilfully because

Ron knew it was better than an ace it was a joker. The auditor did not go about his business in a conventional way and the name was something of a misnomer. It was a euphemism for executioner.

Courts martial comprised three members assembled in a makeshift court arranged by the auditor. There were no rules of evidence. The auditor presented the case for the prosecution and was the only witness allowed at the hearing. At the end of the prosecution's case the defendant was asked to comment on the evidence.

Few could think of anything to say because they knew that once matters had reached that point their goose was cooked. The proceedings were a charade designed to spread the word that it was not healthy to embezzle Sinn Fein money. They knew the auditor was the archangel of death and members of his courts martial were surplus to requirement.

The defendant stood before the court aware that he had seen his last dawn. He would be taken hence and shot in the back of the head like a dog. His body would be left in a ditch or buried in an unmarked grave. The tribunal before which he stood was not empowered to alter his fate.

Some stood with their heads bowed unable to speak because of their fear of death. Others made impassioned pleas for mercy whilst others spoke out in anger. It made no difference the verdict was a foregoing conclusion, as was the sentence.

Michael knew his life was at risk, a situation he disliked and intended to do something about. He never looked to himself as the author of his own misfortune. No, others were to blame and in this instance the person representing the danger was Ron Keegan. He had the Photostat and he had the shout as to whether it would find its way to the Auditor. Not to be trusted Ron, a fucking blackmailer if I ever saw one, Michael thought. I'll deal with him later but is my money safe?

Bank accounts in Eire and the United Kingdom are fraught with danger.

The Brotherhood could access them and it's a simple matter to work out whether one was banking a greater percentage than one was entitled to.

Michael was wondering whether the system he devised after Uncle Pat's death, whereby safe money was banked in Ireland and "surplus" in an over-seas account was as foolproof as he thought. It involved delivering the surplus to an account in the Cayman Islands twice a year.

The risk of being questioned leaving Dublin Airport by treasury officials had been minimised. Contingency plans to counteract such an event involved an arrangement with the bank manager. He was prepared to confirm that the money was "clean" and would produce documentation to support the agreed explanation that a similar amount of cash had been lent to Michael by the bank.

He was never checked and believed the visits to his Cayman account had gone unnoticed. It was a bad mistake to underestimate one's friends in the Patriot Game. Friend today, executioner tomorrow; Michael Lynch knew the score he had overlooked the obvious. Some innocuous little shit in Dublin Airport Security was also on the payroll of Sinn Fein. The contingency plan was no good in these circumstances. There had to be another way and that would inevitably lead to a serious conflict of interest with Ron Keegan.

His behaviour was very strange earlier in the day. Michael recalled that Ron for the first time ever insisted that they leave the hotel together. Michael thought he was being led into a trap and made up his mind to shoot Ron if that were the case. But Ron did not behave as though he was walking next to someone he knew was in the sights of a sniper's gun. On the contrary he was walking so close to Michael that they were touching.

They walked from the hotel and were near Ron's car when he gripped Michael's arm. 'Can you see that fucking dog at my car Mick?'

Michael thought he had misheard Ron. 'Dog?'

'Yes, the one standing there at the driver's door of my car. He's following me Mick …he's been following me for the last three of four days and I can't get rid of him.'

Although Michael could not see a dog the urgency in Ron's voice persuaded him that there must be one. 'I'm sorry Ron where is it?'

Ron took a pistol from his pocket and shoved Michael with such force that he fell to the ground. The bastard's going to do me here and now, Michael thought, reaching for the pistol in his inside pocket. He had fallen awkwardly but he knew he had to roll on the ground to prevent being hit. He heard the report of the pistol and knew that Ron had missed. The sting of the bullet comes before the bang, Michael thought, as he took aim at Ron.

But Ron was not firing at Michael he was facing the other way firing in the direction of his car. 'I think I got him Mick.'

IX

Leprechauns & Banshees

LATER AS RON MADE his way home his mind kept returning to the black dog. It was an eerie creature that had taken to following him or to put it more accurately it had developed an uncanny knack of anticipating his movements.

The first time he saw it was the morning he learned of Fr Murphy's death. The dog was sitting next to Ron's car looking at him when he set out for work. The ugly black mongrel stripped its teeth and looked at Ron with small evil eyes. When Ron got close it growled at him contemptuously turned and walked away. It showed no sign of fear as it looked back at him still displaying its teeth.

***

Ron's mind was occupied with thoughts of his friend Fr Murphy and how he had been murdered in his vestry in horrible circumstances. Fr Edward Murphy would be missed, the person who murdered him would pay and Ron would make sure of it. It was the least that he could do in memory of the man who officiated at his wedding and baptised his five children.

His death in horrendous circumstances came as a great shock to Ron's family. His wife Eileen took the news very badly. Ron had to carry her upstairs to bed where she still remained in a state of shock. The children were also lying in their beds not speaking because they could not come to terms with what had happened. They all loved Fr Ned as they used to call him and he loved them.

***

Ron Keegan loved his wife and anything that upset her upset him. He loved her from the first time he saw her after she came to live near the Keegan family home. She was so beautiful that Ron dared not hope that she would look at him twice. At the time Ron was going through a very bad phase.

There was a family row over Uncle Tom's farm and Ron felt he had been cheated out of it. Ron had lived with his uncle after his wife died. He helped Uncle Tom on the farm and it was settled that Ron would inherit it in due course. 'This farm's yours after my day, Ronald,' his uncle said time and again. 'I've made a will leaving everything to you son.'

He insisted that Ron read the will and there it was in black and white. *One hundred acres and my homestead devised to my nephew, Ronald Keegan, in recognition of the help he has given me in my lifetime.*

'Look Ron it's been properly witnessed by two upstanding members of this community. It's settled and you deserve it', his uncle said.

Uncle Tom was Ron's father's brother. They were the last two males in that Keegan line. Tom had no issue, so it was for Ron or his brother J.J. to "beget a son." Their father was obsessed with the fear that his sons may have inherited the same gene defect that prevented Uncle Tom from fathering children. It was a fear born out of ignorance rather than knowledge. The family doctor pointed out that Uncle Tom's impotency was probably the result of his contracting mumps when he was a boy. This revelation did not enhance Ron's chances in his father's eyes. 'You had mumps when you were twelve so you're like your uncle. It's up to John Joe to carry on the family name.'

***

After Uncle Tom died Ron moved into the house in accordance with the terms of the will. He was happy and felt secure in the knowledge that he could spend his life doing what he enjoyed. Then the solicitor's letter arrived inviting him and his brother to the reading of Uncle Tom's will. Ron thought it was a foregoing conclusion. He had already seen the will and did not remember seeing a bequest to John Joe. It was fair; as the eldest son it was known that he would inherit the family estate. It comprised a bigger house and outbuildings along with three hundred acres of good farmland.

At the appointed time they attended the solicitor's office and the will was read.

> *"To my nephew Ronald, I bequeath the sum of IR£10'000, to be paid free of taxes. The remainder of my estate I devise to my nephew John Joe Keegan absolutely."*

The smug smile that John Joe had been wearing all day grew bigger. Ron thought there must be a mistake. The solicitor had confused the names.

'But that's not Uncle Tom's will Mr Blaney.' Ron heard himself say. 'There must be a mistake I've read Uncle Tom's will and he left the farm to me, not to John Joe.'

The solicitor looked at the will again and then at Ron with a degree of sympathy. 'Yes, your Uncle Thomas did make a will in your favour some years ago. But this is a new one made last year, and it revokes all previous wills. I'm afraid that your uncle's farm goes to John Joe. But your uncle did not forget you; he left you £10'000, a considerable fortune for a young man starting out in life.'

They knew about this and didn't tell me, Ron thought. They let me live on in the house working for nothing. 'But I've been living there for almost a year,' Ron said. 'Uncle Tom promised me; he always said that the place was mine.'

'I'm sorry Ronald; your brother owns it now and what

happens to it is up to him. It's the law and that's the end of it, I'm afraid.'

Both the solicitor and Ron looked at John Joe for guidance. He was seated with his legs crossed adopting what he must have thought was a superior posture. He was pondering playing the role of the benevolent benefactor. After suitable deliberation he spoke. 'It's true that Uncle Tom wanted to leave his place to Ron, but after speaking to my father he changed his mind. That's between them, and I've known about the change of will for some time. Even so, I allowed Ron to live there for longer than I had to, rent-free I might add. Now that it's all official I intend to charge a fair rent. He can live there until I've made my mind up what I'm going to do with the farm. I think that's fair all round.'

Ron was livid, the cheek of him letting me do all the work. Milk the cows, fodder the cattle and now he wants me to pay him. 'I don't think that's fair. I think you should pay me for looking after things unless you are saying that the livestock and machinery are mine?'

'No I'm not saying that. What I'm saying is pay a fair rent or find yourself somewhere else to live.'

***

At the time Eileen was settled in the Murphy household. They were the Keegan's nearest neighbour and had moved into the locality when Ron was about ten years of age. Eileen would come from the North to visit the Murphy's with her parents. She was pretty, and the locals referred to her as a "grand shy girl." Little was known about the family except that the grapevine reported they were relations of the Murphy's from the North.

When Eileen was sixteen, she came to live permanently with the Murphy family. She never spoke about it, and Ron never found out what had happened to her parents.

From that time Ron was smitten. He could not take his eyes off her long dark hair and her beautiful friendly face. But he held no hope of ever winning her affections. He was a big awkward country lad and she had natural grace and beauty.

Ron was happy just to know her and to be in her company from time to time. His mother spoke highly of Eileen and did little to hide her feelings that she should marry John Joe. 'Mother is up to her matchmaking tricks again,' her husband would say, and no doubt he was right.

John Joe was the favourite, but Eileen did not seem to notice and showed the same affection to both. Her friendly disposition was similar to that of her constant companion and cousin "Ned" Murphy, who was also a frequent visitor to the Keegan household.

At the time Edward was studying for the priesthood and was beginning to take on a self-assured aloofness tempered with a proportional showing of humility. "He'll make a grand priest," pious ladies often remarked.

Eileen had a similar genteel presence and the cousins were inseparable. Ron's mother used to tease Eileen. 'Don't lead that man astray Eileen ... he's promised to God!'

'Chance would be a fine thing, Mrs Keegan.'

'Now can you imagine it? Mrs Murphy landing at my

door blaming me for allowing you to take her son away from God?' Mrs Keegan would say in jest.

'Indeed I can. I don't know which would be the worst, Mrs Murphy or God himself.'

'Ah he's a lovely lad though,' Mrs Keegan would say. 'He'll make a grand priest. I hope he won't be too hard on us at confession. My God, won't it be strange telling young Ned all our sins? Can you just imagine it Eileen?'

'I don't think I could do it Mrs Keegan. "Bless me father for I have sinned." "And what sins have you committed my child?" "I've had impure thoughts about you Ned! Do you think you can forgive me?"

Mrs Keegan was highly amused every time the scene was enacted in her kitchen. There would be much laughter as she tried to come up with something better. 'Good God you're some card Eileen. How do you think of them?'

Ron smiled as he remembered the good humour between his mother and Eileen. They got on so well. Of course everyone got on well with Eileen; even Dad laughed, he mused.

***

Edward was ordained and to everyone's delight Killmarch had a son in the priesthood. The Murphy's were ecstatic and their reputation was greatly enhanced in the community. Fr Murphy came home to his village to say his first Mass. The chapel was bursting at the seams as all the villagers came out to gawk.

Eileen accompanied Ron and there were tears of joy in

her eyes as she listened to Ned's first sermon. He spoke well, thanked everyone for their prayers and promised to remember them in his. Mrs Keegan marked the occasion by throwing a big party in honour of Fr Edward Murphy. The whole neighbourhood was invited and the celebrations went into the small hours.

Eileen stayed by Ron's side during the day and later at the party. It was her way to link arms with the person she was with and Ron felt honoured that he was that person. The shindig was in full swing, and they danced and drank together all night. Even John Joe was in high spirits, and remarked that they looked "great" together. The new Fr Murphy was in attendance and also remarked that Eileen and Ron made a "grand couple."

***

The next morning Ron awoke suffering the effects of the previous night's alcohol intake. He could not remember when or how he got to bed. The sun shining through the flimsy bedroom curtains did little to clear the fog in his aching head. Then out of the nebulosity emerged the pleasant memory of his holding Eileen in his arms and kissing her. She responded with more enthusiasm than he expected.

It was coming back to him, as he lay stretching in his bed naked. The touch of a smooth skin against his bare leg sent a sensation through his body. He was not alone and when he looked to see who was in bed beside him he saw it was Eileen.

It was then that he heard the scream. He could still hear

it now, a horrendous human wail renting the morning silence. It was coming from below somewhere in the yard a cry of such magnitude that it caused the hair on the back of his neck to stand. It's mother someone's killing her, he thought, as he jumped out of bed.

He found her at the back of the house with both hands clasped together on the top of her head. She was walking in circles emitting the eerie sound that can only be made by a human being in utter desperation. The biblical expression "there shall be weeping and gnashing of teeth " came into Ron's mind as he saw his desolate mother looking towards the sky pleading to the highest authority. 'No God please don't, don't do this to me, no not this, no not this!'

The sight of his mother in such despair was frightening. He looked around and could see nothing that would account for her anguish. 'Mother, it's all right mother, I'm here.' He shouted running to place his arms around her. 'What's happened mother?'

Tears welled in Ron's eyes. He could remember that dreadful day as though it was yesterday although it was nearly twenty yeas ago. His mother trembling in his arms still crying out to God to change things. She must have seen me in bed with Eileen, he thought. 'We did nothing mother, we just had too much to drink.'

'He's lying there dead at the gate,' she said looking in the opposite direction to where she was pointing. 'Your father, your poor father's lying there dead. May God have mercy on his poor soul.'

***

Fr Murphy said the funeral Mass to a packed congregation. He was too emotional to give the farewell sermon and the parish priest Fr Abbot stepped in to take his place. 'John Joseph Keegan was taken from amongst us at the early age of fifty. We extend our sympathy to his grieving widow and his two sons John Joe and Ronald.'

Then the priest gave a brief account of the life of the late John Joe Keegan senior, and afterwards the choir sang a sad hymn and then they went to the cemetery. The soil was placed over the coffin and people drifted out of the graveyard. Big John Joe Keegan was no more.

The numb feeling does not go away for a long time when a loved one is taken. There is a void, yes a constant void, and that is what I'm feeling now, Ron said to himself as the tears rolled down his cheeks. It was hard for Eileen too, he thought. She loved daddy and one of her lasting regrets was that he was not alive when we got married.

She broke the news to Ron five weeks after the funeral, 'I'm pregnant Ron,' she said nervously. 'I'm going to have your baby.'

The first thought that came into Ron's mind was that daddy was wrong after all. He would have been delighted that the Keegan name was secure, things would have been different if he was alive. There is no doubt he would have changed his will, but as matters stood he left everything to his wife, with the remainder to John Joe after her day.

***

They were married in Dublin a month later and Edward

was born seven months after that. Fr Murphy performed the marriage ceremony, a low-key affair because the family was still in mourning. Mother did not attend and in fact never got over the sudden death of her husband. She wasted away and died within two years.

Ron and Eileen had four more children. The twins, Maria and John Joe, were born a year after Edward, Patrick a year after that and the youngest, Simon, two years later. Five children in as many years were a big responsibility and without Fr Murphy's help the Keegan family would have sunk. He pulled strings to get Ron into the garda. It was not a job he would have thought of doing because he always wanted to work on the land.

Fr Murphy was a frequent visitor to the Keegan home. He was Ron's closest friend apart from Eileen. Of course she was preoccupied with the children and the strain affected her somehow. Although she was the same friendly Eileen on the surface, Ron felt there was something missing in their relationship. She never again showed the same passion in the matrimonial bed as she showed on the night of Fr Murphy's ordination.

'I think I've managed to get you a job you'll like, Ron.' Ned said running his hand over his head.

'It's too late to join holy orders Ned.' Ron joked.

Ned laughed for a long time and then paused and stood up. He walked over and shut the door. 'The Garda Schiconna, Ron. I've a little influence with someone who has a lot of influence, if you follow me?'

Ron was shocked and looked to see if he was serious,

'You must be joking, Fr Ned Murphy, it's all that wine you're drinking.'

Ned sat down and ran his hand through his hair, 'The job's yours Ron. I've spoken to the right people, why don't you give it a go?'

***

The garda was not like Ron imagined it would be. He had a notion that it was going to be something like being a priest. Telling people not to do wrong and setting a good example. He would learn in time that being a member of the Garda Schiconna was like being a member of a special club. The Irish police ruled with an iron fist, and the majority of the population treated them with fearful respect.

There was something about the blue uniform that caused a reaction in people. Ron felt proud patrolling the streets of Dublin because he knew he was cock-of-the-walk. Better still every week the shift landlord gave him an envelope with at least IR£100 in it. Ron was naïve at first, but soon learned that it was his share of the "contributions" donated by members of the public for favours. Publicans, shops owners, scrap dealers, drug dealers, prostitutes and hawkers and others paid for the privilege of plying their trade.

There were two golden rules. The first that contributors were not hassled by the police and the second that the police stuck together through thick and thin. Ron never discussed the internal workings of the police with his wife or Fr Murphy.

***

About two years after Ron joined the garda Fr Ned took him to one side. 'I think it would be a good idea if you joined the Catenians Ron,' he said out of the blue. 'It would be a smart career move boy.'

Ron was not surprised because by then he was more aware of how the power game was played in Eire. The Catenians are the Catholic's answer to Freemasonry. But because there are less checks and balances in the Irish constitution than the British, it wheels considerable influence over both the public and private sector. Many believe that the top tier comprises the powerhouse of Irish political, judicial and executive life. Steeped in mystery and secrecy membership is restricted to those destined for great things. 'Did I hear you right Ned?' Ron said. 'You did say the Catenians didn't you?'

Ned was seated in the chair he always used. In fact the children called it, "Fr Ned's holy chair". He moved forward and lowered his voice. 'Yes, you heard right Ron," he said placing his hand on his head. It was one of his little habits to place his right hand on his head and move it backwards slowly until it came to rest at the back of his neck. An idiosyncrasy Ron had not noticed for years. His youngest son Simon had a habit of doing the same thing and that was what caused Ron to notice Ned's habit.

Once it registered, he realised that it was something Ned always did. Ron felt proud of his young son's perception. It became a source of amusement to him. 'Look the young lad's copying Fr Ned.' Ron remarked to his wife.

She laughed patting the boy on the head. 'He doesn't miss a thing our little Simon.'

Now as Fr Ned's hand came to rest on his neck he said to Ron, 'It's the way to get ahead in the garda you know. What do you say?'

Ron thought about it. Of course, membership of the elite club would have advantages. 'I like the idea; I'll see what Eileen thinks.' Ron said, but at the back of his mind he knew that Ned and Eileen would have already discussed it. It was something that irritated Ron. Nothing he could readily put his finger on, but he felt that important decisions about his life were being made behind his back. 'Oh she's all for it, Ron, I mentioned it to her earlier,' Ned said enthusiastically. 'She thinks it would be a grand idea.'

It was something Ron had hated in his youth; the way favours were distributed in Ireland. If you weren't in the right club you were out in the cold, and that applied to over ninety-percent of the population. Later in life Ron changed his altruistic philosophy and concentrated on looking after his own interests. If you can't beat them, join them, he thought, looking at Fr Ned. 'Will they let me join?'

'Of course, I'll sponsor you and I think I can persuade someone to second it.' Fr Ned said, extending his hand. 'Congratulations Ron, you've made a good choice.'

***

Three months later Ron was sworn into the Catenians at a special ceremony. It was not his idea to get so deeply involved, Fr Ned made all the running. One night after the ceremony Ron and Fr Ned were together in Ron's home.

'Do you love your country Ron?' Ned said out of the blue during one of their many chats.

Ron looked at him somewhat surprised. 'Yes, I suppose I do Ned.'

Ned ran his hand over his head and looked more serious than Ron had ever seen him.

'I mean do you really love it Ronald,' he said intensely. 'What I'm asking you is would you die for it?'

Ron had not given the matter much thought he did not feel that it was relevant to him. He had made a point of not getting involved in discussions involving "The Troubles" in the North. But as a policeman it was his job to arrest terrorists, at least that was the official line. But unofficially it was considered prudent to avoid getting involved in any political arrest unless they threatened the State. 'Ned, I've heard such questions before, but I've never been able to see any logic in them. The short answer to your question is no.'

'Well take me out of my suspense Ron, what's the long answer?'

'I knew you'd have to dig deeper, but frankly Ned I'm not sure what the long answer is. Shall we say that I can envisage circumstances where I would put my life at risk and leave it at that.'

***

What a load of bullshit that was, Ron thought as he drew his Mercedes to a halt in preparation to turn right.

Dusk was falling as he drove into the narrow road leading to his home.

He owned a six bedroom detached house which stood in the middle of ten acres of land. He turned into the long drive, it was dark under the rows of conifers situated each side of the drive. He switched on his headlights and observed the outline of his house in the distance. He wondered if his wife and children would still be in mourning for Fr Ned Murphy.

***

Michael Lynch was in deep thought as he drove along the busy road to negotiate the junction at the exit from Phoenix Park. After his telephone call to Jim Doran he felt more at ease as he followed the road towards Dublin Port. As he passed Old Kilmaimhem Jail he recalled that Padraig Pearce and his followers were shot there following the Easter Uprising in 1916. 'May their souls and the souls of all the faithfully departed from this life through the mercy of God rest in peace, amen.' he whispered as he drove passed.

But his mind was on other things, not the least of which was the car that had pulled out of The Phoenix Park and was following him. To confirm his suspicion he decided to take an indirect route to his destination. "That car is definitely following me and I want to know who's in it," he mused, looking for a suitable place to park.

He stopped at a paper shop and watched the car drive past. He went into the shop and when he came out the same was car parked waiting to pick up the pursuit. He could see two men seated in the front and there was no sign of the third man who was in the back when he saw it earlier.

Then he noticed him standing in a nearby doorway pretending to read a paper. It's the fucking Special Branch, he thought. Who else would stand there like something out of a bad American movie? Michael walked up to the man, 'I'll only play cat and mouse if I can be the cat. Are you agreed?'

'It's not my call Michael,' the man said, with a friendly smile. 'Someone wants to see you at the Castle.'

Michael raised his eyebrow, 'Are you allowed to tell me why?'

'I'm Detective Chief Inspector Price from the Special Branch. I think you'll find that we have something important to discuss with you.'

Michael thought he detected a hidden message in the words. He looked at the DCI Price and realised that the message was not in his words, it was in his eyes. The words were diplomatic, but behind the smile Mr Price's eyes gave a clue that he was no ordinary policeman. Perhaps he can see the same thing in my eyes, Michael thought. That cold look is the hallmark of an assassin and something we recognise when we see it.

The look comes with the territory and is sparked when one is sizing up the next victim. They know about the Cayman account, but that is not the question going through Mr Price's head at this moment. He is wondering how I'll react when the moment comes. 'May I ask who wants to see me, Mr Price?'

'Nothing to worry about. As far as I know something has cropped up in your area. I've not been authorised to give you any further information.'

Michael looked at Price and then over his shoulder at the two men in the car. He knew how the game was played. They did not want a scene in the street, but if necessary would do the job here and now. It was better to go along with the charade and see if a better opportunity presented itself.

The man seated in the passenger seat of the police car would have a gun trained on Michael and one false move was all it would take. 'All right, I can come with you now,' Michael said. 'I'm afraid I'll have to follow you if that's all right?'

'No problem,' Price said, starting to walk towards his friends.

It was the chance Michael needed. It was too good to be true, he thought, as he walked towards his car. I'll loose these three pricks in quick time. Then he heard Price behind him. 'Better still, why don't I join you and then I can show you the way.'

This boy is sharp, Michael thought, a few rungs up the ladder from Ron Keegan. 'Fine, that's a great idea.'

En route, Chief Inspector Price said, 'we're going to have a meeting with the permanent secretary to the DPP. Beforehand we'll spend a while with our Commander to sort out a few things. You know, background stuff?'

Michael was sceptical. The meeting was going to be with the Auditor and everyone knew what that meant. The only reason they were going to these lengths was that they wanted to get their hands on the money in Cayman. That was the reason they were holding the court martial in Dublin Castle. They knew there was a lot of money and they wanted to get their hands on it. Otherwise we'd be on the way to some remote barn, Michael thought, where I would end up with a bullet in the back of my head. 'What's this all about?' Michael asked.

'Can't you guess?'

Michael smiled and looked at Price. 'I don't think this is a good time to play guessing games. Anyway I only play when I'm sure I know all the questions and answers.'

'That's a good system you have Michael. I think you should stick with it, if you know what I mean?'

'You're flattery's embarrassing me Mr Price. Does that mean you're not going to tell me anything?'

Price thought for a moment. 'Fair enough, the meeting's about three things. The first is Fr Murphy, the second is Ron Keegan, and the third I'm not at liberty to tell you.'

'Well, two out of three isn't so bad I suppose,' Michael said. 'I'll open the box.'

'The Fr Murphy saga is a reminder to us all that the Unionists are not as daft as we like to think.'

'The Fr Murphy saga! Don't you mean the Fr Murphy murder?'

'I'd call it a saga that started several years ago when the Murphy clan came from the North and bought a place near the Keegan family. You know Ron's parent's farm?'

Michael waited for Price to continue. But he was savouring the moment smug in the knowledge that he had stimulated his listener's curiosity. Michael broke the silence. 'So the Murphys and the Keegans lived next to each other and...?'

Price then added that in the 1950s the Murphys left Co Antrim in Ulster where they were known as McRea and had strong Orange links. They changed their name and religion, and when they arrived in the South they were devout Catholics calling themselves Murphy. Not because they'd abandoned their Orange roots; quite the contrary! What they were after was to get one of their ilk into the republic to spy. 'Care to venture a guess as to who that was?'

'Even with my limited knowledge it's becoming clear that it was the Reverend Fr Edward Murphy?'

'Non other. He was a sleeper in the Orange Order programmed to activate once he was ordained into the Holy Catholic Church. A nice bit of forward planning I think you will agree?'

'Jesus Christ that's the best I've ever heard,' Michael said in genuine astonishment. 'Fr Murphy, spiritual mentor to Ron Keegan is a ringer!'

'Was a ringer, I think, is more appropriate in view of the fact that he is currently prostrate in the city morgue.' Price said pointedly. 'Poor Ron he's in a bad way, he doesn't know whether he's coming or going. It's all come as a big shock to him, the news about his wife Eileen and all. Do you know her?'

This fellow knows how to put his prey at ease. A very clever little question Michael thought. 'No never met the woman, Ron didn't discuss his personal affairs with me,' Michael said. 'I suppose you're going to tell me that she's a ringer as well?'

'Yes, that's exactly what I'm going to tell you. We've traced her back to an orphanage in the North. Seems Catholics wiped out her family in the North and she never forgave or forgot. Poor old Ron he had no idea as far as we can find out.' Price said into both index fingers, which he was holding to his mouth. He was obviously weighing up every word and Michael was beginning to see why.

'So Ron Keegan married an Orange spy. She must have been very good or very committed?'

'A Loyalist through and through,' Price said. 'Yes, they were literally in bed with us and I'll leave it up to yourself to guess who was fucking whom.'

Michael's mind was analysing the new situation and the outline of a plan was coming into shape. 'I'm more concerned that he might have slipped me a crippler, you know what I mean if they turned Ron we could all be on file couldn't we?'

'Depends on what he knew I suppose,' Price said. 'He was firing blanks did you know?'

Michael was confused. Was Price referring to the incident earlier when Ron shot at the dog? Jesus, it was difficult to keep up with this fellow, his laid back couldn't care less attitude was just a front. It's the money they're after, they know about my Cayman account and he's softening me up, Michael's mind was racing. Keep calm, there must be a way out of this mess, don't let him bamboozle you with his half idioms and insinuations. 'Firing blanks you say?'

'Yes, he was impotent. Poor bastard never knew, thought he had fathered five or six children.'

'Fuck off, you're having me on! Nobody could be that stupid.'

'Ah here we are Mick … park her over there if you don't mind.'

***

The car was parked and Michael got out and looked at the dark cloudy sky. Price's two colleagues were standing at the back of the car waiting for instructions from Price. Michael could not consummate the plan that was forming in his mind because there were too many variables. Price had done a good job of confusing the issues. Some would see his frankness as a good sign.

Michael Lynch was not so sure. There is really only one sort of person that can be relied on to keep a secret and Michael was beginning to think that he fitted the bill. A person that is going to be dead when you leave is not going to betray any confidences. That could explain Price's frankness.

Now all four men were standing beside Michael's car and he was in the middle. 'Leave your weapon in the car Mick, if you don't mind?' Price said in the same friendly voice.

'And if I don't want to?'

'Sorry mate,' Price said putting his hand into Michael's

pocket and removing the pistol. 'Can we leave this in your glove compartment?'

Michael's heart sank. He knew the routine. They wanted his car keys to prevent delay if they had to dispose of his body and car later. It was exactly what Michael would have done were he in Price's shoes.

***

When Ron Keegan reached his destination he sat in his car looking at the house that was his home these past fifteen years. This evening it was in complete darkness and was enshrouded in an unusual stillness. There was nobody standing at the door to greet him; normally Eileen or one of his children would be calling to him by now. He felt a shiver run down his spine and thought someone was walking on his grave. Death had been on his mind these past few days. It was the black dog that reminded him of a story his mother used to tell after his father died. 'I saw the banshee. God help me I saw her in the form of a black dog.' She would say with a look of horror on her face.

He remembered hugging her, trying to reassure her that it was only her imagination. 'You don't believe all that nonsense mother, they're only old-wives tales.'

'Ron it's true. The black dog came to warn me before your daddy had his accident.' She said squeezing his hand so tight he was surprised at her strength. 'It was the banshee and after I saw her I should have known that something awful was going to happen. That one of us was going to die.'

Poor mother, Ron thought, as he shook his head to get rid of the scary thoughts that were gathering there. I shot the black fucking dog, he's lying dead in the Spa car park. So much for banshees and leprechauns, he thought, as he loaded his revolver. And fuck the bastards for trying to tell me that my wife is an Orange spy, that my children are not my children. 'Eileen! Eileen! Where are you?' he called as he got out of his car.

He walked slowly towards his front door and from time to time looked over his shoulder to confirm that the dog was nowhere to be seen. Then he saw it waiting at the front door where Eileen used to greet him. 'I won't miss it this time,' he shouted halting to take aim.

He felt the sting in the back of his head followed by the sound of a shot. His pistol went off in his hand as he staggered forward one or two steps and stopped. 'Mother! It's you mother,' he said falling to the ground where he died within minutes.

X

The Brotherhood Sign

THE DEATH OF RON Keegan occurred during a time of much bloodletting by Irish Nationalists. There was great suspicion in the movement. People in high places were paranoid and keen to eliminate informers. This coupled with a sustained epidemic of Chinese whispers amongst volunteers and sympathisers made the air extremely volatile. The Fr Murphy affair was an embarrassment and worst than that it demonstrated that Orange Loyalists had penetrated sacred Nationalist institutions.

The IRA hierarchy knew who was responsible for the death of Fr Murphy but it was not sure who had dispatched Ron Keegan. A top sniper from the North had been brought in by the IRA to do the job. The plan was that he would "visit" Ron's home, eliminate Eileen and ambush Ron when he came home.

The decision to kill Ron had not been taken lightly.

There was no evidence that he had any part in the Orange Plot. On the contrary it was known that Ron would never agree to place his wife and family in mortal danger. His weakness was that he loved them too much and would not be able to cope with or accept what had to be done. But it seems someone else had similar thoughts for when the IRA assassin entered Keegan's house he found Eileen and her children had already been murdered. The assassin also reported that Ron Keegan had shot himself.

***

That was the known state of play as far as the IRA hierarchy was concerned when Michael Lynch was called to account.

He remembered sitting in the waiting room in Dublin Castle, and wondering how he was going to appease his examiners. The money sitting in an account in his name in the Cayman Islands was as lethal as the barrel of a gun. They knew about it, and they also knew it was disproportionate to the contributions made to the Brotherhood. Ir£2'550'000 was too much to account for even before they considered the additional amounts he held in domestic accounts.

They took him into the well-furnished office at the centre of which was a conference table surrounded by big leather chairs. There were three men seated at the table, enough to constitute a court martial. The only good news was that the Auditor was not present. But Michael was sure that if things did not go in accordance with the wishes of the three men that the Auditor was waiting nearby to join the proceedings.

As he took in his surroundings a sick feeling came over him. He found it difficult to think clearly because he harboured an inner picture of being taken to a destitute location and there being shot. He wondered how he would face it, whether he would break down and beg for mercy like his uncle or would he accept his fate and ask for a clean kill.

Michael had been a party to many executions and from experience knew that it was impossible to predict how one would react. The picture of hard-men attempting to overcome their fear by attempting in vain to put their minds elsewhere was etched in Michael's memory. He could remember none that succeeded and the tell-tail traces of urine seeping through their trousers left no doubt about their state of mind.

Price introduced Michael to Mr Higgins, from the DPP's office and Mr Rooney head of Special Branch. Both men acknowledged Michael with a friendly smile. 'Sit here next to me.' Mr Rooney said with a degree of charm that belied the seriousness of the situation.

Michael resented the pseudo-air of friendship and the transparent attempt to beguile him. But he was in the net and this was not the time to wriggle. He knew that his chances were limited and that those before whom he sat had already decided his fate. Rooney waited for Michael to sit, 'We're sorry for keeping you waiting Mike, would you like something to drink?'

'No thanks, I'm fine.' Michael managed to say with more confidence than he felt.

Rooney looked down at a file in front of him and said to Michael, 'Something has cropped up and we need a chat with you.'

'Yes fine,' Michael said. 'I hope I can be of help.'

'Good lad, now let's get the formalities over with. I think you know Mr Price? Have you heard of Mr Higgins or myself before?'

'No sir, today's the first time I've met any of you gentlemen.' Michael said. 'Including Mr Price.'

'You're right of course, you report to Ron Keegan, I understand you met him this afternoon?'

'Yes, at the Spa Hotel.'

'How did you find him? I mean did he seem himself?' Rooney said looking up for the first time at Michael.

Michael looked along the conference table. It was disproportionately large to the number of people seated. Then he looked back at Rooney. He had a fixed smile on his face and was waiting for a reply. He must be about sixty, with a slight aroma of evil, Michael thought. 'He seemed different somehow, I can't quite put my finger on it, but yes he was acting strange, Mr Rooney,' Michael said.

'I see,' Rooney hesitated as though he was formulating an important question. 'Do you mind telling me why you met him today?'

He's bending over backwards to be polite, Michael thought. He wants to lull me into a false sense of security before he pounces. He knows well why we met. They think they have me, I've one chance and I must play my cards very carefully. 'That depends in what capacity you are asking the question sir?'

Rooney gave the Brotherhood sign, which Michael acknowledged and then made a different sign to the effect that he was not satisfied that all those present were brotherhood members. That was Brotherhood procedure, and if Michael were amongst friends each person present would give an appropriate sign without further prompting. Price gave the sign but Higgins did not. 'In the capacity of a friend,' Rooney said.

Michael remained silent, proper protocol had not been adhered to and in the circumstances he considered it inadvisable to overlook the breach. Everyone in the room knew he was under considerable pressure and were waiting to see how he would react. If he started blabbing out nervously they would perceive him as a liability and send for the Auditor. His only chance was to remain cool and not permit his interrogator to outsmart him.

It was finely balanced and the key was to project an air of confidence. The least sign of fear would spoil his chance. He looked at Rooney and said, 'At this moment I only feel at liberty to discuss that Mr Keegan asked about the murder of Fr Murphy.' He hesitated looked at each man in turn and added, 'We did discuss another matter but I do not feel I can go into it at this time.'

'Were you able to give him any assistance?' Rooney asked.

'No, I told him I only knew what I read in the papers.'

'Did he mention your contributions?'

Michael gave the Brotherhood sign but again Rooney and Price were the only two to acknowledge. Michael knew that they were working on the assumption that if he were lying he would be so nervous that he would not notice. It would be taken as a sign that he had a guilty conscience.

Brotherhood rules were strict and every member knew that the question of contributions was taboo in the presence of a non-member. Higgins had not given the appropriate sign and until he did contributions should not be discussed. A good trick if one had never heard of it before, Michael thought as he said, 'I'm sorry sir, I don't think I understand your question.'

Rooney was about to speak again when Higgins intervened. 'Good man Captain, you've done very well,' he said giving the secret sign.

Michael acknowledged the sign with mixed feelings. People at Higgins' level were not prone to exposing their association with clandestine subversive organisations lightly. It meant that Michael Lynch would never be able to relate what he had seen to another person or that he had Rooney's complete trust. The latter proposition was by far the least likely and Michael knew it.

Higgins was looking through Michael no doubt sizing him up before he decided how to dispose of him. 'So you discussed the murder of Fr Murphy Mike, and you say there was other business on the agenda?'

Nicely put, Michael thought. You know fucking well what other business was on the agenda and that sly little glint tells me that you think you have me on the ropes. Perhaps I am but I have one surprise punch left and I think this is the time to let it fly; 'Yes there was other business on the agenda. In fact I think that was really why Ron wanted to see me. He wanted to discuss our bank account in the Cayman Islands.'

The three men exchanged quick glances and turned to Michael; 'Are you saying that you and Ronald Keegan had a joint offshore bank account?' Higgins asked incredulously.

'No I mean our account.'

Michael's answer had the desired effect. The three men were bamboozled and he could see their minds working overtime in an attempt to comprehend. They must think I'm trying to buy my way out of this quagmire and of course they're right, Michael thought. They're amazed because I pinpointed exactly what's on their minds.

'I'm sorry Mike, we have no record of that account,' Rooney said. 'When you say "our" account, what do you mean?'

'The Brotherhood slush fund. The account Ron instructed me to open a few years ago.'

'I see.' Rooney said looking down at his file. 'And how much is left in this account?'

'I'm not sure of the exact figure Ron would be better able to tell you that. I guess that there's over five million in it. Yes, there must be at least that much because we've never had occasion to make a withdrawal.'

Michael knew that greed would come to his rescue; he was out of the woods. The fact that there were no withdrawals made his story credible, and people believe what they want to believe.

***

The incident was a watershed in Michael's career. The Cayman account became the cohesion in a bond between those present at Michael's court martial. The opportunity presented was not lost on any of those present and they were prepared to back their new man Michael Lynch on his way to the top.

The morning after Michael's "court martial" the body of Ron Keegan was discovered half eaten by foxes. Jim Doran had done a good job. In less than a year Michael was brought into the higher echelons of the IRB.

XI

Sympathy

MICHAEL WAS PUT IN charge of a new post, called Head of Home Affairs. The role could be roughly compared to that of Minister for Home Affairs in the Irish Republic or that of Home Secretary in Britain. That was how Michael perceived his new post and there was logic in the comparisons.

In the state comprising thirty-two counties of Ireland, the need to have political institutions in place was perceived as elementary in the political equation. The new order under the political wing of Sinn Fein pursued that policy and hence Michael's appointment. It was explained to Michael that although the job did touch internal discipline it was more to do with the internal security of the state.

At first Michael found it difficult to grasp the thinking behind the scheme. Being in charge of the Home Affairs of an abstract state was bordering on the surreal and served no useful purpose. Later it was explained to him that the scheme was born out of a desire to court the electorate. To show that Sinn Fein could deliver on law and order. That it would be tough on crime and anti-social behaviour. These were important issues in the mind of the electorate.

There were "no-go" areas in parts of the North and to a lesser extent in Dublin. In the North the media blamed paramilitaries for the rise in crime and the inability of the Royal Ulster Constabulary to do anything about it. If people felt fear, which they ascribed to the activities of the IRA, votes would be lost. "Remember the golden rule for a successful guerrilla campaign," Michael was told. "If you lose the sympathy of the people you lose the war."

Michael began to see several advantages to being in charge of law and order. People were discontented with the legal systems of both the North and the Republic. The soaring crime figures and the inability of the police to do anything about them created the right conditions. The IRA could fill the gap and extend its protection services to ordinary people.

***

Michael was given permission to inaugurate a self-financing unit with the specific task of law enforcement. In the Republic the scheme got off the ground with little difficulty. The nod was given to garda members to co-operate by providing details of active criminals through liaison channels. In the North the task proved more problematic, but eventually people in "no-go" areas were provided with a forum where they could air their grievances.

Culprits were dealt with harshly. First offenders were given the option to make good the wrong they had done, after which they would receive punishment. In most cases that comprised a severe beating and a warning not to commit further offences. For second or subsequent violation offenders received similar punishment and were ordered to leave the neighbourhood. The definition of neighbourhood was the territory under the control of the IRA.

***

When Denise Ward-Riley arrived in Panama she was labouring under the illusion that she was going to carry out a straightforward transaction with the Panama National Bank. She had her grandpa's death certificate, a copy of his will and a safety deposit box key.

The friendly bank-clerk confirmed that the bonds were in a safety-deposit box in the bank vaults. Provided one was in possession of the key that fitted the box, the bank, would hand over its contents after checking the identity of the key-holder.

The first hint that there was a problem emerged when Denise indicated that she wished to cash-in the bonds. The clerk explained that they were not negotiable in Panama and added that as far as he knew they had no value outside the Irish Republic. He told her he could put her in touch with a person whom he knew, and who might be able to assist her. She agreed.

The next day a meeting was arranged with the person to take place in her hotel room. Afterwards she had second thoughts about the wisdom of inviting a stranger to her room. But it was too late and the man was due within the hour.

In fact he arrived half an hour later and turned out to be nothing like the person Denise had conjured up in her mind. He was good looking, in his early thirties, smartly dressed and spoke with a barely perceptible Irish accent. 'Miss Ward-Riley?' he said with a friendly smile, when Denise opened the door. 'I'm Damien Price; we spoke on the telephone.'

Price knew his stuff. He was able to give Denise the full history of her grandfather's bonds including details of his service in the IRB. Two hours passed, by which time Denise was completely relaxed in the company of the helpful stranger. He was returning to Ireland in a few days and suggested that Denise accompany him. He would ensure she met the right people and got the going rate for her grandfather's bonds, 'It's the least I can do for the granddaughter of a friend of my grandfather,' he said. 'They were both of the same mind about the English invasion of their country.'

She knew better than to put her trust in a stranger, but this man was different. He looked her straight in the eye and she felt she could trust him. Two days later they stood arm in arm at Panama Airport waiting to board a plane for Amsterdam.

***

Denise thought she should be experiencing pangs of guilt but to her astonishment she felt none. She was happier than she ever felt and she knew the reason. The only difficulty she had was trying to pinpoint the moment her life changed. Three days ago if someone predicted that she would give herself to a man other than Patrick O'Connell she would have been insulted. At that time she thought the bond of fidelity that existed between them was unbreakable.

But that's what happened and it happened more than once. Damien Price had opened a door into her heart that she did not know was there. She believed he did not do this by beguiling her with sweet-talk or by taking advantage of her situation. It happened because she wanted it to happen and she did not regret it.

The long haul to Amsterdam passed too quickly. Denise hoped it would last forever as she snuggled into Damien. She was lost in a pleasant romantic mist and did not want the spell broken. 'We'll be landing in less than an hour,' he said, as he withdrew his hand from her breast. 'I think we'll spend a night in Amsterdam before going on to Birmingham.'

'Yes, I'd like that,' Denise said, looking adoringly into his eyes.

They booked into a hotel from where Denise telephoned her parents. She told them that she was at Birmingham Airport waiting to catch a flight to Dublin. I couldn't tell them I'm spending a night in an Amsterdam hotel with someone I just met, she thought, as she hung up the telephone. In fact she spent three days and three nights in a hotel room in Amsterdam consumed in lustful copulation with Damien.

***

During the flight from Amsterdam to Birmingham Denise learned that Damien wanted them to pass through customs separately. It was the first sign that distant clouds were gathering in an otherwise blue sky. Denise refused to permit her instincts to spoil her newly found happiness and ignored the warning signals emitting from somewhere inside her head.

The nightmare started when an insignificant looking customs officer singled Denise out of the throng of people passing through the green channel of Birmingham Airport. She was unable to see his eyes behind his dark spectacles, but the irritating smirk on his face was enough to betray his despotism. As he went through the routine of eliminating plausible excuses in the event of contraband being found in her luggage, she stood at the low wooden counter.

'Read this notice. Did anyone assist you to pack your luggage? Are you carrying any luggage that does not belong to you? Do you understand that you may be prosecuted if you are found importing any illegal substance into Great Britain? You have entered the green channel, do you know what that means? Have you anything to declare Miss?'

'No nothing;' Denise said nervously.

'Please open your case Miss.'

The officer rummaged expertly through the contents of the case until he found what Denise began to suspect he was looking for, the package in which was contained the Irish Republican bonds. He looked suspiciously at it and then at Denise, 'May I see your passport Miss?' he said extending his hand.

'Yes, of course Sir,' Denise said, handing it to him.

'Thank you Miss Ward-Riley,' the official said after examining the passport. 'I have to inform you that you are being arrested on suspicion of drug trafficking.'

XII

The Bordello Spy

ROBERT CHAMPS WAS BORN in Glasgow in 1930. As a young boy he harboured notions of joining Rangers FC along with his friend George Goody. It never happened and in 1949 both were lance corporals in the Army Intelligence Corps, stationed in West Germany. They left the army in 1953 and went their separate ways. When they renewed their friendship in 1965 Robert was a detective sergeant in Coventry City Police and George Goody was a millionaire businessman in the same city.

***

In 1969 Detective Inspector Robert Champs was required to resign from the Warwickshire and Coventry Constabulary. The Chief Constable, under powers conferred on him by the Police Act 1964, dispatched him. Many believed that Champs was lucky not to have been prosecuted but he did not share that feeling.

Robert Champs found it difficult to understand what had gone wrong. His problem started as the result of a routine complaint by a member of the public, which spiralled into a full blown disciplinary inquiry headed by senior officers from an outside force. Detective Superintendent Cox, assisted by Detective Chief Inspector Guest of Birmingham City Police conducted the investigation.

The decision to call in "outsiders" was made as a result of pressure exerted by the Home Secretary, 'Use your powers to get rid of this bad apple Chief Constable,' he said, in a tone that left no room for negotiations.

When Champs was told that the Home Secretary had taken an interest in the case, he was not surprised. He thought the intervention was a signal that the government was behind him. That his friends at MI5 had come to his aid and persuaded the Home Office to do the right thing and rescue an agent in difficulty. After all, the problem he was facing came about because of the nature of the operation he was engaged in.

***

The complaint was made by the single parent mother of a fifteen year old girl who alleged that her daughter had been forced into prostitution whilst on the run from a young offenders institution. She complained after being spoken to by Champs about the attempted blackmail of George Goody. The blackmail hinged on her asking for a substantial amount of money in return for not prosecuting Goody for having unlawful sexual intercourse with her young daughter and leading her into prostitution.

If the matter had ended there Inspector Champs would not have featured. But he was implicated in the second prong of the complaint, which was that he a police inspector threatened to arrest the mother for blackmail instead of pursuing the more serious complaint of corrupting a minor.

***

When Goody and Champs met in Coventry in 1965, it was inevitable that they would resurrect their close friendship. Coventry had been lucky for Goody and at the time he had several friends amongst influential members of Coventry City Council. He had nailed his mast to the ships of Councillors Waugh and Meffin, who between them had control over the allocation of lucrative contracts emanating from Coventry Corporation.

Favours done were favours remembered. Goody looked after the people who looked after him. He was pointed in the right direction and by the time he shook hands with his old army comrade he was a multi-millionaire. His construction business was thriving and it was impossible to put a price on the invisible assets of his company. The goodwill he had built up in Coventry Corporation alone was the envy of other businessmen in the city. If it were possible to quantify it there is no doubt that it would have added considerably to his fortune.

George maintained strong links with the Scottish (Div) Orange Order. He held an innate hatred of Catholics, particularly those who were moaning about the way they were being treated in Northern Ireland. The answer to their problem was simple in George's eyes. All they had to do was cross the border and join their brethren in the South. But he knew they had no intentions of doing that because if they did they would have plenty to moan about. They would have no free "National Health, poor education and less free handouts from the state.

On 11th July every year George went to his Lodge to prepare for the short voyage between Broadsea Bay in Scotland to Larne in Northern Ireland.

On such occasions he would dress in traditional Orange attire and join the flotilla taking thousands of Scots Orangemen to Ulster to celebrate their forefather's 17th century victory at the Battle of the Boyne. They would march onto Irish soil beating drums, playing flutes and bagpipes and be greeted by Ulster Orangemen in similar attire and doing likewise.

***

Back in Coventry over the years George had found a kindred spirit amongst some Freemasons. He was high on the list to be elected Worshipful Master of his Lodge, but he was disappointed to learn that English Masons had put clear water between themselves and associated Orange Lodges. Worst still, there was no objection to Catholics joining Lodges in England. It was as though the English had forgotten the "Glorious Revolution" of 1688 and the antics of King James.

Still there were those who remembered. George made it his business to seek them out and encourage them to do the right thing. If Catholics got their way the celebrations of 12th July would become a thing of the past. That could not be allowed to happen. Once they got their way in Ulster they would zoom in on Scotland. Catholics there were waiting for their chance to pounce and would follow the example set by their Irish cousins.

***

Goody was disappointed when he met his old pal Champs in Coventry and learned that he was a lowly detective sergeant. Champs said on leaving Scotland all those years ago that he was going to London to join British intelligence. Goody had no doubt that his friend was doing the right thing. Espionage was Champs' big interest and he had the makings of a great spy.

He had always wanted to be a James Bond and when they joined the army it was Champs that talked Goody into joining the Intelligence Corps rather than the Black Watch.

Champs had an inordinate interest in the methods of the Gestapo. He admired Walter Schellenberg the Nazi spymaster and studied his methodology. Champs admired the way Schellenberg perfected the art of utilising trained prostitutes in bordellos to surreptitiously extract information from clients. Champs even persuaded Goody to accompany him on a visit to 11 Giesebrechtstrasse, Berlin. There in 1939

Madam Kitty Schmidt ran a high-class bordello for Schellenberg. 'This is it,' Champs said pointing to the derelict building. 'Kitty made a fortune here. She did a lot of good too helping Jews to escape from Blackshirt harassment. The SS found out and made her spy for them.'

'Is that why you brought me here?' Goody asked impatiently. 'You want me to marvel at this dilapidated shambles?'

'As a member of the Intelligence Corps, you should feel privileged to visit this shrine.' Champs said holding his arms up as though he was going to embrace it.

***

During their army service Champs would return to the subject whenever he saw an opening. He explained how Kitty was recruited after she found out that the SS was onto her and she was attempting to escape Berlin. How her plan was frustrated at the last moment when the SS confronted her with a dossier outlining her activities. She was given two choices, either work for the Nazis or be executed for aiding Jews. She opted for the former and agreed to resume her career.

To all outward appearances things were the same as before. Nobody suspected that she was working for the Gestapo or that ten third-floor rooms had concealed microphones linked to recording devices in the cellar. The rooms were allocated to twenty SS specially trained high-class prostitutes. Their job was to encourage selected clients to betray their secrets during pillow talk.

Word of the service on offer soon seeped down the Berlin grapevine. High ranking army officers, visiting officials, embassy staff and foreign dignitaries frequented the establishment. In the relaxed atmosphere tongues were loosened. Few could resist bragging about their importance to the beautiful Gestapo agents.

***

The thing that appealed to Champs was the way human frailty could be used to the advantage of the State. It was a treble-edged tool in that it had the potential to uncover traitors, provide intelligence and blackmail those caught in its web. Champs pointed out that the Russian KGB had adopted and refined the methods of the Third Reich. Beautiful Russian female spies called "Swans" were trained to trap heterosexuals, and males called "Ravens" to ensnare homosexuals.

Champs saw it as exploiting "human frailty." He harboured a notion that a similar system could be of use to Western Intelligence Agencies. In their last conversation before Champs set out for London he indicated that he would impress his examiners by suggesting that British Intelligence should adopt a similar system. He would cite the "Auntie Vera " (William Vassall) spy scandal and point out that it was the use of Ravens that enabled the Russians to "turn" Vassall.

What Goody did not know when he said goodbye to his friend at Glasgow Railway Station was that Champs was going to London on spec. MI5 was not expecting him nor was it in the business of employing ex-non-commissioned officers of the Army Intelligence Corps. Nor did Goody know that Robert Champs would spend three months in London attempting to persuade officials that he was the up-and-coming James Bond, before he was sent to Coventry.

***

Champs' naivety in believing that his service in the Intelligence Corps would guarantee him a place in MI5 struck a sympathetic cord in the official instructed to reject his application. Before informing Champs that there was no suitable vacancy in British intelligence the official telephoned a friend in Coventry City Police.

Champs took the advice imparted by the official and left London to join Coventry police. He was successful and within a year rumours, started by him, were in circulation about his association with MI5. These coupled with exaggerated accounts of his exploits in the Army Intelligence Corps gave him kudos in the small force.

Other happenings within the police world fuelled speculation. The Home Office was putting pressure on chief constables to bring their forces into the twentieth century. The police national computer was in the pipeline and criminal intelligence was seen as the answer to spiralling organised crime.

Over-imaginative senior police officers in Coventry began to see Champs as a Home Office mole. They thought he had been planted to report on the strength of opposition to the proposed amalgamation of Warwickshire and Coventry police and to report back on the force's attitude to crime intelligence. He fuelled speculation by qualifying his denial with throwaway remarks. 'Of course the Home Office have a spy in the camp but it's not me.'

***

Within three years he was promoted to sergeant in the new crime intelligence department. He was given an office in Coventry Central Police Station and a remit to organise channels of communication for the transmission and dissemination of criminal intelligence. It was an autonomous temporary position to be reviewed when the question of the proposed amalgamation of Coventry City Police with Warwickshire Constabulary was decided.

The Home Office forced the amalgamation, which led to the birth of the Warwickshire and Coventry Constabulary. Once again lady luck came to the aid of Robert Champs and he was promoted to detective inspector and placed in charge of the Criminal Intelligence Department of Coventry division. His department was expanded to reflect his extended responsibilities. He now had three sergeants and fifteen constables under his span of control, supported by three civilian clerical staff.

***

Champs left the day-to-day running of his department to his sergeants and seldom questioned their judgement. In return they turned a blind eye to his inordinate obsession with vice. He called it the "Human Frailty" section and gave strict orders that it was never to be discussed unless he was present. He reinforced his instruction by warning that any violation would be treated as a breach of the Official Secrets Act 1911. The department was known as the FH section and files contained therein were only for the eyes of Inspector Champs and MI5.

The mention of MI5 was enough to confirm the suspicions of many that Champs was in reality an undercover agent. He made no effort to correct the misapprehension; on the contrary, he dropped hints designed to fuel speculation that he was in fact a spy. And from his point of view there was truth in the rumours.

His FH section was not confined to gathering information about the activities of the criminal fraternity. He had learned much from his research into the way Nazi and USSR agencies obtained and utilised intelligence. He saw information as a universal tool. Its ability to persuade reluctant supporters to come on side was as strong as its ability to recruit reluctant informers. Knowledge about the habits and weaknesses of those with power to grant or withhold favours was as potent as that about the enemy.

***

George Goody, at the time, was obsessed with the state of play in Northern Ireland. The Civil Rights movement was causing him nightmares. He wanted to hear that the establishment was aware of the situation and doing something about it. He listened eagerly as Champs explained that things were in hand and that he was part of them. 'I knew it,' Goody said jumping up, 'I fucking knew you were part of British Intelligence!'

'That's not for me to confirm or deny George, as you very well know,' Champs said slyly. 'Let's put it this way, MI5 were impressed with my research.'

'Say no more Bob,' Goody said raising the palm of his hand, 'I've been thinking about that too.'

'We're still toying with it George. M has reservations about public reaction if news of such an establishment ever leaked.'

'If you wait for official sanction you'll be waiting forever. Maybe I can help? As you know things have being going extremely well for me here. My wealth and talents are at your disposal. Do you know what I'm saying?'

'Go on George?'

'I can provide the premises if you can square it with the boys in blue. Do you think you can do that?'

'I'm sure I can George, but I'll have to get clearance from M.'

Champs would get his intelligence if he went along with what George had in mind. There were two things that drove him; a hate of Catholics and a penchant for young girls. He could see a way of satisfying both through his old army friend's obsession with Kitty's dilapidated bordello in Berlin.

Goody's plan involved a bloc of council high-rise flats in Hillfields, Coventry. He could acquire the tenancy of three flats on the top floor and turn them into "entertainment" suites, 'You know Bob, use them to gather intelligence, like Kitty's in Berlin.'

'It's a great idea George, I'm sure M will go for it.'

A week later Champs announced that M was fully behind the scheme.

'I thought he'd like it,' George said pretending to believe what he was hearing. 'Have you squared it with your colleagues?'

'That's no problem, just get the place up and running.'

***

Champs role was to ensure that the police turned a blind eye to the activities in the new entertainment suites. George paid for the refurbishment and for the installation of sophisticated recording equipment. It circumvented the problem of Champs having to show the expenditure on his department's budget. It also ensured that Goody was in full control of the venture including income.

As the enterprise mushroomed it became difficult to keep matters under control. Questions about the new entertainment suite in Hillfields, Coventry, were being asked. Champs managed to keep the authorities at bay with a mixture of blackmail and bullshit. Some senior police officers and local officials were happy to turn a blind eye in exchange for a blind eye being turned to their patronage of the establishment. Champs persuaded others that the operation was part of a legitimate undercover sting.

Police officers under Champs' span of control were told to protect the status of the new "Intelligence Gathering Centre." Selected officers were trained to deal with information and complaints from members of the public. The officers were primed to show kindred revulsion and moral outrage at complaints that a brothel was in operation. 'Thank you for your help, we are on top of the problem and will move in when the time is right,' was normally enough to satisfy complainants.

The crime intelligence department found it difficult to handle the amount of criminal intelligence emanating from the brothel. Champs submitted reports to MI5 about the activities of subversive elements in the Midlands. George Goody took charge of monitoring Irish clients. He was looking for intelligence about the activities of Irish nationalists in the area. He submitted the names of Coventry Irish businessmen who were contributing to "The Cause," to his contacts in Belfast.

Champs never received any recognition from MI5. He took silence as an indication that his intelligence was being gratefully received. In the Army Intelligence Corps, if an officer did not like something one would hear about it. Silence was a signal that things were going well and being noted by the right people. In that way MI5 either deliberately or unwittingly fed Champs' ego and gave him the confidence to continue.

Goody was responsible for recruitment. He imported a madam to take charge of the day-to-day running of the entertainment suites. Like Kitty in Berlin she guided special clients to wired rooms. Girls on the run from home or young offenders' institutions were high on the list of "recruits." Scouts combed cafes, nightclubs, railway stations and similar establishments in Birmingham, Brighton and London looking for suitable girls. It was decided not to inform them that they were part of an undercover operation or to give them special training.

Champs kept foremost in his mind that the core business was gathering crime intelligence. He was not surprised how readily customers let their guard down. It was amazing that men, who in other circumstances would withstand the rack, were prepared to blabber and brag to prostitutes. It was as though they saw the encounter as part of an egotistical tour. They were in what Champs called a "vulnerable state."

Then it happened; men from a hitherto unheard of department from New Scotland Yard sent in undercover officers. It was unheard of that members of an outside force would cross police boundaries without informing the local constabulary. The Chief Constable was furious, not with the London vice Squad, but with Inspector Champs.

***

At first Champs did not connect the two incidents. He believed that he had disposed of the first and was unaware of the second. A vulnerable state, he thought, as he listened to the chief.

When George Goody came to him and said he was being blackmailed, Champs assured him that he could fix it. As the story unfolded, he recognised that there was a serious problem. Goody had been stupid; he had fallen in love with a fifteen-year-old girl who had been recruited whilst on the run in London.

She came to Coventry and was taken to the bordello where her first client was George. He saw her every night thereafter and forbade Madam Spice from introducing her to other clients. After a few weeks the girl wanted to return to London and George volunteered to provide her with a flat there. All she had to do was keep seeing him to the exclusion of all others. She agreed, and that arrangement would have continued if George did not arrive unexpectedly one night to catch her entertaining a client.

Inspector Champs did not have to be told what happened next. He knew George and he knew his temper. 'How bad is she George?'

'I admit that I give her a few slaps, you know me Bobby,' he said. 'But that's not the problem.'

'Okay, how much does she want?'

George shrugged his shoulders and explained that she was not the one making the demands; it was her mother. He ignored the look of alarm on Champs' face and continued to explain that after the tiff they made up and she promised not to do it again. But when he next visited her a woman who turned out to be her mother confronted him. She was vitriolic and after telling him exactly what she thought of him demanded £10'000 cash or she would report him to the police.

When the mother came to Coventry to collect the £10'000, Champs met her. He told her who he was and that he was investigating a complaint of blackmail made by a prominent businessman. The woman was about 35 years of age, smartly dressed and spoke with a degree of confidence that he did not expect. 'I don't think blackmail is a word I would use in these circumstances,' she said coldly. 'No, I think compensation for deflowering a minor is more appropriate.'

Champs was finding it difficult to pin her down. She was elusive and had a quick tongue. There was something about her that told him his police warrant card had not found its mark.

'I see where you're coming from,' he said pausing. 'Mr Goody says that your daughter told him she was eighteen and that he was not the first man she was with. Even so he's prepared to pay £500 to avoid embarrassment. I'm not sure how one quantifies these things, but I think it's a fair offer?'

'Is he a friend of yours inspector?'

The question had implications and it annoyed him, 'I'm not sure that's relevant,' he said sharply. 'As a matter of fact I do know him, but that's not why I'm here.'

'Are you a member of the Coventry vice squad?'

Champs was not accustomed to members of the public questioning him. No, it was his job to question them and this lady was too cocky for her own good. It was time to show her who was boss. 'Look madam, I'm not here to answer your questions,' he said coldly. 'No, I'm here to investigate an allegation of blackmail, or to use the modern term, making unwarranted demands with menaces. I've shown you my warrant card and told you this is an official investigation.'

'Very good Inspector,' she said, calmly. 'Are you going to arrest me?'

'No, the complainant wants this resolved with as little fuss as possible,' Champs said. 'But if I have any further complaints I may be forced to act.'

'You won't have any further complaints about me officer,' she said pointedly. 'Have you the £500 on you or do I need to speak to Mr Goody?'

It worked, Champs thought, but it always does.

'I have the money here madam.'

'Would you like me to sign for it?'

'No, that won't be necessary. All I want is your word that you won't bother Mr Goody again.'

'You have it Inspector. I'm sorry did you say your name was Champs?'

'Yes, Inspector Champs.'

***

Now as Robert Champs sat in front of his Chief Constable, he could see the same £500 on the table with his fingerprints all over it. 'Have you ever heard of a Ms Shepherd, Inspector?' The Chief Constable said looking over his half-rimmed spectacles.

'No sir, the name doesn't ring a bell.'

'If I were you Inspector I'd pay more attention to bells,' the Chief said with a wry smile. 'I can hear bells knelling all round me, warning bells and the closer you get the louder they clang.'

'Really Sir?'

The enquiry team had submitted an intermediate report directly to the Chief Constable. Normally the Chief would not get involved so early because disciplinary matters are in the domain of his deputy up to the point of an official hearing. The fact that the Chief was involved at this early stage gave Champs to understand that the Home Office had instructed him to quash the complaint. 'Ms Shepherd, Inspector, that's who I want to know about.'

'I'm sorry sir,' Champs said earnestly. 'Ms Shepherd, who is she?'

'She's the lady you gave this money to on behalf of your friend Mr Goody,' the chief said picking up the bundle of notes. 'Now if he were the victim of a blackmail why did you pay the alleged blackmailer?'

'Yes, I see your point Sir.'

'Where's the crime report covering Mr Goody's complaint?'

'I sorted it out myself Sir, there's no crime report.'

'I won't embarrass you by pointing out that Standing Orders require officers to record all crimes,' the chief said flatly. 'We have much more serious matters to discuss.'

***

An hour later Robert Champs was no longer a police officer having agreed to resign in exchange for not being prosecuted. He was driven from police HQ, Leek Wotton, to Coventry where he was supervised as he collected his personal belongings. He was unable to secretly palm three tape cassettes he wanted to take with him. They were in a secret compartment in his desk and the superintendent was watching him like a hawk. I'll get PC Bayliss to get them later, he thought, as he walked out of his office for the last time.

***

In 1970 Robert Champs was appointed general manager of two bordellos in strife-ridden Belfast. One was off the Malone Road and the other off the Antrim Road. It may be taken as a marker of how desperate the security agencies were to find out what was happening on the ground, that on this occasion Champs had the tacit backing of MI5 and the Royal Ulster Constabulary.

George Goody "fronted" the financial aspects of setting up the enterprise. Financial donations were made anonymously by several well-connected people in Northern Ireland and assurances were given that the operation would not be hassled by the authorities. 'You have a verbal permit to carry on for the foreseeable future,' George was assured. 'Obviously if things go wrong and this gets into the papers you're on your own.'

The Chief of police was prepared to permit his officers to turn a blind eye. He reasoned that Northern Ireland was virtually under martial law, which enabled him to leave such matters in the hands of the armed forces and intelligence agencies. The official line from both was to the effect that they could not give official sanction to the operation but unofficially they supported it. Two agents from MI5, and captain of the Army Intelligence Corps were unofficially appointed to liaise in the gathering of intelligence.

***

Robert Champs was furious. It was typical of British Intelligence to leave the dirty work to someone else. Where were the trained agents capable of eliciting information from their customers? Like the last time, it was left up to him to take all the chances.

Champs' job included maintaining lines of communication with security officials through his handler. He had limited access to intelligence but he knew the location of cameras hidden behind two-way mirrors and microphones concealed in bedposts. Security technicians had stolen his idea to run cables to a central recording point and with this knowledge he was able to tap into the system and monitor activities in some of the rooms.

He was required to sign the Official Secrets Act and warned that to communicate anything he saw or heard in the course of his duties to an unauthorised person would land him in prison. It was also pointed out that in the event of his being imprisoned he would serve his sentence in the same prison as many of his old customers.

***

Against that Champs had to pay homage to his masters in Orange Lodges who got him placed. Goody used up several favours in order to get his man appointed, at least that is what he told Champs. However, the real reason was that Goody needed a man he could trust to intercept intelligence relating to the activities of Loyalist paramilitaries before it reached the authorities. From his perspective it would be counter-productive if his side was caught in the trap set for Catholics.

The official line that Britain wanted to interview terrorists, of whatever persuasion, did not sit comfortably with the way George saw things. Loyalist paramilitaries were on the side of righteousness and should not be subjected to the same scrutiny as nationalists.

People had gone to great lengths to ensure that Loyalist political parties in Ulster were not tarred with the same brush as Sinn Fein. George knew that political parties with paramilitary wings did not get good public or political relations. He was going to ensure that Loyalist politicians would not be embarrassed, a thing that could happen if intelligence returned from the bordellos was not censored.

It was a complication brought about by his failure to anticipate that the British Government could not be seen to be taking sides. Sir Edward had made it clear that his participation was strictly on the understanding that all intelligence gathered would be handed over to MI5. He refused to give an undertaking that intelligence gathered on Loyalist activities would be ignored.

Goody saw it as typical of the English to apply the rules of cricket to everything they did. He did not trust them and knew that in their hearts they wanted rid of Ulster. He knew they would give it back to the "Fenians" tomorrow if they could. But they can't give it back, not whilst the "Fenians" held a bomb in one hand and a gun in the other, he mused.

XIII

※

A Loyalist Plot

THE INTELLIGENCE DEPARTMENT OF the IRA heard that Fenian bonds were being circulated in the Irish Republic. Its initial reaction was that British Intelligence was engaging in its felicity for dirty tricks. But given that Eamonn de Valera, first leader of the Irish republic, called in official Fenian bonds more than fifty years ago it was a trick that would not succeed. The bonds were no longer negotiable and had little value as collectibles.

Michael Lynch was given the job of finding out what was at the bottom of the rumours. Sinn Fein, IRA Senior Command wanted to know what was happening and in particular whether its territorial sanctity had been breached.

It was verified that Grandpa Riley had informed Central Council when he acquired the Fenian bonds. At the time it was thought that he had merely purchased a sample for sentimental reasons.

Through contacts in Miami, Lynch established that Riley had purchased a consignment of bonds, which he placed in a safety-deposit box in a Panamanian bank. The story did not make sense until further enquiries in America suggested that Riley had been conned. The bonds were forgeries. That raised more questions than it answered.

Answers began to emerge when it became known that Riley was not the only person taken-in. Rumours that bonds impregnated with heroin were being sold at discotheques in Dublin and Wexford were investigated and found to be true. The obvious implication that someone was out to discredit the Fenian movement in the Irish Republic called for immediate action. Lynch was given a week to get to the bottom of what was going on.

***

Lynch suspected a Loyalist plot to discredit the IRA in the Republic. A bond sold at a discotheque in Dundalk was analysed. It was a forgery professionally copied onto high quality absorbent paper and impregnated with heroin. Its estimated street value was between IR£300 & IR£500. The political wing of the IRA called an emergency meeting.

The meeting was conducted in boardroom style and assertions had to be backed by fact. The assembly listened to Michael's report after which he was ordered to wait in an ante-room. He was in Sinn Fein HQ, Dublin and aware that it was the control centre of Irish terrorist activities. Presently he was recalled to the committee room, 'We consider that something must be done about this state of affairs Michael,' the Chairman said. 'We're putting you in charge of the operation.'

A Special Unit was authorised and Lynch was told to leave no stone unturned. There was consensus that the bonds were probably forged by Loyalists to raise funds for paramilitary organisations. The Chairman concluded, 'If people think that we're circulating these bonds we'll lose the goodwill of the population. '

***

The Australian branch of the IRB was requested to re-examine papers taken from Grandpa Riley's home after his death. That was when the letter intended for his family was found and sent to James in Vietnam. Lynch enlisted the assistance of an Irish American activist to bribe an employee in the Panamanian Bank to inform him when there was movement of the bonds. Arrangements were also put in place to monitor the movements of the Ward-Riley family.

When Denise Ward-Riley arrived in Panama to collect the bonds there were two men and a woman waiting for her. One of the men was a member of the Ulster Defence Association (UDA) and the other a member of the Provisional IRA. Michael Lynch dressed as a Catholic priest, wearing thick rimmed glasses was so well disguised that his mother would not have recognised him. Nor would the mother of his female companion have recognised her daughter disguised as a nun.

***

Amanda DeCourcey was twenty-five years of age, beautiful, with long black hair and green eyes. She joined the IRA to avenge the death of her brother by Loyalists terrorists. It was not the fact that they had killed him that persuaded her to take up arms, but rather the way they did it.

Her brother's crime was that he was a lover of music with no political affiliations. He was murdered because he happened to be a member of a show-band hired to perform in a club in Co Down. When in the Republic late one night they were ambushed. They were not granted a quick clean death, but instead were interrogated and tortured before been beaten beyond recognition. Amanda wanted revenge and she moved to Dublin where she joined the IRA.

Michael Lynch spotted her potential. Her stunning beauty was enough to turn men's heads. Her innocent eyes and friendly smile were sufficient to put to rest any doubts or suspicions in the mind of her prey. If she dropped her handkerchief men would rush to pick it up and if she were stranded by a broken-down car male motorists would stop to assist her. She was perfect for the role Michael Lynch had in mind and she lived up to his expectations. She lured her prey with a degree of animal instinct that made even Lynch regard her as "keen".

In Panama, Amanda, dressed in a nun's habit, was not there to turn heads. She bribed the desk clerk to book her into the hotel room adjacent to Denise. There she set up monitoring equipment and when Damien Price entered Denise's room his movements and conversation, were picked up by Amanda, in sound and vision.

As soon as the itinerary was known Michael Lynch went to Panama Airport and booked a ticket to Birmingham. He booked Amanda on the same flight as Denise and Price. When he boarded his flight he was in possession of information confirming UDA involvement in the Fenian bond drugs racket. More importantly he knew that the UDA man with Denise was travelling incognito and purporting to be Detective Chief Inspector Price of the Garda Special Branch and the IRB.

XIV

Harry the Chat

THE BIRMINGHAM SERIOUS CRIME Squad was the brainchild of an adorned Detective Chief Superintendent called Harry the Chat. He was ascribed the nickname by his subordinates because of the friendly chatty way he had of getting what he wanted. Most high-ranking police officers had a military attitude towards junior ranks. Harry was different; he preferred to talk his officers round, to make it seem as though they were doing him a favour.

His nickname did not reflect all his characteristics. Harry was ambitious, lubricious, and extremely intelligent. He had perfected the art of concealing the unseemly side of his character, but on occasions he would come from behind his mask and strip his teeth. What was then on show was a man prepared to go to any lengths to get what he wanted.

***

When born in Birmingham in 1927, Harry brought joy to his childless parents. They had almost given up hope of producing an heir, so when Harry arrived his parents were overjoyed. His life was set out for him; he would inherit his father's terraced house and be trained as a silver polisher in the Birmingham Jewellery Quarter. If things had run their normal course he would have followed in his father's footsteps, 'I have Adolph Hitler to thank,' he would say when reminiscing about what life might have been like in the absence of World War 2. 'Hitler woke up the working classes.'

At such times Harry would be alluring to the effect the War had on everyday life in Britain. Although he would pass off his remark as a joke, deep down he was not so sure. He had come to realise that men returning from the Second World War were not prepared to put up with the same treatment as those returning from World War 1.

***

During his national service, between 1945 and 1947, he was a signalman in the Royal Signal Regiment stationed in Verdon, West Germany. The War was over when Harry arrived at his posting but only just. In fact there were those who believed it was not over, and reckoned that in the near future British soldiers would be fighting the Russians. Mr Churchill was not going to stand for the way the Soviet Union was behaving!

It was a sobering thought for Harry. He had no desire to go to war, but he knew that was a decision over which he no influence. Others had the say as to whether he would be sent to war; people he did not like because they shouted orders and were not interested in his point of view. At 18 years of age Harry was not in control of either his army or personal life.

On the personal front, his fiancée's father had refused to grant his daughter's hand in marriage. Harry was not good enough, but that was not the reason he gave. It would not have been seemly for a vicar to come straight out and say, "my daughter is too good for you". Instead he used the old procrastination trick, knowing that Alice would meet someone more suitable whilst Harry was away in the army.

***

When he met Alice, Harry was a shy sixteen-year-old lad ignorant about the ways of the world. She was an attractive innocent fifteen-year-old upper middle-class girl. Their innocence was the only thing they had in common. Harry became painfully aware that he was punching above his social class when he learned that the girl sitting beside him at the pictures was a vicar's daughter. She spoke without a Birmingham accent and lacked the brashness of the girls in Harry's social circle. He was afraid of them but with Alice he felt at ease.

She did not mind that Harry came from a lower class, 'Daddy says we are all the same in the eyes of God,' she would say when Harry mentioned the difference.

'He sounds like a very fair man, your father,' Harry would reply.

They were happy in each other's company and when they were not together Harry would daydream about their future together, about the time when they would marry and live happily ever after. Reality came in the form of a letter from the Ministry of War informing him that the day was drawing close when he would have to serve his country. He was obliged to indicate in which of the armed forces he intended to do his National Service.

Alice was devastated and cried when she heard the news. They kissed and wept and swore undying love for each other. They got engaged and announced their intentions to marry before Harry went to war. Alice met Harry's parents who were overjoyed at the prospect of their son marrying, "A lady," as his mother put it.

***

He felt nervous as he walked up the drive to the vicarage. He was wearing his best suit and wanted to give a good first impression to his future father and mother-in-law. Alice had broken the news to her parents and they wanted to meet him in their home as soon as possible. 'They'll love you,' Alice reassured him. 'Daddy's a real softie and you'll love mummy.'

The moment of truth had arrived and Harry looked nervously at the well- spoken lady who opened the door. 'You must be Harry,' Mummy said pronouncing every syllable, as she looked him over from head to toe. 'Won't you come in we are expecting you.'

He followed her into the big drawing room where a

man with grey hair dressed in formal attire sat at a table. He did not stand up to greet Harry, who stood awkwardly in front of him. 'Peter, this is Harry the young man Alice has been seeing,' mummy said in a voice that betrayed her disappointment.

Harry did not like the atmosphere in the room, nor did he like the fact that Alice was nowhere to be seen. He had a keen eye and could see that the table had been set for four. He suspected that the bad atmosphere was the telltale residue of a row that had taken place shortly before his arrival. It did not look as though a fourth person, Alice, would be joining them.

***

Harry did not know that Alice was in her room sobbing. She could not face him or her parents. It had all gone terribly wrong at the last moment. When she first announced her intentions to marry to her parents they were surprised. 'It all seems so sudden dear,' her mother said. 'Do we know the young man?'

'No mummy, I don't think so.' Alice said, and went on to explain that she had not intended to marry so soon but because Harry was going into the army events overtook them.

Her parents seemed to agree pointing out that they had spent their first years of married life in the army. 'You remember Alice, daddy was an army chaplain. You were a captain weren't you dear?'

'Yes, that's right dear,' daddy said putting his arm

around Alice and hugging her. 'The army's a good life, we're very happy for you.'

That was a week ago and they were keen to meet Harry. 'Invite the young man over for tea Alice,' mummy said. 'When can he come?'

The date was set for the following Saturday and during the week mummy fussed and daddy reminisced about life in the Officers' Mess. It was all going so well until an hour before Harry was due to arrive. Mummy had spent the morning preparing the room and setting the table for an introductory tête-à-tête with her prospective son-in-law.

It was all so wonderfully exciting and Alice could not stop talking about Harry. She was still singing his praises when she realised that her mother had stopped what she was doing and had sat down with a vacant look on her face. It was the face that said something is seriously wrong. 'Did you say National Service dear?'

'Yes mummy, Harry has to do his national service like everyone else.'

'Yes, but he's going to Sandhurst isn't he dear?'

'Is that in Aldershot Mother?'

'No not there, Alice. It's the Officers' Training Academy in Kent. Harry is going to be an officer isn't he?'

There were more questions and things went from bad to worse. Daddy, who always took Alice's side in family disagreements, looked pale and bewildered. He agreed with Mummy that there had been a terrible mistake. Alice could not marry a private soldier. She had been properly educated, brought up to be a lady not a common housewife. It was all so upsetting and caused Alice to run to her room and lock the door. It was a thing she had done on previous occasions when things weren't going her way. Daddy would always come to rescue her, but this time no one came; 'We forbid you to marry this boy,' her father shouted after her. 'Stay in your room.'

***

Harry felt uneasy. No it was more than that he was being made to feel inferior. He knew he should break the silence but he could not think of anything to say. There was an invisible wall between he and his future in- laws. They were barely attempting to conceal their disapproval of him and had managed to manoeuvre him into a situation in which he felt silly. He became conscious of his inability to put into words what he felt. To explain that he was aware that he was not what they wanted for their daughter, but he would work hard and provide for her. All he wanted was a chance to prove himself, but the words would not come out.

As Harry stood self consciously at the table the man spoke. He could barely bring himself to look at Harry and when he did his cold eyes forewarned what was coming. 'I understand you've been seeing my daughter,' he said like a judge about to pass the death sentence, 'and that there's been talk of marriage?'

'Yes sir,' Harry said. 'We…'

'My wife and I do not think Alice is old enough to get married,' the man interrupted. 'We're not prepared to give our consent Harry. That's your name, isn't it?'

'Yes, I mean why don't you agree?'

'We cannot give our consent,' the man repeated. How can I put this without hurting your feelings? Alice has been brought up to be a lady, do you understand?'

'But, we're in love sir, 'Harry heard himself blurt out. 'We're…'

'Love is a passing thing son, you'll get over it,' the man interrupted impatiently. 'Now let me explain a few things to you. First Alice is a minor and she may not marry or consort with a person without our consent. Secondly, we do not approve of this relationship. It's not that we don't think you're good enough. I want to make that quite clear. But we do not want you to see her again whilst she's a minor. She'll be 21 in five years time or thereabouts. You'll have to wait.'

'But sir…'

'Harry this interview is ended, I'm very busy and would like you to leave my home please. I must press on.'

Harry walked home in a daze and turned to his father for comfort. 'They don't want people like us son, we're not good enough. I was going to warn you but I thought Alice was different.'

***

Harry did not hear from Alice again. She did not turn up for their Saturday rendezvous and he was too frightened to contact her. He was bitter and humiliated at the way he had been treated. It was a feeling he would know again. During his army training he saw similarities between the attitude of army officers and Alice's father.

He came to resent the snobbery and high-handedness of commissioned officers. He did not like they way they treated other ranks as disposable inferior "things." Their patronising upper-class ways sickened Harry because he realised that they were not play-acting. They believed it was their duty to keep the lower classes in their place and to treat those not born with a silver spoon in their mouth as their lackeys. Harry was proud he did not see himself as a serf fawning at the feet of his lord and master.

***

At the end of his national service, when Harry stood on the deck of the troop ship leaving the port of Bremerhaven he was not the same obliging lad they knew in Birmingham Jewellery Quarter. He had changed and what made him change was the way he had been treated by upper-classed snobs.

There was a time when Harry believed he had found the answer to his problems in the Good Book. In the Bible the parable about talents explained that it was for each of us to cultivate the talents bestowed on us by the Lord. The parable did not say that only those born with a silver spoon in their mouth were eligible.

Harry followed the Good Book and applied for a commission in the army. He was sent for by his sergeant major and was told that he was wasting his time. The sergeant major was direct. 'You are not officer material,' he said.

'Look around you young man, and ask yourself whether you come from the right background?'

Harry looked and began to understand how the system was stacked against him. Commissioned officers were recruited from amongst the rich and upper classes. A sub-lieutenant's salary was not enough to sustain him and it was necessary to have a rich relation to subsidise the cost of mess fees and uniforms. It was a clever little trick Harry thought, a nice way someone thought of to keep the lower classes in their place.

Harry spent long and laborious nights thinking of ways to beat them at their own game. Then it dawned on him that there was a way. It was not to be found in the armed forces. The police force was the only establishment that had not been cornered by the ruling classes. There was no collateral rank structure: it was the same for everyone. Chief constables start out as probationary constables and worked their way up the slippery promotional ladder. The chance was there for everyone and all Harry wanted was a chance.

***

Harry saw Germany disappear into the distance and he was not sorry. He walked from the deck towards his bunk and looked up at the sign, "Officers and their ladies," with an arrow pointing to the luxurious end of the ship. "Soldiers and their wives," with an arrow pointing in the opposite direction. That's it, he thought, officers and their ladies - soldiers and their wives. My wife will be treated like a lady and not subjected to this mindless snobbery and humiliation.

The humblest constable could aspire to become chief constable and that was an aspiration Harry held when he took the oath to serve without fear, favour or affection in Birmingham City Police. "A citizen locally appointed and having authority under the Crown for the protection of life, the prevention of crime and the apprehension of offenders."

He knew exactly what he wanted and how to get it. He was going to get to the top and use all he learned in the army to do so. He knew that in order to succeed it was necessary to make friends with the right people. Those with power to influence his career whether directly or indirectly, it did not matter, so long as they could help to achieve his ambition.

During his initial police training Harry managed his instructor with charm. It helped him come within the top three students in his final examination. He did likewise with his first shift sergeant and secured an excellent report at the end of his probation period. Later when he became a sergeant he made it his business to find out what pleased his inspector. As he ascended the police ladder he perfected the art of singing his own praise through his subordinates. He had acquired the reputation of being an all round people manager destined for the top.

In 1970 when he became detective-chief superintendent in charge of Birmingham CID, Harry had his nickname. His job now was to impress the Chief Constable by impressing the Assistant Chief Constable (Crime.) On his way to the top Harry had surrounded himself with a retinue of officers whom he blended and prepared for power. He was ruthless in weeding-out those whom he considered unsuitable. He wanted managers, system manipulators and most of all trustworthy officers of whatever race or creed provided they were white.

He would explain that he was not racist and if one permitted oneself to be confined to the parameters he set there was logic in his argument. Harry expected members of his entourage to confine themselves to his parameters; that was the way he had climbed the slippery promotional ladder, and what was good enough for him was good enough for them. It was the price of membership and those who did not subscribe were not wanted.

***

In the twenty years since Harry joined the police he cast his net beyond the powerbrokers within the police service. He served as Worshipful Master of his Masonic lodge and used his power to grant favours to those who could grant favours. When he was crowned head of administrational and operational detectives in 1970 it symbolised a fact he had been aware of for some years. He knew that he was one of the most powerful men in Birmingham. The irony was, he thought, that nobody else knew how powerful he was. He had built an empire under the noses of the City Fathers and they were completely unaware of it. They thought they were controlling him, but in reality it was the other way round.

***

Harry's Empire as it became known comprised a network of well placed senior officers in key positions. The complaints and disciplinary department, staff officers to assistant chief constables, divisional detective superintendents, and chief inspectors owed him allegiance. They served the same role as parish priests do to their bishop. It was their job to ensure that the flock was kept in check and to pay homage to their bishop. That system was in place long before Harry was ordained Detective Chief Superintendent. What was not in place was the tight control Harry maintained over his Empire.

It was achieved through a department that was conceived in Harry's mind before he was ordained. He knew that human nature being what it is he would lose control of his Empire if he did not keep control over others as ambitious as he was. That to maintain power it was necessary to have in place a system staffed by people in whose interest it was to maintain the status quo.

The police service was organised in such a way that there were several lines of communication to the Chief Constable. The Special Branch, Crime Intelligence, Complaints and Discipline and Uniform Departments came readily to mind. It was too much for one pair of eyes and Harry saw a need for a special department manned by senior officers who owed allegiance to Harry's Empire. His plan was to convince the Chief that such a department was essential to the efficiency of the Force.

It was a tall order, which Harry feared he might not be able to fulfil. Then it struck him that the Flying Squad in the Metropolitan Police held the answer. All that was needed was to "chat" the Assistant Chief Constable into believing that he had thought of it. It should not be too difficult, Harry mused, after all, he comes from the Met.

The seed was planted for the Serious Crime Squad. It grew and when Harry concluded his maiden speech, as the Detective Chief Superintendent, to the captains of his Empire he received a standing ovation. At the time he lived with his wife, whose name was not Alice, and two children in secluded Lady Byron Lane, Solihull, alongside judges, civil dignitaries and captains of industry. He was a rich man in his own right, much richer than his police salary could have made him.

***

The Serious Crime Squad was Harry's powerhouse. From there he was able to exert influence over Birmingham City and beyond. Birmingham was Harry's home ground and he was content to confine his activities within its boundaries. But success is difficult to confine and over the years the Serious Crime Squad encroached beyond the limits Harry had foreseen. Favours were done and returned with many other police areas.

Perhaps because Harry did not exhibit the dominant characteristics of most post-war senior police officers he was perceived by his "troops" as one of the boys. He did not project the arrogance, lack of imagination or intellectual insensitivity commonplace amongst ex-army police officers. He made it his business not to adopt the attitude that is symptomatic of a person accustomed to military power and blind obedience. Harry saw that it did not sit comfortably with the expectation of young police officers in the late 1960s, many of whom had no military experience. His approach was more in line with the way they expected to be treated and it commanded more loyalty.

Despite this, the blind side of Harry's management technique was traceable to something he overlooked in the army. He failed to realise that when he reported for National Service in 1945 he was joining an army that laid claim to defeating Hitler. The word failure had been removed from its vocabulary. Things would go from good to better and the institutional attitude was one of non-failure.

The right formula was in place and the job of army managers was to leave well enough alone. It was not permitted to question the fundamental tactics that led to success. The machinery was in place and Britain stood proud amongst nations. The effect of this on Harry was twofold. In the first place he felt secure provided he was part of the British establishment. In the second, he did not countenance the possibility that terrorists could seriously threaten stability on the British mainland.

XV

✺

The Junta

EVERY ELITE CLUB HAS an inner sanctum within which the shakers and movers busy themselves. In the Serious Crime Squad such people were known as the junta. They were the archangels who sat at the right and left side of Harry who was God the Father. In 1970 the junta was ahead of the game preparing for a big event. The new West Midlands Police was on the horizon and its horizon reached from Coventry to Wolverhampton. The proposed amalgamation of the several forces would bring about 6,000 police officers under the command of one chief constable.

The headquarters of the new force would be situated in Birmingham, the home of the Serious Crime Squad. Some felt it was a time of uncertainty, but those who knew Harry knew that he was calling in favours. He was working hard to ensure that on amalgamation day he would be named the Detective Chief Superintendent of the new West Midlands Police. When that happened, the jurisdiction of the Serious Crime Squad would extend far beyond its current boundaries into new horizons.

The Junta was well represented on the Steering Committee set up to guide the new force through its transition. Clandestine meetings were held with potential players from the different forces affected by the amalgamation. Coventry would be the second biggest city in the new force and it was there that Detective Chief Inspector Ballivor, a known troublemaker, was stationed. In the parlance of the Junta he had brought attention on himself. The word went out to, "get the goods on him" and his protégé, Detective Constable Bayliss.

***

At the time trainee Detective Constable John Bayliss was meeting Chris the Hat, from whom he collected sealed envelopes to be passed to Ballivor unopened. There was a break in the routine when John attended his initial CID training course at the Detective Training School, Tally-Ho, near Birmingham. It was an opportunity too good to miss and one day John was informed that a superintendent from Birmingham City Police wished to see him. John had misgivings about police superintendents especially those who called unannounced.

This one was friendly and greeted him with an outstretched hand. John might have fallen for the old "I'm your friend" trick in his younger days, but now he treated smiles with caution and ignored outstretched hands, 'Don't worry John, you're not in trouble,' the Superintendent said, displaying a sugary smile. 'The Detective Chief Super wants to have a chat with you, if you don't mind?'

***

Within half an hour John was in Harry's office being seduced by his friendly chat. His avuncular tone delivered in a slow Birmingham patois soon put John at ease. Harry addressed John by his Christian name and an onlooker would not have guessed that it was their first meeting. Harry sat on a large leather swivel chair behind an enormous desk. John's quick wit prompted him to say something sarcastic but he decided not to say anything about the small man on the big chair. The Superintendent, whose name was Malcolm, sat on a smaller chair giving John encouraging smiles and nods. He was playing the role of prompter and John realised that he was expected to take his cue from him.

Although the atmosphere was full of smiles and sweetness there was a hint in the air that the mood could change if Harry perceived any dissension from his audience. The small man oozed an air of self confidence that left no doubt that he was accustomed to getting his way. It was as though the price of his patronising attitude was compliance. He knew he was a fair man and he knew everyone else knew it as well.

One could see him wielding influence in his Masonic Lodge and exchanging favours for favours. He was setting out his stall now and John imagined himself in a room with many open doors through which he could escape. Harry was effectively closing doors as he spoke and by the time John realised it; there were only two exits left. Harry had done his homework and knew things John thought that only he knew.

Then the verbal balls started flying out of Harry's mouth and John could feel their effect. The meeting was to give him an opportunity to correct a great wrong. It was to do with Seamus Ballivor and Chris the Hat. They are IRA activists who are using John with or without his knowledge. He could be arrested with them today if Harry wished. That was not what he wanted but his decision depended on whether John was prepared to co-operate.

The prompter had stopped smiling and prompting. John was on his own and he was having difficulty comprehending what was being said. Harry had anticipated John's incredulity. There was no need for John to say anything Harry was providing the questions and answers. He explained that it was only natural that John would find it difficult to believe that his boss was an undercover spy working against the interest of the State. That was the very loyalty upon which treachery was founded. 'The Blarney Boys are past masters at it,' Harry said sincerely. 'You're not the first or the only one they have fooled.'

Harry explained that up to now John could be forgiven for not realising what was going on. But the fact remained that it could be proved he had assisted the enemy. Now, the only way John could exonerate himself was to co-operate, 'I'm willing to give you a one-time opportunity to exonerate yourself,' Harry said leaning forward so that John could hear him all the better.

Harry was going to give John an opportunity to choose which of the two remaining doors he wanted to enter. One led to arrest and a long prison sentence, the other to a fruitful career in the police. John knew the technique and had seen police officers use it time and again to browbeat prisoners. The choice was always the same, put a bigger fish in the pot than yourself.

Harry had not played all his cards by a long shot and knew precisely what he wanted. John was not the object of his nemesis; he was just a means to an end. But it was necessary to bring him to heel and to indent on his mind that there was a greater power. The message was clear; do what I want and I'll let you sup the milk of life, but if you refuse you'll spend the rest of your days eating shit. He had not acquired his nickname by compendious delivery; his cant was designed to project an air of understanding and fellowship, 'If you do me this favour I'll look after you,' he said sincerely. I'll see you're promoted within the year.'

Door number one was illuminated and looked inviting. Malcolm was smiling again, 'Is that possible sir?' John asked humbly. 'I haven't passed my promotion examinations.'

'That's not a problem son,' Harry said, waving his hand to dismiss John's concern. 'We know you've difficulty with theoretical examinations, but Malcolm will take care of that. Your promotion is necessary to enable us to get you away from Ballivor when the time is right. If you work for me your future is guaranteed. If you refuse I have no alternative but to arrest you. What do you say John?'

That illuminates door two, John thought, and I don't like what I see, 'Are we sure that Ballivor and Chris are IRA, Sir?'

'I've told you they are,' Harry said flatly. 'I've also told you that you are part of their act. I think I've been fair with you John, and you know enough to make a decision?'

'Yes of course sir, I'm at your service sir.'

'I knew I could count on you John,' Harry said resuming his avuncular tone. 'I want to know all about your meetings with Chris the Hat?'

'What do you want to know sir?'

'Everything John, everything.'

***

John told him almost everything from the first meeting to the collection of envelopes. He decided not to mention the gun. They could not possibly know about that, he thought. 'What about DS Priest John?' Harry said leaning forward.

John had forgotten to mention Priest and the fact that he was supposed to have given Chris the gun. But perhaps he didn't give it to him, John thought, 'Ballivor got me to breathalyse him sir.'

'I thought as much,' Harry said. 'Now I'm going to tell you something that'll leave you in no doubt that you've made the right decision. Priest was on to Chris and that's why you were asked to breathalyse him.'

'I see sir.'

'I hope that explains to you why he was not demoted. I look after my people John. Detective Sergeant Priest is now back in the Serious Crime Squad being chauffeured by his own driver.'

Harry was demonstrating his power. John knew that when Priest appeared before Coventry magistrates he pleaded guilty to refusing to provide a breath sample and was disqualified from driving for one-month and fined £10. He got off lightly and now John knew why.

'They also used you as a go-between to prevent them being associated if things went wrong.' Harry said, bringing the subject back on track. 'The envelopes you collect from Chris probably contain IRA intelligence. Do you know what's inside them?'

'No sir, I was ordered to deliver them to Mr Ballivor intact. They never discuss them with me.'

'I thought as much. I think with your help we can find out what's in them.'

Malcolm was still smiling and nodding at appropriate moments. John took the cue and said, 'I'll help all I can sir.'

'Malcolm will be your handler in this matter,' Harry said, extending his hand to John. 'I want to welcome you on board.'

The meeting was over.

***

Harry asked Malcolm to stay when John walked out of the room. It was part of their plan to demonstrate to John that Harry was telling the truth, 'Is it all set up Malc?' Harry asked, as soon as John left.

'Yes sir, Sergeant Priest will be in the car waiting with his driver.'

'Who is his driver Malc?'

'I'm not sure, he was allocated by traffic with Priest's new car.'

***

Three months later the night before the promotion examination Malcolm sat with John at Birmingham City Police HQ. He was provided with a copy of the examination paper and model answers. He was sworn to secrecy and wrote the examination from the answer sheet. The next day he took the official examination in the knowledge that the paper would be switched for the one he wrote the previous night. He had performed his part of the bargain and it was payback time. He had given the envelopes he collected from Chris to Malcolm before Ballivor got his hands on them. The contents of the envelopes were not discussed with John. They were returned in the same state, and Ballivor never suspected that the Birmingham Serious Crime Squad had sight of the contents.

XVI

Keystone

DETECTIVE SUPERINTENDENT MALCOLM SMITH was in the inner sanctum of Harry the Chat's Empire. He had latched onto Harry when they were detective sergeants at the same nick and it paid off. As Harry ascended the police rank structure he pulled Malcolm along with him. The arrangement was to their mutual benefit. Malcolm realised that without Harry's help he would have found it difficult to sell himself. Harry was his springboard and in return he watched Harry's back and never questioned his reasons. He realised that Harry was the keystone to his success and knew that if the keystone was dislodged the whole structure would come tumbling down.

None of this had escaped Harry's keen eye and it was because of it that Malcolm Smith currently occupied a strategic position in the Complaints Department of Birmingham City Police. The reason was to ensure that complaints against Serious Crime Squad members were contained within Harry's domain. Malcolm's position also gave him considerable power to monitor police activity against Serious Crime Squad subscribers.

***

Ballivor fell outside the jurisdiction of the Birmingham Police Complaints Department, but not beyond its influence. The proximity of Birmingham to Coventry had been brought closer, in police terms, on the amalgamation of Coventry City Police and Warwickshire Constabulary. The new force called the Warwickshire and Coventry Constabulary had Elmdon Airport within its boundaries. That was going to change when the proposed new West Midlands Police came into being. Coventry was going to be part of the new force, which meant that Ballivor would come directly under Harry's control.

***

Meanwhile Harry was becoming impatient with Ballivor's antics. 'There's more to him than meets the eye.' he would say. 'Look into him Malcolm, I want to know what he eats for breakfast. Better still find out whether he was breast-fed.'

That meant he wanted Ballivor's antecedents checked from the day he was born. His record showed that he had served in the Royal Air Force before joining Sussex Police. His personal records could not be accessed, but a helpful officer in Sussex found Ballivor's report seeking permission to apply for a transfer on promotion to Coventry. The officer provided anecdotal evidence that Ballivor was born in England but moved to Co Meath, Ireland, with his parents when he was five years of age. There he received a standard Irish education before returning to England when he was aged sixteen.

This information supported what was already known, but Harry was incredulous. He studied a report Ballivor submitted about Priest and concluded that a person with standard Irish education did not write it. A check with Airforce records proved unhelpful because of security restrictions. It was all too convenient as far as Harry could see. He could see the hallmarks of a government undercover operation. Ballivor was a Home Office spy masquerading as an IRA infiltrator.

***

Harry had not kept the lid on his activities for so long by overlooking the obvious or for that matter, the not-so-obvious. The report about Priest contained clues and provided an insight into Ballivor's modus operandi. There were other signs, but Harry knew enough to realise that he was under threat. Malcolm must not be allowed to know what was worrying Harry. It was much better that he perceived Ballivor as an IRA infiltrator.

***

If word spread that Ballivor was a Home Office "plant" it would cause great concern amongst senior police officers.

Many including Malcolm would distance themselves from Harry. After all, the Home Office has the last say and if the extent of Harry's activities became known in the wrong quarters he would be defrocked. The Whitehall machine would retire him with a smile and a golden handshake, but those close to him would not be so lucky. Their careers would either come to an abrupt end, and at the very least they would be permitted to serve out their time doing some menial task behind a desk.

That was a long way off and Harry had a plan. The Whitehall smart-arses lacked the low animal cunning of a seasoned detective. They had gone too far in covering up their man's true identity and in the process left a trail of evidence that would satisfy a court that Ballivor was a member of the IRA. If Ballivor was charged with membership of the IRA, his friends in Whitehall would desert him like rats abandoning a sinking ship.

***

Harry ensured that IRA infiltration of Midland's police forces was pushed high up the list of priorities. Word spread that someone sympathetic to the IRA was leaking secret information about police operations to Irish terrorists. Harry warned that the media was not to get wind of the threat. He did not want every Irish officer in the police to fall under suspicion.

Soon senior police officers through the Midlands were secretly combing their personnel records looking for IRA infiltrators. Irish born police officers and officers with Irish connections were under suspicion. Senior detectives from the Junta visited all the police forces earmarked to come within the new West Midlands Police spreading the word about IRA infiltration.

Ballivor was put under surveillance. Malcolm was happy that on this occasion the right man had been singled out for special attention. The envelopes passing between Chris the Hat and Ballivor were enough to secure a conviction but Harry was taking no chances. He insisted it was too soon to pounce on Ballivor. 'Where there's one there's others Malc; find them.'

***

Jane Hogan was an obvious choice. She lived with Ballivor and it was an unusual alliance. Chief inspectors do not co-habit with ordinary policewomen. At the very least she must have information that would convince Harry to move against Ballivor. Malcolm did not like her but then he did not like women.

He had never come to terms with the reason his marriage broke down. He courted his wife for three celibate years and on their wedding night had convinced himself that he would be able to consummate the union. When the moment came he was unable to get an erection, and despite the patience and love of his wife in the ensuing five years the marriage was never consummated.

The perplexing thing was that he was physically capable of sexual excitement and ejaculation. Alone in their marital bedroom, he found that if he wore his wife's silk underwear he would become erect and enjoyed masturbating whilst looking at himself in the mirror. It was whilst he was so engaged that his wife unexpectedly returned home one day, and caught him standing in front of the mirror dressed in her silk stockings and panties masturbating.

He cringed as he recalled that she entered the room without his knowledge and must have heard him saying to his reflection, 'I love you. I love you.'

His wife was sitting calmly on the bed looking into the en-suite. He did not notice her until he turned to walk into the bedroom. He was mortified and realised that his secret was out. He looked at her and for a moment the thought entered his head that if he murdered her there and then no one need ever know his secret. She sat on the bed with the air of someone who had a great mystery explained to her. As far as Malcolm knew she was still a virgin. 'I want a divorce,' she said acidly. 'And I want you to leave my house immediately.'

'Yes, of course ... whatever you say dear.'

No other words were exchanged between them and their respective solicitors had the marriage annulled on the ground of non-consummation. That was five years ago and Malcolm now got perverse enjoyment out of causing distress to women. On this occasion he would use John Bayliss to do his dirty work.

***

Bayliss bragged about the time he "had" Jane whilst they were on duty. Malcolm could not be sure whether

Bayliss was exaggerating but he accepted that something had happened. If it happened once it would happen again, provided the right circumstances were created. Malcolm came up with a simple plan. On promotion to uniform sergeant, John Bayliss would be posted to his old shift where Jane still worked. His job was to seduce her and get her to talk about Ballivor's activities.

***

Jane Hogan was not surprised when newly promoted Sergeant John Bayliss was introduced as the new sergeant on her shift. The introduction was hardly necessary because most members remembered him. It had not been long since he had left the shift to join the CID.

Jane watched with amusement as she saw Ballivor's predictions unfold. They had discussed the matter at length and she was fully aware that John was promoted for the purpose of getting her to betray Ballivor. In his enthusiasm to snare Ballivor Malcolm failed to consider that Jane might be part of the infiltration.

Events unfolded as Ballivor predicted and Jane pretended to be flattered by the amount of attention lavished on her by John. Promotion had changed him though. He carried himself with a degree of aloofness that he must have believed was commensurate with his new rank. He adopted a pedantic style with officers under his span of control, including Jane. For her part she found his superior attitude amusing if not pathetic. But she had a job to do and she played her part.

John was under pressure from Malcolm to deliver. John arranged the shift allocation so that he was on patrol with Jane when they were on night duty. He drove to the Seduction Post and set about convincing Jane that he was in love with her. She rebuffed his advances and he had to report failure to Malcolm.

XVII

The Code

A CODE TO BE used by members of the Junta was devised by Harry to reduce the risk of secrets being leaked. Sensitive and surreptitious operations to do with IRA infiltration were not to be discussed in police buildings or on the telephone. An invitation to meet at the Thistle Hotel signified that an urgent matter had arisen. The degree of urgency was communicated in the terminology of the invitation. The person receiving the call would be put on notice that an emergency had arisen by the opening remarks of the caller.

"Sorry I missed our lunch appointment yesterday," meant the meeting was extremely urgent. "I want to confirm our appointment for today," meant the meeting was desired as soon as possible.

Malcolm telephoned Detective Superintendent Bill Guest to confirm their meeting for that day. Bill then knew that Malcolm wished to discuss a matter of importance with him at the Thistle Hotel as soon as possible. They met for lunch and Malcolm explained that he wanted an illegal tap put on Ballivor's telephone. Bill agreed and suggested that Detective Sergeant Priest be put in charge of monitoring the calls.

Once agreed the matter would only be raised thereafter on a need to know basis. The task of obtaining and installing an illegal telephone tap was that of Guest. Harry had laid down a rule that he must be informed before taps were activated and be given sight of intelligence obtained from them.

Bill became aware of Harry's obsession with Ballivor and was a little concerned. For whatever reason Harry shrugged off intelligence reports that the IRA was planning something big in Birmingham. 'It's a Fred Carno outfit,' he would say with an air of finality. 'Concentrate on Ballivor.'

***

Bill Guest was not the type of man to press a point that he knew would upset his boss. He knew that Harry owed favours to several well-connected members of the Birmingham Irish community. There were rumours that he had accepted favours in return for favours; favours that would normally involve a pecuniary outlay, but where Harry was concerned the price was exerted in other ways.

The most common method was to give the subscriber a connivance licence to perform some illegal activity. In order to maintain that understanding the control of criminal intelligence had to be in the hands of the licence grantor. That was why the Bomb Squad and Special Branch were part of the Serious Crime Squad.

Bill was present when the Chat and the Assistant Chief Constable hatched the idea of bringing the Special Branch and Bomb Squad under the control of the Serious Crime Squad. The idea was unconventional and made little strategic sense. It flew in the face of Home Office guidance but that did not dampen enthusiasm for the plan. The cohesion in Harry's Empire was maintained by keeping a tight lid on information. It would be too risky to give the Special Branch or the Bomb Squad the degree of autonomy recommended.

***

The problem was that it would be impossible to protect Barons if intelligence went unchecked to the Special Branch. Bill had misgivings he was not the type to lightly ignore Home Office circulars. He could see the danger in the new proposal; personnel not positively vetted would have access to secret intelligence files. The Home Office circular was clear that the name of informers and the information supplied was to be graded as top secret and only made available to personnel that were positively vetted. That was not provided for in Harry's scheme where information would be freely available to every member of the Serious Crime Squad including civilian support staff.

***

Harry was becoming more obsessed with Ballivor. He perceived him as a loose cannon on a mission to expose corruption in the Serious Crime Squad. In reality he was a Home Office spy using Irish factionalism as a convenient cover. Harry could read the signs and had a plan to turn them to his advantage.

The IRA had no reason to infiltrate Birmingham City Police. But that would not be an argument that would persuade a jury to acquit Ballivor in the face of overwhelming evidence that he was a member of the IRA. It mattered not whether the Home Office or MI5 sent him. Whichever sent him sent him half-cocked and had not thought through the consequences.

When he stands trial for being a member of a proscribed organisation, and conspiracy to cause explosions in the United Kingdom, he will be found guilty on the evidence extrapolated from the careful cover story they provided Harry mused.

***

Six months passed and John, now Detective Inspector Bayliss, was about to be briefed on his next mission. The telephone tap on Ballivor had been a success and there was enough evidence to secure a conviction. Chris the Hat would stand beside him in the dock and Sergeant Priest would be the first witness to take the stand.

John and Sergeant Priest had become friends. Priest would laugh when they referred to their first meeting.

'Would you believe that this pissed-up shit breathalysed me?' He said to his driver as they helped John into the car.

'This is your chance to get your own back skipper,' the driver said with good humour. 'He's as pissed as a newt.'

'Can't hold his ale, that's his trouble Cliff,' Priest said. 'Come on inspector, pull your last leg into the car.'

'Where to skipper?' Cliff said, turning into Hagley Road towards Birmingham City Centre. 'I mean do you want me to drop you before I take him to Coventry?'

'Yes, it's two o'clock and I want picking up in the morning at eight. Sorry to piss you about mate.'

Cliff didn't mind; he was doing the job he wanted. He would be paid overtime as a traffic constable for the extra hours he worked. The later the better, he thought as he came to a halt outside Priest's home.

'Here we are skipper. See you in six hours.'

'Don't remind me, I'm off to bed.'

Cliff drove to John's address in Coventry. 'You're home sir,' he said, shaking John. 'Come on, I'll see you to your bed.'

He deposited John on his bed and conducted a search of his house. In a drawer he found three cassette tapes which he placed in his pocket. He left John asleep and drove back to Birmingham. He went to his room in the Railway Hotel, New Street.

'Good night Mr Duffy,' the night porter said as Cliff got into the lift.'

XVIII

IRA by Any Name

HARRY WAS ACQUAINTED WITH several prominent members of the Birmingham Irish community whom he knew he could trust. He knew that most objected to the way Ulster Unionists had gerrymandered and treated the Catholic nationalists as second-rate citizens. But he also knew that these people were opposed to the violent campaign being pursued by the IRA. He also suspected that many were more sympathetic to the notion of a United Ireland than they felt comfortable about saying in his presence.

He understood their position but that was where he drew the line. He was not a politician and refused to discuss the rights and wrongs of the situation in Ulster. Birmingham was his concern, not Ulster, and provided the Irish left Birmingham alone he did not wish to become involved. That was the line he sold to his Irish Catholic friends, but in his Masonic Lodge he had to deal with Ulster Protestants.

They had a different story to tell. They warned against having any truck with Irish Catholics and not to be confused by the rhetoric emanating from the lips of Fenian murderers. Nationalists were all tarred with the same brush, the Official IRA, the Provisional IRA, the Irish National Liberation Army or the IRA by any name was the same. The name mattered not because they all wanted the same thing.

If proof was needed it could be found in the written Irish Republic constitution. What they wanted was Ulster and they were prepared to cause havoc throughout the United Kingdom to get it. Harry listened and delivered whatever chat suited his audience. But deep down he felt far removed from the bigotry and squabbling that had been a feature of Irish history for longer than anyone could remember.

The important thing was that at this point in time there was no evidence of an IRA plot being hatched in Birmingham. He was more concerned about the strange reports reaching his desk purporting to herald warning of mysterious plotters at large. He realised there was something afoot but it was unlikely that the IRA was at the bottom of it.

The brothel in Coventry, the disappearance of women; Ballivor and Chris the Hat they were all beginning to take on the shape of a Home Office set up. Harry looked around his impressive office and felt proud. I've come to this through hard work and by outsmarting those who thought they were smarter than I was, he mused. Mr Ballivor …Let's see how smart he really is.

NETTLEGRABBERS

Harry had a nose for intrigue and he got the scent of Ballivor before their first meeting. He smelled a well-heeled aristocrat with a pedigree longer than his bank balance. Harry knew their hallmark and their ability to play the chameleon, but they could not fool him. If Ballivor is the product of Irish peasantry, I'm the Queen of England, he thought, looking at Ballivor's report. Harry may have turned one blind eye to events in Ulster but he maintained a careful watch on the Irish community in Birmingham with the other. Ballivor was not one of their ilk and he had a plan to prove it.

The plan had been tried and tested on previous occasions. It involved catching them at their own game and their game on this occasion was Irish terrorism. They are using the current situation to create specious reasons to snoop into affairs that were none of their business. But in order to do so they had to masquerade as terrorists and leave cryptic clues to hide their trail.

That was the flaw in their scheme and it would be thrown into their faces when Ballivor stood before Birmingham Crown Court charged with conspiracy and being a member of a proscribed organisation. They had overlooked the obvious.

***

The realisation that there had been a misunderstanding dawned on Sir Edward on a cold morning in February 1972. The decision to permit Irish nationalists to operate freely, "for a strictly limited period," in Ireland was made on the understanding that a firmly held leash would control them. That those making the request maintained the ability to call a halt to activities as soon as their objective was achieved or if things got out of hand. Sir Edward looked at the chronology of events in Ulster and compared it to the resulting political backlash in Westminster.

It was difficult to see that the prospects of a united Ireland were still alive in late1971. The nationalists had lived up to expectations and the Unionists had more than enough to sustain their stance against a united Ireland. But the plan had backfired because nobody had envisaged that the Provisional IRA would gain a foothold in such a short length of time. In truth Sir Edward still could not believe that they did so without the aid of Unionists.

Ulster was not like other parts of the United Kingdom as far as policing and security were concerned. The RUC carried arms and there was a visible military presence. The RUC Special Branch, with the help of British Intelligence, had the personnel and equipment to keep surveillance on almost every Catholic in the Province. It did not make sense that an illegal band of terrorists were capable of causing the amount of disruption that was taking place. There had to be a missing part of the jigsaw and Sir Edward had a good idea who was holding it.

He had been hoodwinked and he did not like it. Worst still there was little he could do about it. Ulster Protestants were lubricious, he thought, as he contemplated the possibility that there was a correlation between the death of seven soldiers in Aldershot and the decision to give the nationalists enough rope to hang their cause, three years before.

The news that a bomb had exploded near the officers' mess killing the soldiers came as a great shock because it marked the first blast on English soil in the current campaign. It raised serious questions about the efficiency of the intelligence service and if it ever came to light that there was an element of collusion the backlash would be enormous.

Plausible excuses were given but deep down Sir Edward suspected that those in whom he had placed his trust had let him down. The Unionist faction had played a part in facilitating the bombing of the Parachute HQ and whether their part was through design or omission made no difference. He could see them rejoicing at the impact the atrocity would have on public and political opinion. Unionists probably felt the incident would put an end to talk about a United Ireland; but to Sir Edward it was a wake-up call.

He knew that the monster was out of control and that those that believed otherwise were deluding themselves. He listened with concealed scepticism to reassurances that the leash was intact and had been tightened. That apart from a few loose ends everything was under control.

Sir Edward was not going to be hoodwinked again and he put the full weight of MI5 behind the quest to harness the monster. He went further and coerced the head of MI6 and other well-placed officials to do likewise. The situation was serious and the great fear was that information about the role of the intelligence services in the debacle would be leaked.

Ulster Loyalist mobsters and Republican gangsters had shanghaied the hiatus created by the connivance of the Northern Irish security services. The Ulster Protestants gangs exploited the fear created in their communities and Catholic "pseudo-patriots" did likewise. That was the way Sir Edward saw the situation.

The Provisional IRA was fed off the fear and patriotic aspirations of Catholics whilst the Ulster Defence Association and similar mobsters did likewise in their localities. There was no doubt in Sir Edward's mind where the mistake was made. He knew it had been determined in the higher echelons of the British establishment. Ulster Orange Lodges brokered the deal whereby the decision was made to permit a nationalist backlash in Ulster. If push came to shove, Sir Edward also knew that he was a party to that "understanding" and that he would be ruined if it ever came to light.

***

'We are walking in a bed of nettles gentlemen,' he said at a meeting of mandarins convened to discuss the Aldershot bombings. 'Yes, the nettles have grown in our garden because we have neglected our duties.'

There was a grim silence and no voice of dissension could be heard. Sir Edward looked at every person assembled and each in turn, nodded in agreement. 'I take it that we are all agreed that something must be done,' he continued. 'I do not subscribe to the somewhat optimistic view that the IRA has finished its campaign on the mainland.'

By the time the assembly dispersed Sir Edward had achieved what he set out to achieve. He had put sufficient pressure on the influential gentlemen present to make them realise that they could be called to account. The prospect frightened them and whilst in a state of fear he was able to get their financial support for his plan. Those invited to the meeting had not been chosen at random, but rather because of their position to further a plan Sir Edward had devised to get to the bottom of the Ulster conundrum. Gone were the days when he would listen to anyone tainted with the brush of Ulster prejudices. Decisions henceforth would be grounded on proper intelligence gathered from both sides of the political divide.

Sir Edward suspected that the same trick that had been played on the intelligence services had also been played on others. Police officers, low- grade civil servants, reporters and no doubt countless others had been taken in. The answer to the Irish problem in England was not to be found amongst the labouring-class Irish who had left their country to find employment. They were the curtains behind which the real protagonists hid. They provided the perfect cover and it should have struck him sooner. Spies operate on the same system of concealing themselves amongst ordinary members of the community. Their stock in trade is not to draw attention to themselves but to conduct their business in secret.

***

The reports emanating from the Coventry brothel were too controversial to be acknowledged. There was something distasteful to the British palate about consuming information tainted with salacious activity. Brothels were illegal, and prostitutes along with their clients were pariahs. It just was not morally or politically correct for MI5 to be seen to be part of such a scheme. That was the attitude Sir Edward was obliged to adopt when one of his young officers suggested that the scheme had merit.

The officer was thirty years of age and ambitious. He was the son of an army major known to Sir Edward and who would not thank him in the very likely event of the matter being splashed across the front pages of "The News of the World".

That was then, but recently the situation had changed and Sir Edward authorised the tapes to be transcribed. 'Sit down Henry,' he said to Major Sweet's son. 'Was the exercise worth it?'

Henry Sweet was an Oxford graduate with a likeable personality. His build was proportionate to his six foot three inches. His dark hair was well groomed and contrasted pleasantly with his well-tanned high cheekbones. In the old days he would have been "officer material," but today he joined MI5 shortly after graduating. He had not been tested fully in the field but Sir Edward harboured no doubt that Henry would exceed expectations. His mind was as sharp as his physique and he projected an air of confidence that showed no element of self-importance.

'There is something sir,' Henry said. 'We have picked up a passage in a conversation which may be significant.'

Sir Edward was impressed. The passage in itself gave little away but to a keen ear it contained a warning. To complicate matters the warning could not be discerned from a single conversation; it was necessary to listen to several conversations that took place over a period of time.

The male participant was a Jack Murphy, and he was concerned about the mother of the prostitute he always selected when he visited the bordello.

'Tell your mother to change her job,' he could be heard saying.

'Whatever do you mean?' The girl asked.

'I'm serious, tell her it's not safe there. That's all I can tell you.'

'And what do you think it means Henry?' Sir Edward said.

'It could mean several things sir. 'I'd like to go to Coventry and check it out.'

***

Sir Edward agreed, but before he would permit the agent to go, he arranged for the police to raid the bordello. The Chief Constable of Warwickshire and Coventry Constabulary was unaware of the entertainment suites. Sir Edward pointed that the Home Secretary would not be impressed if he learned of the Chief's ignorance. 'You owe me a favour Chief Constable,' Sir Edward said. 'I'll be in touch.'

By October 1972 Henry Sweet had gathered sufficient

intelligence to show that a priest in Coventry was operating an IRA cell. It was enough to convince Sir Edward's wavers that he had been right. The Aldershot bombings were not a "one-off" as had been suggested.

Sir Edward noted that intelligence emanating from the Coventry bordello was restricted to IRA activity. There was no intelligence about Loyalists. He asked for the file on Robert Champs and after studying it came to the conclusion that he was not hearing the full story. He decided that the time had come to use a similar scheme in Northern Ireland but on this occasion he wanted sight of all the intelligence. He saw it as a way of cutting through the invisible walls that had been erected to prevent MI5 getting to the bottom of what was happening on the ground in Ulster.

The suspect priest fitted the profile Sir Edward had of serious Irish terrorists. He was not a loudmouth rebel-song-singer. In fact he was not Irish nor had he been born a Catholic. From the pulpit he preached love and understanding of all human beings, even those who differ in religion and culture. 'We are all God's children,' he would say. 'God loves us all and we must love each other.'

***

Two bordellos and a laundry under the control of British intelligence were up and running in Northern Ireland when the question of arresting Fr Brown and his disciples was discussed. Fortunately, Brown had been followed to London, where he was observed visiting premises linked to the IRA. It was enough to enable MI5 to distance itself from the operation and hand it over to the local police. Sir Edward was not convinced that the local police would deliver and he sent for the Chief Constable of Warwickshire and Coventry Constabulary.

'Of course I understand that it will be difficult Chief Constable; these things always are,' he said rejecting the Chief Constable's protests. 'You have two weeks to arrange it. I'll make sure our people are up to speed, meanwhile you make the necessary arrangements for their appointment.'

Two weeks later Detective Chief Inspector Ballivor took up his post in Coventry and Jane Hogan joined the senior training course at Ryton-on-Dunsmore. On 13th April 1973 the priest was arrested and later convicted, along with six Coventry Irishmen and one Birmingham Irishman of conspiracy to cause explosions in the United Kingdom.

XIX

※

IRA English Department

IT WAS JUNE 1973 and Michael Lynch was not a happy man. Things had not unfolded as he expected. His plans were being thwarted and he knew the reason. There were traitors and informers, the curse that had plagued Irish nationalism down the centuries, he thought.

To Michael the expression embraced infiltrators, loud-mouthed volunteers and slippery two-faced serpents who would sell their mother for the price of a pint. Out of the three categories, he harboured begrudging admiration for the first, an intolerant acceptance of the second and an innate disgust of the third. But in practice he viewed informers of whatever hue equally dangerous.

The campaign in Ireland was not living up to expectations. Sensible people were beginning to see that if its purpose was to promote a United Ireland it was failing. The reality was that in early 1973 the prospects of a United Ireland were more remote than they were in 1967.

It was a state of affairs that had the capacity to undermine the core reason that some Irish people were sympathetic to the Provisional IRA. The great fear was that if their sympathy could not be maintained, the IRA would find it extremely difficult if not impossible to exist. Out of that fear the decision to extend the campaign to the English mainland had been hatched.

The English Department was originally constituted to swing British public opinion behind a United Ireland. The "troubles" in Ulster were too remote to have any real impact on British public opinion; it was necessary to do something nearer home. What was needed was the echo of bomb-blasts in England to serve as a reminder that the IRA could extend its campaign beyond Irish shores.

It was known from the outset that for such a strategy to succeed it must restrict damage to buildings and utilities. British public opinion would swing inwards if innocent people were injured or the Irish question was perceived as a war against England rather than a struggle for freedom.

The aim was to sell the campaign as a means of publicising the plight of downtrodden Catholics in Ulster. To make the British population understand that there was no other way of making its government listen to reason. Once the message was spread in England that the democratic principle of one-person one-vote was not applicable to Catholics in Ulster, the population would force the government to act. The essential ingredient in the English campaign was to confine activities to the bear minimum necessary to keep the "Cause" in the media and through it in the public domain. The Coventry lesson of 1939 still applied today; if you kill the English in their country, you also kill your cause.

***

Dolores Flynn, Belfast Catholic schoolteacher, was in charge of a Belfast ASU seconded to the IRA English Department. Michael Lynch met her in 1971 and they became lovers. Since then their relationship progressed to the stage where they were discussing marriage. They planned to combine their assets and leave Ireland to start a new life together in America. That was in the not too distant future but meanwhile there was work to be done.

***

The vibrations of the arrest and conviction of its cell leader in the English Midlands could still be felt in the IRA's English Department. The probability that the Coventry curate was betrayed by a tout or informer was too strong to ignore. The current plan to cause explosions in London was premature in Michael Lynch's opinion. But Dolores would have none of it. She had sent her ASU ahead to prepare for the big day and felt that the risk was acceptable.

She was adamant that the operation should go ahead as planned on 8th March 1973, Referendum Day in Northern Ireland. On the evening of 6th March she was poised to go to London where she would meet the advance party. The ASU comprised top explosive handlers and experienced bomb placers in the Nationalist movement. They had been handpicked and trained for the operation by Dolores. Her reputation as a cool operator was known in the Nationalist community and the only voice of dissension was that of Michael Lynch.

She countered that the risk of her being caught was minimal because she was not the person who was going to place the bombs. Her job was to ensure that her ASU did its job and got out of the country safely afterwards. The operation was top secret and information had been distributed amongst operators on a strict need-to-know basis. The police in London would be caught on the hop and she would be in Dublin by the time the first bomb exploded.

***

Lynch could not point to an unacceptable risk and the night before she set out for London was spent lovemaking and discussing their future. The next morning Lynch drove her to the centre of Belfast and watched her board a taxi to take her to the airport. It was the day before the referendum, the result of which was a foregoing conclusion.

Of course the people of Northern Ireland would vote to remain part of Britain, Michael thought, it was a charade designed to give legitimacy to the intransigent stance of the Orange Order. Dolores was right; the only way of making the nationalist's voice heard was to amplify it with the sound of a bomb. The important thing was to ensure that the bomb did not injure or kill ordinary civilians. Michael blew a kiss to Dolores as she waved to him out of the taxi. He watched her until she was out of sight and then he drove towards the M1 en-route to Dublin.

***

Dolores and her team would fly into Dublin Airport the following day. If everything went to plan she would land before the first bomb exploded in London. They would watch television together and celebrate when the newsflash announcing the blast was shown on TV. It would be the top story of the day in the English speaking world. The cleaver spin-doctors in Whitehall would see their planned headlines about the Ulster referendum relegated to the second or even third division.

Michael smiled to himself as he imagined an Oxbridge snob briefing the Secretary of State for Northern Ireland about how to present the result of the referendum. "You must emphasise, minister, that the people of Ulster have spoken and want to remain part of the United Kingdom." Perhaps the briefing had already taken place because the result of the referendum was already pre-determined, as was the result of every election held in Northern Ireland.

Dolores would know the precise time and place of the first explosion in London. She was a cool operator, ran a tight ship and there would be no slip-ups. Maximum interruption with minimum casualties was the order of the day. "Spread confusion not carnage," was the buzz phrase at Sinn Fein HQ.

A coded warning would be given in advance, and the IRA would claim responsibility once the ASU was safely out of England. A Sinn Fein spokesman would explain to the English people why their lives were being disrupted. The main thing was to get the message across in such a way that people understood the reasons.

***

The next day Michael waited in the arrivals lounge of Dublin Airport for the 12.30 p.m. flight from Stanstead. The flight information screen showed that the flight was delayed. Its ETA was changed to 1.30 p.m. later to 2.30 p.m. and it eventually landed at 3.20 p.m. He stood at the entrance to the arrivals hall and watched the first passengers off the flight enter the hall. Dolores was not amongst them and Michael was still waiting when the last few stragglers came through.

There was excited mutterings from arriving passengers from which Michael realised that something out of the ordinary had happened. He looked around and saw several members of the Irish Special Branch watching people waiting to meet passengers off the Stanstead flight. Something was wrong.

The English police would have contacted the Irish SB to check the identity of anyone left waiting for passengers who had missed the flight. Michael went to a stranger and smiled, 'Paddy I've been sent to meet you,' he said to the surprised man. 'Come on your coach is waiting outside.'

***

The news that a cell of IRA terrorists was under arrest in

London broke in the late afternoon. Michael was incredulous and refused to believe that Dolores was amongst those arrested. They had discussed every possible scenario and it was unimaginable that she had fallen into a trap. But as time went on and the British police released more information, he was forced to accept that she would not be coming home today or for many a long day.

Members of the hierarchy of Sinn Fein were furious. They had stolen the limelight but were not getting the publicity they craved. News headlines that a major IRA campaign designed to cause carnage in the streets of London had been foiled, were exactly what Sinn Fein did not want. It would have the opposite effect on British public opinion to that intended. 'We've been outmanoeuvred, the police must have been forewarned,' Michael's boss said striking his desk. 'Find out, who is responsible Michael. You have a free hand on this one.'

***

Michael Lynch did not have to be told that they had been outsmarted. He had suspected for some time that subliminal forces were at work and now his suspicions were converted into certainty. The arrest of Fr Brown in Coventry held the key. 'That's it,' Michael said aloud as the answer came to him. 'Murray he lived in Birmingham not Coventry.'

Alphonsus Murray was the odd man out and whether he knew it or not, held the answer. He was at the time serving twenty years in Wakefield prison and Michael Lynch went about arranging a visit. It took three weeks and several favours to secure the visit but it was worth it. Murray provided names amongst which was one that knew about the Coventry cell and had information about the London campaign.

It was Big Tom McDermott, a self employed builder whose pedigree in republican circles was well respected. He was used on several occasions to provide safe houses for people on the run and to store armaments.

The word went out to check McDermott's antecedents and it was discovered that his pedigree was not as long as had been thought. He had connections with Orange Lodges and deeper enquiries revealed that his trusted lieutenant Patrick Kelly was in fact William Craig, a high-ranking member of an Antrim Orange Lodge and ex-member of the UDA.

XX

Ball of Twine

THE TWO AUSTRALIANS WERE God-sent as far as Lynch was concerned. In all probability they were part of a scheme British intelligence had devised, but it made no difference. Patrick O'Connell was an explosives expert and his unusual talents would come in very handy for what Lynch had in mind. Peter Duffy still had enough of an English twang to convince an Irish ear that he was a member of MI5. The time had come to use them but not for the purpose they thought.

When Amanda DeCourcey was briefed she smiled at Michael. 'Jesus you are some ball of twine Mr Lynch,' she laughed. 'I thought my mind was twisted, but that's the best I've ever heard!'

'So you're game,' Michael said. 'You'll seduce him.'

'Only if I can kill him afterward,' Amanda said seriously. 'When can I have my bit of fun?'

'Yes, I forgot about that,' Michael said scratching his head. 'Look you'll have to wait for a while, we need this guy alive for some time.'

***

'Come in Mr O'Connell,' Lynch said extending his hand to greet Patrick. 'Is it Okay to call you Pat?' Patrick looked at Michael Lynch and nodded to affirm that it was okay. Before taking the seat proffered he glanced around Lynch's business like office. It had the hallmark of a well-run nerve centre and reflected Lynch's pseudo-friendly informal manner. On inspection Patrick could see in his host's eyes that he was a man accustomed to giving orders and getting his own way. Someone who had disciplined himself to study the character and mindset of those with whom he interacted in order to avoid futile personality clashes.

Lynch had developed this skill because he had the power of life and death over many of those with whom he came into contact. He knew that it was important to him not to permit personal idiosyncratic preconceptions to fog his judgement. 'I'm pleased to meet you at last Mr Lynch,' Patrick said gripping Lynch's hand firmly but not too tightly.

Michael explained that both Patrick and his man Duffy had passed the IRA security checks. They were now full members of the Provisional IRA and subject to military law. He had decided to promote them straight into IRA intelligence with additional duties as staff officers. They would report directly to him, he was their commanding officer and they would only take orders from him.

Lynch explained that Duffy's mother had been traced to a geriatric home on the outskirts of London. She was acutely affected with senile dementia and would not know him. 'Give him this,' Michael said handing Patrick an envelope on which was written an address. 'It's the address of the home where she's staying.'

'Is it possible for him to see her?' Patrick asked.

'Yes, we've thought he would want to. One of our female operators has to go to London and he can accompany her.' Lynch said, 'they can spend a weekend there as a courting couple.'

'I must say I'm impressed that you were able to trace Peter's mother sir,' Patrick said. 'Has there been any news as to the whereabouts of my fiancée?'

'We're looking into it and there may be something. But first things first Pat,' Lynch said changing the subject. 'We need your expertise to design a bomb. What I have in mind is something that will explode the moment someone attempts to make it safe. Do you think you can help?'

'Yes I believe I can design a device to that specification, but first I am anxious to know about my fiancée?'

'Yes of course you do, but first things first if you don't mind Pat?'

Patrick could see the suspicion in Lynch's eyes. He smiled in an attempt to ease the tension, 'I expect you were briefed by your contacts in Australia, sir. Would it not be quicker if you asked me to explain anything you are doubtful about?'

'Okay, where's Mr James Ward-Riley at this precise moment?'

'Somewhere in Birmingham looking for his sister.'

'Can you make contact with him?'

'Yes.'

'Is that through the man, wearing a pork-pie hat, you meet at Dublin Airport?'

'Yes.'

'That's great,' Lynch said smiling. 'There's something he can do for me, if he has no objections?'

'If it helps find his sister, I'm sure he will oblige.'

'We think that Denise may be in the hands of Unionists, Pat,' Lynch said with an air of concern. 'If you do exactly as I say you might have a chance of getting her back alive.'

***

Six weeks had elapsed since the arrest of Dolores Flynn. Michael Lynch was busy. Big Tom McDermott made the mistake of activating the trap set for him. He made enquiries through IRA intelligence about Peter Duffy, who had recently booked into the Railway Hotel, near Birmingham New Street railway station. Denise's brother, James, had kept his side of the bargain and booked into the hotel under Duffy's name. He spread sufficient suspicion that he was an Irish terrorist to reach the ears of the Birmingham Special Branch.

Peter Duffy was not in Birmingham; he was undercover in Northern Ireland minding Amanda DeCourcey. But that was not what concerned Lynch; it was how to make McDermott pay for his treachery. He signed his own death warrant when he informed IRA intelligence that the Birmingham Serious Crime Squad had approached him about Duffy.

Like most men with something on their conscience McDermott felt it would stand him in good stead to report the approach in case he fell under IRA suspicion in the future. If all things were equal he would be right, but on this occasion the variables that aligned pointed in the opposite direction. The police would not have trusted him with such sensitive information unless he was in their camp. The secret is not to follow the logic of the con man, Lynch thought, as he listened to Big Tom.

'I'm sure Michael,' Tom said uneasily, 'the name of the man is Peter Duffy. He was seen in Belfast and followed to Birmingham where he booked into the Railway Hotel.'

'It's interesting Tom,' Lynch said engaging Tom's eyes. 'But that name means nothing to me.'

'It looks like I made a journey for nothing then,' Tom said, shifting uneasily in his seat. 'It's just that I thought I should tell you personally in case there was something going on.'

'You did the right thing Tom,' Michael said. 'Are you sure the police are not having you on?'

'No they were serious, I thought they were going to arrest me.'

'Why would they arrest you Tom?'

'I don't know, you know what the bastards are like. They hate us all.'

'Look Tom,' Michael said seriously. 'Be careful, we don't

want to lose you, they might be trying to set you up or something.'

'Yes, your right Michael. I'll be on my guard from now on.'

'Well, thanks again Tom, I'm sorry to have to cut this short but there's someone waiting to see me;' Michael said looking at Amanda DeCourcey waiting outside his door. 'Need a lift back to the airport?'

'No, I'll get a taxi, my flight to Birmingham is not for another three hours.'

'I'm very grateful Tom. You're one of our best men,' Michael said, offering Tom his hand. 'This is my appointment Tom ... Mary say hello to Tom.'

'Hi Tom,' Amanda said as she walked into Michael's office.

'Did you clock him Amanda?' Lynch said as soon as Tom left. 'Remember his face, he's an informer.'

***

Peter Duffy was assigned to protect Amanda DeCourcey on a delicate mission in Northern Ireland. The fact that a connection had been made between Northern Ireland and his supposed visit to Birmingham meant Loyalists wanted to know who he was. It was so important to them that they were prepared to risk their man in Birmingham. Big Tom was their man and in the normal course of events he would be found with a bullet in the back of his head. But perhaps that's what they want, Michael thought, the time had come for the IRA to be less predictable.

Michael Lynch was sure he had his man but experience taught him that when dealing with British Intelligence it was not wise to take things at face value. It could be a ruse to protect Duffy and his comrade in arms. It was time to apply the test of fidelity and to do that he needed the approval of higher authority. 'For Christ's sake Michael make up your mind,' his boss said irritably. 'If we eliminate everyone you suspect there'll only be the two of us left.'

'You're right, of course sir,' Michael said. 'I have a plan I want to go over with you and if you give me the go-ahead we will flush out our man or men for that matter.'

'Fine … you know I can't give you the go-ahead without the permission of the Army Council. If things go wrong we'll both be for the high jump. No, I think you should draw up your plan and present it yourself to the Council. I'll arrange a meeting for a week today. The rest is up to yourself.'

'Thank you sir,' Michael said as he gathered up his papers. 'I'll be here a week today.'

It was typical of his C.O. not to take a chance. Michael had become frustrated at his boss' inability to see that Unionist politicians were running rings around the Republican movement. The public relations side of the current campaign was becoming a disaster not only in Britain but also in the Irish Republic. British spin-doctors were winning the propaganda campaign and the Irish government was emulating their methods. If something were not done soon the IRA would be out of business.

***

After Michael presented his synopsis and his plan to the Army Council there was silence. The fifteen men assembled looked to the Chair for guidance. He was a bulky man experiencing difficulty in breathing and showing signs of poor health. In his day he was a towering man full of vitality but today he looked as though he would not see another Christmas.

He was a Protestant academic with a philosophical approach to life and the plight of Irish nationalists. He had no doubt that one-day a United Ireland would happen because it was inevitable. Perhaps not in his lifetime or for that matter in the lifetime of any of those assembled. The important thing was that they could go to meet their maker in the knowledge that they had done their part.

Now as he contemplated the implications of Michael's delivery, those who knew him had no doubt that he would give them wise counsel. The Chair would not blame young Michael Lynch for the thoughts that were going through his head. He was young, ambitious and thought that the world's wrongs could be righted in a day. That if the enemy were eliminated, out of the ashes will grow an emerald green land ruled by altruistic Irishmen! Dream on young man, for when you awaken you will find that nothing has changed. And that was precisely what the Chair wanted … all change no change!

For the Chair represented the last bastion of the old Irish aristocracy. The landed gentry that managed to retain their lands and position despite the events that brought about the Irish Republic. The authors of the written Irish Constitution enacted in 1937, claming sovereignty over "the whole island of Ireland, its islands and territorial seas." (Article 2.)

The article was included to appease the sizeable portion of the population that objected to the division of Ireland into North and South. Its inclusion was quixotic but it served its purpose in more ways than one. Firstly, it retained the nationalist focus on the old enemy England, which in turn deflected attention from the second and by far the most important reason which was contained in Article 10 of the Constitution.

Article 10, had to appease those who had their eye on the main chance. They were the people who suffered and fought in the quest for an Irish Republic. The people who felt they had earned a share of the spoils of victory. The landed gentry of Ireland had reason to fear that they would lose their estates. The Official IRA was the new militia and its members were high on the list of those who felt they deserved a share of the new democracy.

But they were inexperienced in the ways of government and control. They had not addressed the question and laboured under the illusion that their victory would automatically entitle them to status in the new Republic. They envisaged that once the British had departed the New Ireland would transform itself into an egalitarian State. That government of the Irish by the Irish was going to prove to be the panacea everyone knew it would be.

By the time it dawned on the masses that they were worse off it was too late. The written Irish Constitution was similar to the unwritten British Constitution. Of course there were apparent differences, but to the astute these were superficial and lacked any mechanism of enforcement. What good is a right if it cannot be enforced in a court of law? That is the question that was on the lips of those who saw through the charade.

It was a question that had been anticipated and better still it had been catered for. When the Irish constitution was enacted in 1937 the initial transitional phase from British to Irish rule was over. Leaders capable of causing civil disruption were installed in sinecure public situations or held appointments in state institutions. The inclusion of Article 10 .1, of the constitution was achieved without objection. Few bothered to look beyond the opening sentence to the words, "... subject to all estates and interests therein for the time being lawfully vested in any person or body."

The Irish landed gentry retained control of the judiciary. He who interprets the law makes the law; Article 10.1, ensured the legal rights of those who owned land prior to independence retained it afterwards.

The Chair could trace his lineage back to Wolfe Tone, one of the first Irish Protestants to call for Home Rule for Ireland in the eighteenth century. That ensured that his name was beyond question. Irish Republicans place great store in the descendants of their heroes and it would be unthinkable to question the motives of the Chair.

It would be unpatriotic to permit ones mind to dwell on the possibility that there existed a link between Irish and English aristocrats. That the birth of the Irish Republic did not change the close relationship that existed prior to its occurrence. It was easier to assume that the bond had been broken and Irish aristocrats supported the quest for a United Ireland.

The Chair knew different. To him the notion that British influence would cease in Ireland was unthinkable. The existence of Ulster ensured that the Irish government protected the interests of its Protestant citizens. That hard line nationalists did not confiscate their lands as happened in several ex-British colonies.

The proposals put forward by the IRA intelligence officer were exactly what he wanted. Keep the struggle alive and you keep Northern Ireland part of the United Kingdom. 'We are grateful to our intelligence department for the candour and frankness with which it has brought these matters to our attention,' the Chair said in a strong deep voice. 'I agree with the analysis that the Orange Order has masqueraded in our clothes and has used our institutions to defame us. It has always been so and we must take a considerable amount of the blame. But that is for another day, for today we are asked to approve a course of action that would go some way to addressing our problems. I agree that the proposal to eliminate the Birmingham cell be approved. I am very impressed by the proposed method of achieving that objective, but because of its originality I feel compelled to ask for comments before the scheme is approved.'

The member for South Armagh stood up. 'It sounds good in theory but it will put the lives of some of our own people at risk. Can our intelligence officer tell us what measures have been taken to reduce or eliminate the risk?'

'The booby-trap was designed by an expert,' Michael said. 'We are satisfied that the bombs will not explode prematurely unless they are tampered with between the time they leave our safe house and the time they are placed at the target. If the handlers follow proper procedure at the target the risk is the same as it has always been. But if someone attempts to make the bomb safe, such as someone working for the enemy, the bomb will explode.'

'If that has been tried and tested, it has my vote,' the member from South Armagh said. 'Of course, you know that the media will have a field day?'

'Yes, I'm afraid that's the price, but on balance I feel it's worth it,' Michael said looking at the chair.

The Chair looked around the assembly and received nods of approval from all those assembled. 'We approve your plan Mr Intelligence Officer,' he said. 'It is restricted to the English Midlands.'

The Chair looked at his notes and waited for silence. The second prong of Michael's plan was controversial in Catholic Ireland. The notion of permitting a member of the IRA to infiltrate a brothel in Ulster was less palatable than permitting booby-trapped bombs to explode in England. 'Are we sure that British intelligence is using bordellos in Ulster?' the Chair asked incredulously. 'Even if they are, how does that concern us?'

Michael was prepared for difficulty in this area. He knew that he would not get official backing to infiltrate Amanda DeCourcey into a brothel as a prostitute. He lied by maintaining that his plan was to use her to trap Orange recruiters operating on the streets of Dublin to entice young Catholic girls into bordellos in Ulster. He argued that he was motivated by a desire to put an end to the practice and to demonstrate once and for all who was behind the exploitation of young Irish girls.

By explaining his plan in those terms he knew that he had cut the ground from under those who were opposed to it. After his delivery he looked around the assembly to see whether anyone was going to object. No one did and when the proposal was put to the vote it received conditional approval. Michael Lynch was given funding and authority to investigate whether security agencies in the North were utilising bordellos in the manner reported.

Although the authority, in theory, stopped short of sanctioning Michael Lynch's ulterior plan, in practice he had the backing he needed. The authority to carry out an investigation implicitly gave him carte-blanche to do whatever was necessary to get to the bottom of what was going on. To do that effectively it would be necessary to employ the services of women who were willing to work as prostitutes in the Northern bordellos.

Michael Lynch was aware that despite the grandiose titles ascribed to different echelons of the republican movement's political and military wings, that in reality there was little control. Once the go ahead had been given the means of achieving it were to a large extent in the hands of those responsible for carrying out the task.

Orders flow downwards but there is inadequate channels of communication for two-way traffic. It is a fundamental flaw in the management of guerrilla warfare and one that is almost impossible to correct. To do so would mean that operators would have to know the names of those issuing instructions and that would create a greater weakness. The cell or ring system is designed to turn clockwise and the role of the hour hand is to erase any traces left by the big hand. Once an instruction is issued it passes down the chain, and is almost impossible to rescind. Michael Lynch knew he could distance himself from any flack caused by misinterpretation of his instructions.

***

When Amanda DeCourcey went to London with Peter Duffy she expected him to behave like most men in her life did, to fall for her female charms and come under her spell. They shared the same room in a good bed-and-breakfast establishment off Caledonian Road, London. To her amazement, Duffy was the perfect gentleman and showed her a degree of respect she had not experienced in many years. He was attentive, good looking and she felt completely relaxed in his company.

After they visited his mother he was pensive and had an air of sadness about him. The poor woman was near the end of her life and did not recognise him. Yet there was a strange look in her eyes as he spoke to her. Perhaps they imagined it but afterwards they both were of the opinion that she knew who he was. But by the time they left his mother she had lost the small glint of recognition and just stared into space. 'She's being well cared for,' he said, 'that's what she wanted, to be well cared for in her dotage.'

***

Whilst Amanda went about her business Peter Duffy visited his old haunts in Harlesden, NW 10. No one recognised him and he was able to pass himself off as an Australian tourist. In that capacity he went to the inquiry desk of Harlesden police station and spoke to the officer on duty. Whilst he was there he made a mental note of the security precautions protecting the building. In less than a minute he had enough to plan an attack on the police station later if he decided to do so.

It was Peter & Amanda's last night in London and they marked the occasion by eating at an expensive restaurant in Piccadilly. Amanda was not relaxed because her mind kept wandering. She looked at Peter and realised that he reminded her of her dead brother. Not necessarily in looks but in his mannerisms and the way he treated her. If things had been different she could see herself falling for Peter Duffy in a big way.

But that was fanciful thinking and deep down she knew that she had sold her soul to the devil. The job she was about to undertake was not one that was conducive to building a loving relationship. The main purpose of her visit to London was, in the words of Michael Lynch, "to familiarise yourself" with Peter Duffy. In other words Peter was earmarked to be her pimp whilst she sold her body for the sake of old Ireland.

'I feel melancholy Peter,' Amanda said from the small en-suite bathroom. 'Do you fancy me?'

Peter did not show his surprise. He was preparing to sleep on the floor where he had spent the previous two nights. He had not slept very soundly because he was aware that Amanda was naked in bed in the same room. He saw her when she had undressed in front of him and she was beautiful. She did it as though it was the most natural thing in the world. What he did not know was that his behaviour had confused her. She never imagined he would sleep on the floor whilst she lay naked in bed in the same room, but she said nothing.

Peter had to exercise restraint not to succumb to the great temptation he felt. He knew from his days in Vietnam that women had the capacity to detach their minds from their body. Under pressure they would permit their bodies to be used for the sexual gratification of men they resented. He had been guilty, along with most of his SAS comrades, of taking advantage of Vietnamese women who were good at pretending. Their bodies went through the motions but their minds were elsewhere. He felt considerable shame and little gratification afterwards.

He had tasted forbidden wine and he did not like the taste. He was ashamed; he felt he was no better than his father was. He used Peter's mother to appease his lust. The thought struck Peter one night in Vietnam as he lay with a young girl who was pretending that she loved him. She, like his mother, was the victim of circumstances and was doing what she had to do to survive. Amanda DeCourcey did not fit squarely into that category but there were similarities. She was doing it to avenge the death of her brother and using her body because it was her best asset.

Peter had the vision of the young Vietnamese girl in his mind. The fear she showed because she thought that she had displeased him when he got out of bed and got dressed. He tried to reassure her that she had done nothing wrong.

'I sorry if I make you angry,' she pleaded pulling him back into bed. 'I very sorry … I want to make you happy.'

'No! No!' Peter shouted. 'I'm sorry, I'm sorry for everything, you've done nothing wrong.'

He emptied his pockets and wallet of every cent he had and handed it to the girl.

'This is for you,' he said handing her almost five hundred Australian dollars. 'Go back to your family and forget this life.'

The girl took the money and looked at it. 'Thank you Peter. Thank you very much. When will you come to see me again?'

He did not go to see her again, nor did he go to see any of the thousands of prostitutes plying their trade in Vietnam. He felt he had done something to purge his soul even if that something made no difference.

***

Now he could see Amanda DeCourcey coming into the bedroom wearing a transparent negligée. She had left the bathroom light on, either deliberately or accidentally; it made no difference, the effect was the same. It meant that he could see through the transparent garment. 'I asked you a question Mr Duffy,' she said standing over him. 'Do you fancy me?'

'Yes, who wouldn't?' He said standing up and taking her in his arms.

***

The next morning as they boarded their flight to Dublin, Amanda still felt the warm glow she experienced whilst making love to Peter. It was good and a feeling she had not known for many years. 'Peter I just want to say this before we leave England,' she whispered squeezing his hand. 'I want to thank you for letting me be a woman again.'

'And what a woman you were,' Peter said trying to lighten the mood. '...No that's the wrong thing to say, Amanda. What I meant is that I also want to thank you for being a woman.'

They passed the hour's flight to Dublin in silence. Amanda knew that it was too much to hope that he would respect her as a woman. She was a terrorist committed to a dangerous immoral mission that placed her beyond the limits of decency. How could he feel any respect for me, she thought as she resigned herself to what she had promised to do. "Pull yourself together Amanda," she said to herself. "Don't let sentimentality spoil your chance of revenge".

***

Three weeks later Amanda was en route to Belfast in the

company of Martin Boyle. He worked for Robert Champs as a "talent spotter" and Michael Lynch had fed Amanda into his net. Her job was to find out why Dublin prostitutes were being recruited by persons with Ulster Orange Order connections.

Michael had refused to act on speculation and wanted to know whether there was a correlation between the disappearance of Patrick O'Connell's fiancée and the prostitute racket. The bordellos were not far removed from the Fenian bond narcotic ploy and if they could be attributed to British Intelligence it would go a long way towards rectifying the state of IRA public relations. That was the first pillar upon which Michael Lynch intended to mount his counter-attack. The second involved devising a scheme to lead the security services in the English Midlands on a merry dance.

At the time Michael Lynch was not aware that the bordello investigation would prove so fruitful. He could not have known that the scheme originated in Coventry. He was to find out through a weakness that existed in the bordello scheme about which MI5 had apparently overlooked.

The Champs/Goody connection was the weak link and it would be exposed by the activities of George Goody. He was one of the members of the Orange Order that persuaded British security mandarins to facilitate the use of prostitutes. It had not been easy. The result was that two brothels and a laundry, for the purpose of gathering intelligence, were up and running at the time Amanda DeCourcey was recruited.

***

The bordellos proved to be more of a success than was anticipated. The idea of the laundry was to enable intelligence officers to distance themselves from the bordellos in the event of the scheme leaking into the public domain. Officially the reason was that terrorists would send their stained clothes to be laundered. This permitting forensic examination that could pinpoint the name and addresses of those involved in terrorism. Surprisingly a number of contaminated articles of clothing were presented for cleaning and the scheme proved worthwhile.

The idea of recruiting prostitutes in Dublin seemed on the face of it to be flawed. It was suspected that Dublin prostitutes would have an affinity with the Provos, and word of the scheme would reach the IRA. That bothered Michael Lynch; he reckoned that British Intelligence had calculated that word would reach the IRA sooner or later.

He had not fathomed out that from a British viewpoint the sooner the better. They knew that if bordello personnel were restricted to British prostitutes it would look too suspicious. The correct approach was to employ ordinary prostitutes and to superimpose specially trained women amongst them.

It was a good idea but one that overlooked the fundamental principle upon which the scheme was founded. Pillow talk was the name of the game and whilst it was easy to teach prostitutes to listen it was not possible to stop their clients from talking. It would prove to be an area where there was no difference between Protestants and Catholics, security or para-military personnel. Clients who have hired the services of prostitutes assume that there is an implicit confidentiality clause in the agreement.

XXI

Big Tom

ALTHOUGH GEORGE GOODY LIKED to brag he did not like to be thought of as a bragger. He had mastered the art of indirectly informing his listeners of his wealth and achievements without listing them. He found he could achieve his objective by moaning about being overworked, overtaxed and frustrated at the number of decisions he was called upon to perform. "Look at the amount of tax I had to pay last year. They want me to take on this million pound contract, but I'm too busy," were two of his favourite openings.

The listener would offer advice or be drawn into discussing George's wealth. Before long George would have his audience and relate the oft-told tale of how he grew from rags to riches.

It was his way to show his friends, especially those that could return favours, a good time. Trips to bordellos in Paris were on the agenda for buyers and engineers he wished to impress. It often tipped the balance in his favour when tendering for big contracts. A nod here and a wink there could mean the difference between success and failure. George knew the men to court and their weaknesses.

Perhaps it was not surprising that when the bordellos opened in Northern Ireland he felt it was his patriotic duty to take his clientele there. After all, he could lay claim to being part of the scheme and knew the management. The opportunity to find out what was on the minds of some of his customers did not escape him.

Tom McDermott was not one of Goody's customers in the sense that he brought contracts to his table. Their business association was the other way round and Goody brought subcontracts to McDermott. The arrangement came about through their mutual contacts in Orange Lodges. McDermott had technically speaking been an Orange Lodge sleeper sent to Birmingham in the early 1960s to infiltrate the Birmingham Irish Catholic community. At the time things were quiet in Ireland and people in whose interest it was to ensure that they did not remain so used the lull in nationalist activity to regroup.

There were two schools of thought. On one hand there was the view that Northern Irish Catholics were satisfied with their status. Since the end of the War the standard of living in Britain had improved significantly. The same could not be said for citizens of the Irish republic; their living standards were bordering on third-world conditions. Whereas Northern Catholics were eligible to benefit from the new British welfare system, their Southern cousins were left to fend for themselves. There were better employment prospects in Ulster and better unemployment benefits. The British National Health system and the enactment of the Education Act 1944 placed the question beyond doubt. The fact was that the North even with its shortcomings offered a much higher standard of living than the South did. Catholics were not fools; they knew which side their bread was buttered.

George Goody had a different theory. He was one of the hard-line Scots who believed that lurking in every Northern Catholic was a nationalist longing to be reunited with his brethren in a United Ireland. That Catholics believed that they owed it to their forefathers to rid their land of every Saxon invader. It was a fervour that could not be washed away by material gains and sooner or later it would surface.

Goody knew that the Orange Order had a duty to prepare itself for the battle that was coming. Sooner or later the nationalist monster would raise its ugly head. Catholics were always whining about something and the problem was trying to convince Westminster that their whine was a longing for an end to British rule in Ulster.

***

Goody and his associates knew why Catholics were not given equal voting rights. If they were they would import their brothers from the Republic and overwhelm the ballot box with Catholic votes. Then they would look for proportional representation and the voting system that was put in place to prevent Catholics ever taking power in the North would be ineffective. The status quo was the key to ensuring that the Northern Irish constitution remained intact.

When the IRA announced a cease-fire it caused shock waves in George Goody's world. The Nationalists were beginning to wake up to the notion that bombs and bullets served them ill in their quest for a United Ireland.

Hitherto Nationalists had refused to sit in the British House of Commons, a policy the wisdom of which was perverse to say the least. Now that had changed and Nationalists were in the British Parliament directing world opinion to the flaw in the cradle of democracy.

The same flaw that was the foundation upon which Protestant supremacy relied. The gerrymandered voting system that prevented Catholics winning at the ballot box could not withstand public scrutiny in its own right. To survive it needed sustenance and that was provided by the terrorist activities of the IRA.

***

In the inner sanctum of the Orange Order, Goody bragged openly about his role in reminding the British government that it owed a duty of care to Ulster Loyalists. He had provided them a face-saving reason to refuse to negotiate with Nationalists. The deed was done and the sound of bombs and bullets was the price. George was not numbered amongst those who argued that things had gone too far. The further the better as far as he was concerned. The threat of a United Ireland had been removed when the IRA commenced its latest campaign.

***

'Big Tom McDermott!' George Goody said with exaggerated warmth. 'How did it go in Ireland?'

Tom owed a great deal to George who never let him forget it. The success of Tom's business depended on George's good will. And Tom's high standard of living depended on the success of his business. It was in his interest to keep George happy and to do that all he had to do was follow orders.

At first it seemed improbable that Tom would ever get involved in Irish republicanism beyond pretending to be a Southern Irish nationalist. He was given a new name and told to go to Birmingham and mingle with Birmingham Irish Catholics. He was provided with money and contracts to enable him to start his business. It was easier than he expected to pass himself off as a Catholic.

That was a long time ago and since then he married and had three children. He had successfully infiltrated Birmingham Irish Catholics and was known as a man who could provide work and who was sympathetic to the notion of a United Ireland.

Then Goody came on the scene and advised Tom that he was his new boss. He demanded reports, but there was little to report. Tom felt it was necessary to exaggerate his republican activities and to tell Goody what he obviously wanted to hear. Then things began to change. There was trouble in Ulster and the Nationalists began to show their true colours.

***

Four years had elapsed since George announced that he had persuaded the Order to send a man to assist Tom. 'He's one of the best Tom,' George said. 'We've taken him out of Ulster and he's going to be your second-in-command.'

For once George was not exaggerating. Kevin Kelly was good and in a very short time was organising nationalist activity in Birmingham. He moved amongst the Catholic community with natural ease. The surprising thing was that he did not conceal his Ulster Protestant background.

He penetrated the nationalists by saying what they wanted to hear; that he agreed with their cause and was on their side. He organised raffles, dances and other fund raising events in Irish pubs and clubs. Within six months of his arrival large donations were being sent to Sinn Fein in Dublin.

Like all good deputies Kevin Kelly made sure the glory went to his boss. As far as Dublin was concerned the credit for organising the Birmingham Irish was due to a hitherto unknown nationalist called Tom McDermott. It must have stimulated their curiosity for within a year of the arrival of Kevin Kelly a man from Dublin came to see Tom in Birmingham. He arrived unannounced and his name was Jim Doran a high-ranking officer of the Provisional IRA.

Doran was cagey and obviously intended testing Tom's commitment. After a fortnight Doran announced that he wanted Tom to organise and take command of an IRA cell in Birmingham. George Goody was ecstatic. 'We have the Fenian bastards now,' he said. 'I'll have to tell Harry the Chat.'

That was the first time Tom heard of Harry and he would later learn that Harry was head of Birmingham CID. He assigned Tom a handler, Detective Superintendent Malcolm Smith of the Birmingham Serious Crime Squad. He was put in charge of supervising Tom's activities.

***

In the beginning there was little contact with Dublin. Doran would appear and give Tom menial tasks then he would disappear. There was a gradual increase in the number and importance of tasks allocated to Tom. First he was instructed to set up five safe houses in the City and later he was given packages to look after. They contained clocks and wires but no explosive substances.

Tom reported everything to his handler and was instructed to permit things to develop. It was important to gain the trust of Dublin, to encourage them to use the facilities of the Birmingham cell. That was Tom's main task according to his police handler. Kevin Kelly would look after the organisation of the Birmingham cell at operational level.

Tom was content to leave "operational stuff" to Kelly. He was the only person with a military background in the cell. In fact his military experience extended to his activities in Protestant paramilitary organisations in Ulster. There he learned how to manage subversive groups and to enforce discipline.

***

George Goody often said that where discipline ends anarchy begins. It was an argument he used to underline his belief that the Provisional IRA had little control over the activities of its members. Pseudo-officers with grandiose military titles lacked the training and skills to control operations in an organisation that relied on untrained volunteers to survive.

The name of the game as far as Goody was concerned was to ensure that the IRA played its part in preventing a united Ireland. And the best way of achieving that was to make sure that IRA atrocities continued to wreck the Ulster Civil Rights campaign. Tom McDermott had been groomed and placed to do the job. But was he getting cold feet? Why had he asked for this meeting?

***

When Goody greeted him, Tom was mindful that he had ended up between a rock and a hard place. He had asked to meet Goody to discuss recent developments because he was worried about the way Fr Brown had been betrayed in Coventry. Tom knew that despite what others may think he was not stupid. Granted, he was not the smartest player in the game but he was cute enough to realise when he could be heading for a fall. The arrest of Fr Brown in Coventry did not sit comfortably with what Tom knew.

Goody liked to brag by selling himself as a Knight in shining armour of the Orange Order. In that mood he sometimes said things that he must have thought would go over Tom's head.

Early in their relationship Tom realised that George's tongue loosened in keeping with the amount of whisky he consumed. Not only that his penchant for bragging increased as well. He would relate stories about how he had played a role in setting a Cell in Coventry to prove to British intelligence that the IRA was active in England. Whether his words were those of a babbling drunkard or something more sinister did not matter to Tom until recently.

From Goody's lips Tom formed the opinion that Fr Brown was a Protestant clergyman deeply resentful to the notion of a United Ireland. He was encouraged by the Orange Order to change religions and seek ordination as a Catholic priest. He agreed and eventually ended up as the curate of a Coventry Parish. In that capacity he was accepted without question into the local Irish nationalist community and formed an IRA cell. The police were tipped off and evidence to indict Fr Brown and six other men came to light. Fr Brown was currently serving twelve years in prison.

Tom McDermott saw himself in Fr Brown's shoes. Their roles were comparable in many respects. The only difference was that on this occasion things had been allowed to go further. The Orange Order wanted to fix things so that the British population would see Irish nationalists in their true colours. Whereas Fr Brown merely possessed maps and documents Tom was in possession of explosives, guns and ammunition. It was enough to send him to jail for the rest of his life.

But that was only one side of the coin. On the other, Michael Lynch was not a man to cross. Lynch was nobody's fool nor was he the sort that would forgive or forget. On balance Tom felt it safer to stay on side with his Orange friends and the police. That was the only ray of light in his situation. The police knew what he was doing and why.

***

Tom hoped this meeting would serve to remind his police handler that Goody was calling the shots. If things went wrong the police would verify that Tom was acting on their instructions and those of Goody. Tom and his family would be whisked away to safety under the witness protection scheme. 'It went well George,' Tom said. 'Dublin seems happy and so they ought with the money I took over and all.'

'Yes go on … what about Duffy and the campaign in England?'

'They don't know Duffy but they told me something big would happen soon in Birmingham.'

'That's great!' Goody said. 'We need one of their big fish in the net. Up to now they've been playing cat and mouse with us. No that I mind Tom, sooner or later they'll find out which one of us is the cat.'

George was referring to the methods used by the IRA to test their man in Birmingham. It was as though they did not trust him and he was still being tested. Their favourite trick was to get word to McDermott that a parcel had been hidden and ask him to collect it. Gelignite and firearms were smuggled into England via Holyhead Port and concealed in Anglesey.

Tom would receive maps and grid references through his letterbox informing him of the location of the dump. The information would arrive in three separate consignments, none of which was capable of leading to the location without the other two. He was required to acknowledge receipt of the first before the next was sent. The worrying thing was that a considerable arsenal of guns, ammunition, detonators, gelignite and other bomb making paraphernalia was building up in Tom's garage.

Tom's handler was kept up to date but in the absence of a suitable terrorist with whom they could match the material there was little they could do. Tom was instructed to give Kevin Kelly responsibility for looking after the "dump" until something cropped up. The thing everyone wanted to crop up was the missing component…an IRA Volunteer.

In the meantime George Goody had decided that the time was right to reassure Tom. His police handler had reported that he was concerned about the state of McDermott's mind. The pressure was obviously too much for him and consideration was being given to handing over responsibility to Kelly.

It was a stupid idea that failed to take into account that McDermott was the person known to Dublin. If he faltered the whole operation would fold. The only answer was to reassure McDermott, and if that did not work to point out to him that he would be arrested for being a member of the IRA. George decided that it was time to show Big Tom a good time.

**

In the Belfast bordello McDermott was having a good time. George had instructed that Tom was to be "treated like a lord" and sounded out by one of the trained agents. Things were going to plan apart from one snag. Tom had taken a fancy to a girl who was not qualified in the art of gentle persuasion. She was Amanda DeCourcey an untried and untested young woman who had recently been recruited in Dublin.

Robert Champs was in a quandary. On one hand he had been told by his MI5 handler not to use Dublin girls until they were cleared. On the other, Goody had told him to encourage McDermott to make full use of the facilities. 'Show him the catalogue, and get him fixed up with a good interrogator.'

McDermott was out of his depth in the bordello. He was a big awkward shy man and he refused to pick one of the trained girls from the catalogue. 'That's not the way I do things,' he said. 'I don't go with prostitutes. What sort of a club is this anyway?'

Robert Champs then realised that McDermott was obviously naïve and unaware that he was in a brothel. 'I'm only having you on, Tom,' Robert said closing the book. 'What do you think this is… Argos?'

Tom relaxed and downed another whisky. 'There's plenty of stock on show anyway,'he said nudging Robert, 'I'll have another drink and see what's on offer.'

'Let me get your drink,' Robert said calling Amanda. 'Give this gentleman whatever he wants …it's on the house.'

'Whatever you say Mr Champs,' Amanda said. 'And what will it be sir?'

'I'll have a large Powers if you have it?'

The smile froze momentarily on Amanda's face just long enough for Robert to notice. She recovered quickly and made her way to the service hatch to collect McDermott's whisky.

'That's my sort of woman Rob, 'Tom said, 'Yes sir, if I could spend a night with her they could hang me in the morning.'

'Have you seen her before Tom?' Robert asked casually.

'No, not in this life anyway,' Tom said bursting into a fit of laughter at his own wit.

As she waited at the serving hatch Amanda was worried. She forced herself not to look back to confirm what she already knew. It was the same man she met leaving Michael Lynch's office in Dublin. The informer.

'Here's your whisky sir,' Amanda said turning to leave.

'Don't rush off,' Robert said studying Amanda's reaction. 'This is Tom. He's new here, make him feel at home.'

'You don't have to stay if you don't want to,' Tom said offering a big hand to Amanda. 'I'm able to look after myself.'

'No, I'd love to stay,' Amanda said, 'I'm new here myself and I know how you feel.'

'There's something I have to discuss with Amanda,' Robert said. 'Can I take her away for a few minutes?'

***

Robert took Amanda to his office. He wanted to know where she had seen McDermott before. She convinced him that she had never set eyes on him. Robert believed her and let his guard down. He told her that Tom was a very important man from Birmingham and not to be fooled by his appearance. 'I tried to get him off with one of the girls but he's taken a fancy to you.' Robert said earnestly, 'If you do me a favour I'll make it worth your while.'

'What sort of favour do you mean?'

'Take him to a room and try and find out things. You know, get him talking about himself, what he does and that sort of thing.'

'Jesus, Mr Champs I'd be no good at that,' Amanda said. 'I've never done anything like that in my life.'

'You'll be fine, you'll be just fine lass, there's really nothing to it,' Champs said. 'All you have to do is get him talking and pretend to be interested.'

'You make it sound so easy. How do you know he'll tell me things?'

It's my job lass, I'm not a brothel manager you know, I work for the ... No never mind just do as I say will you?'

'Jesus, Mary help me, Mr Champs,' Amanda said crossing herself. 'I'll do it, but don't blame me if it goes wrong.'

***

Peter Duffy was ordered to rent a cottage in Northern Ireland and live there as an Australian sheep farmer on extended holiday. That was shortly before Amanda was recruited to work in the bordello. Duffy was instructed to visit the premises "to get his face known" before Amanda was recruited. The plan was that when she arrived Peter would be her regular client and receive her reports.

The cottage he rented was in a remote area of Co Antrim and belonged to a Protestant farmer. In years gone by it was a labourer's cottage, which had fallen into disuse. The farmer had made a poor attempt at refurbishing it but it had electricity, septic tank and a well. It was situated on the southern side of Antrim in a relatively peaceful location about an hour from the border.

After spending a week there Peter noticed an increase in activities. The postman arrived one morning with a letter addressed to someone Peter had never heard of. Then a man from the electricity board came to check a non-existing fault and the following day a police constable visited to check if Peter was settling in.

Peter feared he had become the latest subject of suspicion in the files of intelligence gatherers in the area. It was the last thing he wanted. The cottage had been selected because of its remoteness. It seemed the perfect place at the time from which they could carry out their plan.

***

Peter was glad that an end to his tour in Ireland was in

sight. He did not know what he expected from Ireland before he arrived but whatever it was, it was not how things had turned out. In a relative short time he had acquired access to a fortune and fell in love. Jim Doran had proved to be a shrewder operator than he first appeared. And Amanda DeCourcey had agreed to be Mrs Peter Duffy.

The only thing that remained to do was to find Denise Ward-Riley. Even on that matter progress was being made. Amanda held part of the jigsaw puzzle without realising it. It dawned on her in a conversation with Peter that the woman he and Patrick was looking for was the same person she saw in the Panama hotel with the man calling himself Damien Price. Lynch had later told her what he saw at Birmingham Airport and after putting two and two together it became obvious that the IRA was not holding Denise.

It was planned that when Denise was found, James, Denise, Patrick, Jim Doran, Amanda and Peter would set off together for a new life in Australia. Lynch had agreed that the latter four could decamp as soon as the present operation was concluded, 'I might come with you,' he said. 'It depends whether I can bring Dolores with me.'

Peter had misgivings about Lynch. He doubted that the lure he used to get Amanda to prostitute herself was genuine. But there was a chance that Denise was being held against her will in a brothel in Belfast. And a chance was enough to get Patrick and James' vote. Peter reluctantly went along with the plan because Amanda advised him not to cross Lynch.

***

When Dolores Flynn was arrested in London Michael Lynch lost interest in everything else. He wanted revenge and went about getting it by utilising the insight into human nature that he had acquired from his Justice Department.

Peter Duffy's latest report from Amanda was confirmation if confirmation was needed that Tom McDermott was working for the Orange Order. He would pay dearly for his treachery. To shoot him would be too kind. Lynch's plan was to allow Tom to live a long life so that when he woke every morning he would regret that he underestimated Michael Lynch. 'We have a deal Peter,' Lynch said through his joined fingers. 'You all can leave Ireland as soon as this is over.'

'And the money?'

'Yes you've earned it. Tell me where you want it and I'll make sure it's in your account within a week.'

Peter had just delivered his latest report from Amanda. News that Tom McDermott was seen in the Ulster bordello explained everything. The red hand of Ulster Loyalists had greased the palm of security agencies from Belfast to Birmingham. Amanda had excelled herself, not only did she spot McDermott she also learned that the bordello was crawling with British agents. The leaders of Sinn Fein now had enough and would have to give Lynch the go ahead. 'Keep up the good work Peter,' Lynch said. 'I think we…'

'What do you mean. Don't you realise the danger Amanda is in?'

'Don't be too hasty.' Lynch said raising his hand to halt Peter. 'What about your Miss Ward-Riley?'

Peter looked down realising that Lynch knew he had him. 'All Right, we'll give it a week but I want Patrick O'Connell and Jim Doran with me.'

'You can have Patrick, but Jim is not available.'

XXII

❈

Two Birds with one Stone

HARRY THE CHAT WAS not pleased. He had gone out on a limb when he turned a blind eye to the accumulation of explosives in his City. It was contrary to every rule in the book for a senior police officer to place the British public in danger. There were other irregularities that could come back to haunt him.

Until recently things seemed to be going to plan. McDermott was a good man and it was just a question of time before an IRA Active Service Unit would arrive in Birmingham. The Serious Crime Squad would arrest them and Ballivor. Two birds with one stone, it was all going to plan.

***

The IRA was not living up to expectations. It had ordered McDermott to set off explosions using local men and gelignite already in his possession. It was a worrying setback but in order to keep the original plan intact Detective Superintendent Guest gave Tom the go ahead to set off controlled explosions.

Harry was out of the country when he heard about the explosions in Solihull and Birmingham. He scanned newspapers and listened to the BBC World Service for information but there was no mention of an arrest. He returned home immediately and now as he looked at Bill Guest his worst fears were becoming reality. Bill was sitting in front of him with a worried expression on his face. "Two gun Billy" was living up to his reputation of shooting from the hip and missing the target.

'I thought we were on top of this situation Bill?' Harry said glancing at a log sheet. 'If we know whose behind this why are they not in custody?'

Bill thought the question was unfair. Harry knew very well what the problem was. The IRA had ordered McDermott to set off bombs at soft targets before they moved in to "flatten Birmingham."

It was agreed to allow McDermott's cell to place disarmed bombs at the targets specified. But there was a problem, a misunderstanding about how to make the bombs safe. We even sent our own men to ensure that the bombs were disarmed, Bill thought, but there must be a fault in the wiring. Several of the bombs went off causing serious damage and the public was up in arms. 'I think we've solved the problem now sir,' Bill said with more self-assurance than he felt.

'Bill, I can't see that we've solved anything,' Harry said. 'Are you sure you're on top of this thing?'

'Yes, I'm as sure as I can be sir, the problem is that we have no control over orders coming from Dublin.'

A look of alarm crossed Harry's brow. It was as though the realisation that things might not pan out as anticipated had just dawned on him. 'Bill, do you realise what's at stake here?' Harry asked in desperation. 'Heads will roll, yes heads are going to roll, and we must make sure that they're not ours.'

Of course Harry was right. The public was up in arms about the apparent lack of success by the police. But it was just a question of time. Sooner or later the IRA would send in their team and when that happened everything would fall into place.

'We have to be patient sir, our whole strategy depends on Dublin sending a team into Birmingham. The only people in the frame at the moment are the ones we are using to bait the IRA.'

'I don't like it Bill, we must have an alternative plan. What if Dublin decides to get McDermott to do the job? What are we going to do then?'

'Sir I think…'

'Look Bill, I don't want you to think. Just answer a few straight questions. Am I right in thinking that McDermott's people believe they're active members of the IRA?'

'Yes sir.'

'Apart from McDermott who else knows the truth?'

'Kevin Kelly sir.'

'Of course, that's right,' Harry said tapping his finger on his desk. 'Bill get some of that stuff off the streets, you know the explosives and guns. Why don't you arrange to have a bomb factory discovered? Yes that will ease tension and make it look like we're having some success.'

'That's a brilliant idea sir, I'll arrange it straight away. It might make the IRA in Dublin think they have to move quickly before we discover the rest.'

***

Bill selected a derelict house, 232 Clifton Road, Birmingham and made sure everything was in place. An anonymous tip-off to the Birmingham Evening Post led to the discovery of the bomb factory. The find was given front-page headlines. It was billed as a significant breakthrough by the police, in the Midlands in the fight against Irish terrorists.

XXIII

The Coventry Bomb

MICHAEL LYNCH READ THE paper with a degree of satisfaction. He contacted McDermott and urged him to be more careful. 'Is it still safe for us to work in Birmingham?'

McDermott assured him that it was but that the longer they waited the greater the risk. Lynch suppressed a laugh as he told McDermott that the plans were almost ready. The delay was because "higher authority" wanted a little job done in Coventry first. Tom was not keen and said so.

Lynch was sympathetic but explained that the decision to set off a bomb in Coventry had been taken. It was to show the British that the IRA's capacity to operate in the City was not diminished by the arrest of Fr Brown. 'Whatever you say Mr Lynch,' McDermott said wearily.

Tom was showing signs of paranoia. He feared he was being sucked into a bottomless pit and there was nothing he could do about it. He contacted his police handler and explained that he did not want to put his family at risk. 'They'll kill us all if they every find out Mr Guest.'

Bill reassured Tom but deep down he knew that McDermott's days as an agent provocateur was nearing an end. 'Just hang in there Tom,' Bill said. 'You know we can protect you.'

Bill was going to use Kevin Kelly on the Coventry job. The problem was that Kelly was unknown to the IRA in Dublin. McDermott would have to be kept sweet for the time being.

***

Once again the IRA had not acted as expected. Harry very reluctantly gave the go ahead for the Coventry bomb. 'It's the last time Bill,' he said with an air of finality. 'I hold you personally responsible for ensuring that there are no slip-ups this time. Do I make myself clear Superintendent?'

Harry emphasised the word superintendent, and Bill knew that the time was fast approaching when Harry would show the other side of his personality. He was worried and would do whatever it took to save himself if there was a backlash.

Kevin Kelly assured Bill that he would personally supervise the "package" and make sure that the detonator was removed. The plan was foolproof. The Coventry bomb would be placed as directed by Dublin, but it would not be armed. A vigilant member of the public would discover it and it would be made safe.

***

When Tom McDermott called Bill and demanded to see him straight away, he came to the meeting prepared to put Tom's mind at ease. He would tell him that his role henceforth was purely administrational. All he had to do was maintain communications with Dublin. Act as a go-between by passing messages to and fro between Dublin and his police handler.

Bill was shocked when he saw Tom. He looked awful, there were huge black bags under his eyes and he was stammering and fumbling his words. 'They, they came to my fucking house Bill. They've given me a gypsy's warning.'

'Calm down Tom, who came to your house?'

'The IRA, that's who. They left the Coventry bomb at my house. At my house if you don't mind, with my wife and children.'

'Don't worry Tom, everything's under control, I've good news. We're not going to use a real bomb in Coventry. We'll make it look like the real thing but it will be accidentally discovered and you'll be in the clear.'

'What about the bomb they gave me?'

'What about it Tom?' Bill said. 'They won't know that we didn't use it, we'll still use the dummy. We'll leak the description of your bomb to the media. The IRA will never know the difference. Do you follow Tom?'

'Yes, I'm with you Bill,' Tom said showing signs of relief. 'When do you want the bomb they left at my house?'

'Right, let me think about that,' Bill said, unpacking the question. 'You must understand that not every police officer in the force knows about the work you're doing for us.'

The next day they met again and Bill wasted no time in putting Tom at ease. 'We've arranged to plant the dummy in Coventry on Friday 15th November. That gives us three days. We'll send an explosive expert to take the bomb away from your home.'

'I thought you said that you were going to make it look as though the real bomb was found in Coventry?' Tom said.

'We are, of course we are. Otherwise Dublin will suspect something,' Bill said. 'I told you Tom, it's all in hand, stop worrying. We'll switch bombs before the news breaks and leak the description of your bomb to the media.'

'Thanks Bill, I'm not myself …it's all the worry. I'll see you Friday afternoon.'

***

Tom McDermott felt better than he had for a long time. He went home early that night to catch up on much needed sleep. The next day was Wednesday 13th November and he went about his business as usual. He had it all worked out in his mind. There would be a two-hour delay from the time a bomb was armed and it exploded. That would give the police sufficient time to get a news flash to the media.

As soon as the news came on the television Tom would

contact Lynch and pretend to panic. He would tell him that things were getting too hot, that the police were onto his cell. He would then persuade Lynch to send someone to take charge in Birmingham. The police would have their terrorist and Tom could move quietly into the background.

That evening Tom went home early and after tea went out to his shed to make sure the bomb was safe. He knew that if it started to sweat the nitrogen was extremely dangerous. It was a cold night and Tom decided that the likelihood of the dynamite becoming unstable was remote. He carefully examined the package and noted the sophisticated wiring and Eversoft Frangex dynamite carefully wrapped.

It was the first time Tom had seen professional industrial dynamite and he realised that the bomb was different. It was more sophisticated than those he had seen before. The sooner Bill took it away the better. Tom swore that this was the last time he would have anything to do with either the police or the IRA. He retired to his living room for the evening and was soon asleep.

Tom did not hear the knock on his door. His wife awoke him and when he looked up he saw Jim Doran. 'How's it going Tom,' Doran said in that over friendly style that never failed to irritate Tom. 'Have you something to drink for a poor old traveller?'

***

Two hours later Tom McDermott was feeling so worried that he thought he was going to be sick. Doran was not alone; he was accompanied by a sullen dangerous looking man who hardly spoke. Doran had told McDermott to explain to his wife that she should tell callers that she did not know where her husband was and did not expect him home until Friday. He told him to get the bomb, after which all three went to a safe house in Aston.

It was not a house known to McDermott although hitherto he believed that he knew every IRA safe house in the Midlands. Doran's attitude had changed and he was almost threatening in his manner. He instructed Tom to name two of his cell members who could be trusted to "place" the bomb in Coventry.

Doran's companion, whose name was never mentioned, went to collect the two men. Meanwhile Tom was informed that the Coventry target was going to be blown a day early by remote control. All the two men had to do was place the bomb at the Coventry telephone exchange. 'Thursday night! We thought it was going to be Friday night.' Tom exclaimed.

'We've decided to bring it forward twenty-four hours. Is there a problem with that Tom?'

'No whatever you say Mr Doran.'

XXIV

The Sound of Silence

PATRICK O'CONNELL REMAINED AT the rented cottage when Peter Duffy went to collect Amanda. It was her last night in the bordello and their last night in Ulster. James Ward-Riley had got word to them to abandon their mission and return to Australia. The message was vague and Patrick understood from it that Denise had been found either safe or dead.

Tonight he was positioned in a foxhole that he and Peter had dug in preparation for an ambush. It was something they had learned from the Vietcong, and he smiled to himself when he realised the irony of the situation. He thought that the foxhole and underground tunnel leading from the cottage was not the only thing he had in common with his old enemy. It was 1.a.m. and Peter was late.

The plan was that Peter and Amanda would follow their normal routine. They would come back to the cottage, collect Patrick and later the three would drive over the border into the Republic. From there they would go to Dublin collect Jim Doran and catch the first Aer Lingus flight to Australia.

Patrick checked his AK 47, and looked out at the silent Irish landscape. There was something eerie about the silence in Ireland; it was different somehow. One could hear nothing except the odd nocturnal animal, such as a vixen announcing to dogs that she was in the neighbourhood. Dogs would bark and the vixen would go in the opposite direction.

***

Duffy had entered the bordello at 11 p.m. to collect Amanda, as he did twice a week. He was her regular client on Tuesday and Friday nights since she came to work at the establishment. Champs had quizzed her about Peter on a few occasions. She answered his questions to his apparent satisfaction but Peter suspected that Champs still had doubts.

That night when Peter entered the bordello compounds he was checked by a security guard. It was not unusual because security at the bordello was always tight. It was one of the things in which Lynch had shown great interest and had obtained details of the layout from Peter.

The irksome thing about tonight's check was that Peter was a regular at the establishment and was known to security. The officer on this occasion was new, self assured and showed a degree of professionalism not common amongst persons of his calling. This guard was a little too smooth, more like a MI5 agent dissimulating his true role, Peter thought.

Peter played the game and hoped that the exercise was to set a trap for a future occasion rather than one that was going to be activated that night. It was Peter's last visit to the bordello and he was not concerned with the future beyond the next hour. By then he would have collected Amanda and be on his way to meet Patrick. When the guard finished asking questions he smiled and allowed Peter to enter.

The clubroom was busy and as soon as Peter entered Robert Champs approached him. 'Peter, sorry about all that nonsense,' he said. 'I just spotted you on my monitor being questioned by security. Come over here, there's someone I want you to meet.'

Peter followed across the room to a table normally reserved for special guests. Tonight there were three tables placed together to accommodate a party of VIPs. There were about ten mixed couples, including Amanda, seated around the tables spellbound by their host. The man had his arm around Amanda's shoulder and was leaning towards his guests to ensure that they did not miss a word he was saying. 'I think Amanda is busy right now,' Champs said. 'I hope you don't mind?'

'Of course not,' Peter said, turning to walk away. 'There's always another night.'

'Don't go, there's someone I want you to meet,' Champs said beckoning to a man sitting amongst the party. 'John, have you a minute?'

Peter Duffy's instincts were seldom wrong and on this occasion he picked up the non-verbal communication that passed between the man sitting with Amanda and the man Champs called John. It was almost an imperceptible nod but it was enough to communicate to John that he had found his mark. He stood up and came over to where Peter and Champs were standing. 'This is Detective Inspector John Bayliss of the West Midlands Police,' Champs said as though he had rehearsed the introduction several times. 'He may have information of interest to you.'

An hour and ten vodkas later Peter thought the time was right to feign the effects the alcohol was having on him. He knew they were playing an old trick on him; lull the opposition into a sense of false security, get him drunk and then see him off. Peter could consume as much vodka again before it would have a significant effect on his state of mind or diminish his physical capacity. He knew that enough was enough and that every drink after ten would be one too many.

'Jesus fella, you're drinking me under the table,' Peter said staggering up to John and placing his arm around his shoulder. 'You know us Australians are not used to this Russian piss. We prefer Foster's.'

John laughed the false laugh of someone trying too hard to be friendly. Duffy was blowing in the breeze, swaying from side to side like a drunken slob. John had done his job, he found out what he wanted to know. There was now no doubt why this man was in the bordello. He was one of the Australians sent to find Denise Ward-Riley.

NETTLEGRABBERS

***

John was the guest of George Goody as he had been on several previous occasions. Usually they went to Paris or Amsterdam to let off steam and enjoy the pleasures on offer in those liberated cities. But this weekend was different. George had invited him to Belfast to do something very important. 'It's worth ten-grand Johnny boy,' he said. 'I want you to find out something for me. You know, to do something that only a man with your training can be relied on to do.'

John owed it to George to do his bidding, as if the £10'000 was not enough. Of course John remembered the night in Birmingham when he had been called to play the role of a solicitor. He was taken to George's luxury flat in the rich side of Sutton Coldfield and introduced to a very beautiful young Australian lady called Denise.

John smiled as he recalled the way she had been set up. The poor bitch had fallen for the old Fenian Bond con, hook-line and sinker. Only George could have made it happen and persuaded the customs officer to play along. John's role was easy. All he had to do was pretend to be a solicitor, instructed by George to defend her, and to convince her that it was in her interest to put her life in Goody's hands.

George had fallen for her as soon as he saw her and decided to change the plan. Initially she was going to be smuggled into Ulster and persuaded to work in the bordello, but when George saw her he wanted her for himself. The sting depended on convincing her that she was completely dependent on him. And to make her believe that the best course of action in her circumstances was to lie low until it was safe to get her out of the country.

John remembered that Denise was no fool and she wanted to fight her corner in court. She could prove that she was not a drug smuggler and she would rather take the chance of being convicted than spend the rest of her life on the run. John did not know what put the idea into his head, but to his surprise he surpassed himself. 'What about your parents?' he said, 'there's not only drugs involved here Denise. Have you considered the question of terrorism?'

When she realised that her parents were at risk she reluctantly agreed to go along with the plan provided John assured her that he would get word to her family. On their next meeting he did just that and also told her that her parents understood and advised her to lie low. He added that the Australian secret service had already visited her parents' home and no doubt their telephone was tapped.

'You must not contact anyone in Australia for the time being.' John lied.

'How long do I have to wait before I can speak to my family?'

'I can't say, it depends. The important thing is to keep you alive and out of jail until we come up with something.'

'Alive, what do you mean?'

'Denise your life is in danger. You've been caught in a spider's web. You know too much.'

'Then I'm doomed,' Denise said. 'I don't know anyone here. Nobody will help me.'

'I think Mr Goody will look after you, but you must do as he says. Is that right sir? John asked George.

'Yes, you can stay here as long as you like lass. I can afford it and I want to help,' George said giving Denise a reassuring hug.

On his first few visits John felt a little sorry for Denise. There was emptiness in her eyes and sadness in her voice that haunted him. She would cheer up when John gave her news of home. He went out of his way to reassure her that her parents were fully behind her. She never asked about anyone else and as time passed she seemed to accept her predicament.

George was happy. There was something about having a beautiful girl under his control that appealed to him. John's visits became less frequent and he thought his role was finished.

When word that Peter Duffy, an ex-Australian SAS soldier, was visiting Ulster bordellos reached George he was concerned. He thought it was too much of a coincidence and went about finding out what Duffy was up to.

Tonight John confirmed that George's suspicions were well founded. Duffy fell for the old trick and John's part in the matter was nearing an end. All he had to do was invite Duffy into Champ's office and that was the signal that Duffy was their man and that he was looking for Denise. Now Champs would take over and there was little doubt that Duffy would be found dead in a remote ditch in the not too distant future.

***

'Let me see if I've got it right officer,' Peter said, using his glass to emphasise the importance of what he was about to say to John, 'If I meet you in Birmingham next week you'll lead me to my friend Denise Ward-Riley?'

'You've got it in one,' John said. 'Let's drink to it.'

'Fair enough me old mate,' Peter said raising his glass quickly and missing his mouth. The contents went over his shoulder and almost caused a commotion.

'Come on,' John said taking hold of Peter's arm. 'Let's take you somewhere to sober up.'

Later when Robert Champs came into his office he saw John sitting on the big swivel chair behind the large mahogany desk. 'Ask George and Amanda to come in please Robert.' John said, 'I have to speak to them.'

'Are you sure John? Where's the Australian?'

'He's out cold on the floor. Everything's fine.'

Robert returned presently with Goody and Amanda. John was in the same position that he occupied earlier. 'Is he our man John?' Goody asked as soon as he came into the room.

'Yes I believe so,' John said.

'Shoot him,' Goody said to Champs. 'Kill the Fenian bastard here and now.'

John felt sick. He could imagine the bullet penetrating the seat upon which he was sitting and blowing his private parts up through his body.

Earlier when he entered Champs' office he was made aware that Duffy was not drunk. He produced a pistol and as soon as John closed the door he felt the cold barrel against his neck. 'You're a smart copper,' Duffy said. 'Do exactly as I say and you might get out of this in one piece.'

Duffy positioned himself on the floor behind the desk with the gun cocked. He ordered John to sit on the chair and when he did so Duffy pushed the barrel of the gun against the seat. John could feel the hard iron under his testicles and knew that if Duffy engaged the trigger that there was no way he could miss. If John jumped up the bullet would catch his anus and if he pushed the chair backwards he was still a sitting target. Now George Goody had given the order to shoot Duffy.

***

When he heard the shot John slumped forward onto the desk aware that he had been hit. He could feel the sting in his testicles as he fell forward. He heard a second shot followed by Goody's cry, 'I'm hit! Jesus Christ, get a doctor, look at me … ' There was silence and then the unmistakable sound of a body hitting the floor.

John could feel the warm blood running down his legs and knew it would not be long before he fell into a coma. He remembered Mrs Knight hanging and prayed that Ballivor would come to save him. He knew he was slowly losing consciousness and was vaguely aware of the sound of Champs' voice pleading for mercy.

John heard another shot and a second body hit the floor. Then he saw a distant light in his mind's eye and he knew he was about to die. His eyes had been closed for a long time and he opened them to take one last look at what he could see of the world. Before him stood the Irish girl with black hair, he had teased earlier at the table. She was beautiful but she had a strange wildness in her eyes as she looked down at the two bodies. 'Get up you piece of shit,' Duffy said, picking John up by the scruff of the neck.

'I can't, I'm not able to stand,' John cried, 'I can feel blood running down my legs.'

'Piss, that's all that's running out of you mate,' Duffy said looking down at John's wet trousers. 'Get a hold of yourself …your coming with us.'

'Let me shoot him now,' Amanda said aiming her gun at John. 'He's been playing the big one all night. Taking the piss out of my accent and bragging about how many Irish he has locked up.'

'No, we need him,' Peter said. 'Lets get moving before the troops come.'

'I'm not leaving until I've been paid for my services,' Amanda said calmly. She went to Champ's body and removed a set of keys from his pocket. She walked over and opened the safe. 'Jesus Mary and Joseph, will you look at all this money?'

'Come on Amanda,' Peter said five minutes later. 'We have enough, we can't carry it all.'

'Here you!' Amanda said to John, 'fill your pockets and then we're off.'

***

Peter led the way out of the bordello, followed by John and Amanda in that order. They followed him across a car park to where Peter had parked his car. As he was about to open the driver's door two shots rang out and Amanda fell to the ground. John ran and hid behind a parked car where he lay on the ground with his hands covering his head. He saw Peter run back, pick up Amanda and carry her to his car. He lay her across the back seat, turned round and fired a shot as he jumped into the driver's seat. Within seconds he was speeding out of the car park pursued by two cars.

XXV

Plan B

HARRY THE CHAT WAS putting the final touches to his plan when his secretary announced that Detective Superintendent Malcolm Smith had arrived for his appointment. Smith was Harry's ace in the hole in the event of things going wrong on the Coventry job. Things had gone wrong and instead of the dummy bomb being planted on Friday night the IRA had outsmarted Bill Guest and set off a real bomb in Coventry the night before.

Harry was trying to piece together the sequence of events that led to the slip-up. Bill Guest was not entirely to blame for the way things had turned out but he was displaying a lack of insight into the workings of the minds of Irish terrorists. He had underestimated them and that was enough reason to distance him from the hierarchy. Malcolm Smith was more resourceful and had warned against placing too much reliance on Tom McDermott. 'Come in Malcolm,' Harry said, 'tell me the latest.'

Malcolm had made notes in preparation for this important interview. He knew that there was no room for mistakes and that Harry was going to put plan 'B' into effect. The plan was originally Malcolm's idea but Harry adopted it as his before Malcolm could finish explaining it. 'Can you see where we're going with this?' Harry interrupted. 'It's based on the premise that apart from Big Tom McDermott and Kevin Kelly all the other members of the Birmingham cell are IRA terrorists.'

'I see,' Malcolm said as though Harry had introduced the topic. 'Go on sir.'

'That's the key superintendent.' The formal address was not lost on Malcolm, he knew it was Harry's way of reminding him who was in charge.

'Are you thinking what I'm thinking sir?'

'Try me?' Harry said.

'In view of what you've just told me sir, I'm beginning to see a way out of our dilemma.'

'And what way is that?' Harry said.

'That apart from McDermott and Kelly, the rest of the Birmingham cell are in effect Irish terrorists and can be arrested and charged.'

'You're not far out Malcolm,' Harry said with a superior grin. 'But Mr McDermott and Mr Kelly may have to stand as well.'

'Really sir?' Malcolm said, 'is there not a risk that they

would use the fact that they were working for us as a defence?'

'That's what I like about you Malcolm,' Harry said warmly. 'You can see the flaw. The only difference between you and me is that I can see a way round it.'

***

Malcolm had to hand it to Harry, he had thought of everything. The basic premise of Malcolm's original idea was still intact but that was all. Harry had honed and modified its application in such a way that Malcolm would have found it difficult to lay claim to being its author. Plan B now involved arresting all known members of the Birmingham cell including Tom and Kevin. They would be given the opportunity to "turn Queen's evidence" and once they did so they would qualify for protection under the witness protection scheme.

Harry had gone further to protect his interests and those of the Serious Crime Squad. He was aware that there was a danger that some of his officers could be accused of acting as agent provocateur. In particular Bill Guest had to be protected. If all things were equal the job of carrying out surveillance and gathering evidence would be given to the Birmingham Bomb Squad. It was a recent innovation introduced to allay public fears arising from the IRA threat. But in reality, like the Special Branch, it was the Serious Crime Squad under a different name. It was too close to home and what was needed here was something much further away.

Harry hit upon the idea of enlisting the services of his

rivals, the Regional Crime Squad. The RCS was a national entity, which had been superimposed on local police forces by the Home Office. Its members were not under the span of control of individual chief constables. Harry perceived the Birmingham Branch as a threat and encouraged his officers not to co-operate with RCS detectives. That was against the spirit under which the Home Office believed that local police and the RCS would interact. To Harry they were outsiders operating on his patch and over whom he had little influence.

Detective Chief Superintendent Blundell, head of Birmingham RCS, was surprised at Harry's request. 'Of course, we'll do it Harry,' Blundell said. 'I agree it's time we shared intelligence on this one.'

Harry had explained that he needed the "expertise of your detectives" in mounting surveillance on a number of suspects whom he believed were involved in bombings in the Midlands. Harry did not mention that he already had taken steps to bring members of the Birmingham cell together on a common purpose. The common purpose was the funeral of the terrorist who had blown himself to pieces whilst planting the Coventry bomb.

***

The IRA had played into Harry's hands by announcing that their dead Volunteer would receive a hero's send-off to Ulster. They announced that when the Coventry coroner released his body, they would wrap a republican flag around the coffin and provide a guard of honour. 'They'll all be there,' Harry announced. 'We'll get photographs of them all.'

Harry was going to use the occasion to identify Birmingham IRA cell members to the RCS. In fact he had done better and got Bill Guest to persuade McDermott to take his best men to the funeral of the dead terrorist in Ulster. He had laid it out on a platter for the RCS. All they had to do was follow the men to the funeral and take photographs. When they returned the RCS would be handed sufficient evidence to convict the members of the Birmingham cell.

'It's foolproof sir,' Malcolm said, 'all we have to do is to make sure that they go to the funeral.'

XXVI

The Empty Safe

SIR EDWARD HAD GONE back to the night he was informed that things had gone wrong in the bordello sting in Ulster. The official reports did not reflect the true extent of MI5's involvement in the operation. The fact that British intelligence had sanctioned the operation could not be allowed to see the light of day. The record would show that information emanating from the sting had been obtained from persons not connected with MI5.

That was the official line but there was a danger that evidence would emerge to prove otherwise. It was always a risk, when one was dealing with self-styled amateurs, that something had been overlooked. Dead bodies, an opened safe and IRA involvement added up to trouble. There was little doubt that the IRA would either want favours or milk the situation for its publicity value.

Nobody in the department knew what had been removed from the bordello safe. That meant that the official policy would be to assume that something incriminating was taken and was now in the hands of the IRA.

After Sir Edward received the call he contacted his counterpart in MI6. The scenario had been envisaged earlier and the call set into motion a cover up operation. A mop up team was immediately sent to Belfast to carry out a damage limitation exercise.

The IRA had shot three agents and there were at least seven civilian casualties. No one knew what had gone wrong. Sir Edward had his suspicions but suspicions were not enough to convince the Orange Order. The IRA was to blame for all Ulster's problems and why should this be any different?

The verbal debrief was more alarming, 'Of course if there was any official documentation, it could be embarrassing sir.'

'Yes, I agree,' Sir Edward said. 'This man Champs did he have anything that could connect him to the department?'

'He had a secret telephone number that enabled him to contact his handler. There is also talk of a diary he kept and that has not been found.'

'In the safe, I suppose?'

'Yes sir.'

'Let me know immediately someone calls the secret number.'

'Yes sir.'

Sir Edward did not like dealing with members of proscribed organisations or their political wings. They lacked any notion of the rules of cricket and were unpredictable. But on this occasion things might be different, the Australians had introduced an element of panache and it may be possible to avoid dragging the service through another scandal.

XXVII

The Duke of Lancaster

TOM MCDERMOTT WAS VERGING on the brink of a nervous breakdown when Bill Guest met him. Tom was sure that the IRA in Dublin was on to him and that his family was in danger. 'Calm down Tom,' Bill said. 'We have come up with something that will put you in the clear.'

'Thank you Mr Guest, I'm in an awful state.'

Bill had listened to how Tom was forced by the IRA to send two of his men to Coventry. They gave him no opportunity to make a telephone call and did not release him until news of the Coventry blast broke. They heard the newsflash on the radio of the car they were driving to Holyhead. 'It went off early,' Doran had remarked when the programme was interrupted. 'What did he say… "A bomb has gone off in Coventry, we'll give you more news as it comes in…" Is that what he said?'

Later they dropped McDermott near Bangor and presumably made their way to Dun Laoghaire via Holyhead. Tom did not get home until Friday afternoon and when he arrived Bill was waiting for him. Tom was one of the few in the country who did not know that the bomber had died at the scene. 'I killed him, he would be alive now if it weren't for me,' Tom said almost in tears. 'I knew something awful was going to happen.'

Bill feigned sympathy and suggested that Tom and his team should go to funeral of their comrade in Belfast, 'We think it'll look better for you in Dublin, Tom.'

McDermott agreed. He was now more fearful for the safety of his family than he was for his own life. The IRA had demonstrated that they could call at his home whenever it took their fancy. And he knew he was being followed. He saw the car at the bottom of his street and another parked nearer his home. The people inside were watching and they followed him wherever he went. 'You must tell the lads to go to the funeral, convince them that it's the right thing to do Tom,' Bill said, pressing his point. 'Have you heard anything from Dublin?'

'No, Bill and to tell you the truth I don't want to hear anything.'

'Now Tom, you went into this with your eyes open, the last thing you want to do is go soft on us,' Bill said. 'If you don't do what I say, I'm afraid we will have to disown you. Do you know what that means?'

'Bill I'll do it, I told you I would there's no need to threaten me.'

'Tom I'm not threatening you, I'm just pointing out the facts of life. We have a dead terrorist, and we're lucky it wasn't worse. If innocent people had been killed in Coventry we might not have been able to keep the lid on things.'

'I suppose you mean that I would have to carry the can?'

'Tom, up to now all the bombs that have gone off in our patch were placed by your cell. Evidence is evidence if you follow me?'

'Yes, Bill I follow you.'

'Well then just do this last thing and we'll get you out of here. All you have to do is go to the funeral with your men.'

'Jesus Bill this is some crock of shit. These people wouldn't be terrorists if I hadn't talked them into it. Are you going to arrest them?'

'Did I say that Tom?' Bill asked. 'No I never said any such thing. But the point is that they volunteered to work for the IRA not the police. They don't know that you work for us do they?'

'Jesus Christ of course not!'

'There you are Tom. They joined the IRA and must be prepared to accept the consequences.'

'Yes if you put it that way I suppose you're right.'

'Of course I'm right …we're always right.'

'Yes even when you're wrong Bill, I know the score.'

'Now Tom, lets get down to brass tacks. Do you need money for fares or anything?'

'No, I'll get the plane tickets to Belfast. It's the least I can do I suppose.'

'Plane tickets, did you say plane tickets?'

'Yes, we'll fly to Belfast.'

'No, don't do that Tom. The Regional Crime Squad are watching the Airports. Go on the ferry from Heysham. Go on the Duke of Lancaster.'

***

It was 2 o'clock and the half-moon had moved westwards across the Irish skyline. Patrick saw Peter's car headlights as they came along the road and swerved erratically into the dirt track that led to the cottage. There were two cars in close pursuit … something was wrong. Patrick peered out of his foxhole and trained the sites of his AK47 on the driver's door of the second car as it drew to a halt behind Duffy.

The third car stopped and three men got out; Peter assumed they were crawling up to the second car but its headlights were on full beam and it was impossible to see. He saw the flashes and heard the shots as Peter's car was sprayed with bullets. Patrick pressed a button on the small box beside him in the foxhole and watched as the explosion illuminated the sky. He could see arms and legs flying in the air along with metal from the second car. Now there were no headlights and no sign of movement.

Patrick pressed the button again and watched as the third car exploded and metal went flying into the air. He crawled out of his foxhole, along the ground to ascertain if there was danger. He opened the driver's door of Peter's car. He was slumped across the steering wheel with blood running from gunshot wounds in his head and body.

Patrick looked at the body of Amanda in the back seat. Her arm was stretched out as though she was trying to give something to Peter. Then Patrick saw the handbag on the passenger's seat and realised that she must have been trying to give it to Peter when she died.

Patrick placed his hand into Peter's pocket and removed his passport. He looked at the handbag and picked it up. It won't be long before the troops arrive, he thought, making his way back to the cottage. He collected his belongings, walked over to the foxhole and pressed the button again. The car in which his friends were dead blew into smithereens, 'May the souls of the faithfully departed rest in peace,' he said with sadness.

***

Michael Lynch looked at the telephone number he found in the open safe in the bordello. Earlier he had watched as Amanda went into the office with Goody and Champs. He knew Duffy had not fallen for the "let's get pissed trick" and that it was just a matter of time. He was a good soldier but the time had come to say good bye. Lynch also felt a tinge of regret about having to part with Amanda. She had found happiness with Duffy but they knew too much.

After he heard the shots in the car park he heard the cars speed away. It was what he knew would happen. Duffy was to be spared so that he would lead the snipers to Patrick

O'Connell. After they left, Lynch entered Champs' office and found the open bordello safe. He looked at Champs' diary and knew he had what he wanted, 'Dolores my love, here's your ticket to freedom,' he said as he put the diary in his pocket.

***

Patrick knew that his best bet was to get onto a main road as quickly as possible. Army helicopters were in the air and he knew that they had thermal equipment capable of detecting the heat of his body in the cold night air. As he crossed hedge after hedge he knew that he was a sitting duck out in the open.

He found a cowshed and hid amongst the occupants for a few hours. Dawn was breaking and rolls of thick fog could be seen across the hills of Antrim. The helicopters had returned to their pads and it was safe to push ahead. He looked in his emergency bag and found what he wanted. He changed into civilian clothes and in less than fifteen minutes he was walking along the road to Belfast.

Several cars passed him having ignored his thumb. Then one stopped about a hundred yards ahead and the driver got out and looked at him,' Don't come any closer mate,' the English accent announced. 'I want to make sure you're what you seem.'

Five minutes later Patrick was chatting to a member of the British army on his way to Belfast. 'It's not the safest place in the world to be hitch-hiking so early in the morning,' the soldier said. 'And as you saw back there it's not the safest place to pick up hitch-hikers either.'

'It looks peaceful enough to me,' Patrick said. 'Of course I'm just an Aussie visitor and a very grateful one at that.'

'There was a lot of commotion back there last night,' the soldier said. 'The IRA had some sort of feud amongst themselves.'

'Really, are you allowed to say what happened?'

'Well, I suppose there's no harm in saying that they blew themselves to pieces. It was a funny thing though, normally they sort out their differences with a gun not explosives.'

***

The sailing from Belfast to Heysham was uneventful. Patrick slept most of the way and was still tired when he booked into the small hotel. Amanda's handbag was full of money. He did not count it but estimated that there was over £5'000 stuffed into the bag. Is that what she was trying to give Peter, he thought, rummaging through the handbag?

'Wait there,' James said when Patrick finally managed to make contact. 'I'm coming up to get you.'

Three hours later they were sipping tea in the lounge of the small hotel.

'I'm going to telephone from here James,' Patrick said. 'I can't wait any longer.'

'It looks good mate, but shouldn't we wait?'

'You tell me?' Patrick said.

'I'm just wondering what might happen if George Goody answers the telephone.'

'It's a good point mate. Let's head for Sutton Coldfield.'

The journey down the M6 was taking forever. There was traffic congestion from Manchester to Stoke-on-Trent and now as they crawled towards Spaghetti Junction in Birmingham James announced that it would take at least an hour to get to Sutton Coldfield.

They updated each other and Patrick mentioned John Bayliss.

'Did you say DI John Bayliss?' James interrupted.

'Yes he's mentioned in Amanda's diary. In fact it's the last entry. Have you heard of him?'

'If he's who I think he is I'm his driver,' James said.'

XXVIII

※

Mrs Goody

WHEN JANE HOGAN KNOCKED on the door she did not know what to expect. Ballivor had taken charge of the operation and refused to permit Patrick or James to get involved. Now the woman peering through the partly open door seemed nervous. She had jet-black hair and did not immediately strike Jane as the blonde she was hoping would answer the door.

'Is Mr Goody in?' Jane asked, with a friendly smile.

'No, I'm sorry. I don't know when he'll be back.' The woman said with a hint of an Australian accent.

'Are you Mrs Goody?' Jane asked.

'Yes, is there something wrong?'

'May I come in, Mrs Goody?'

'Who are you?'

'I'm a friend Mrs Goody from Mr Bayliss' office.'

'Oh you're a solicitor, come in please.'

***

'Are you sure they're married?' Patrick demanded. 'What have they done to her?'

'The answer to the first question is yes and the answer to the second is I don't know,' Ballivor said.

'Can I speak to her?' James asked.

'We haven't told her you're here yet. She's traumatised and Jane thinks she'll have a complete nervous breakdown if we tell her what's happened.'

'I'll kill whoever's done this to her,' Patrick said with uncharacteristic vehement.

'We've managed to persuade the family next door to Denise to take a holiday in France for a week. And they've agreed to allow us to use their apartment,' Ballivor said. 'If you give me your word that you'll do exactly as I say I'll agree to let you watch over her until we know what we're dealing with.'

'Agreed,' James said. 'We both agree.'

***

John Bayliss was in a quandary when he was found walking in circles in the car park where he had seen Amanda shot. He had his hands high in the air and was babbling something incomprehensible when the Military Police patrol spotted him. 'Get down! Get down!' the corporal shouted.

John could hear shots and voices coming from every direction, but the vision in his head was that of George Goody and Robert Champs lying dead.

The next day he was taken to the airport where he was placed on a flight to Birmingham. He went home and slept the sleep of the discontented. Twenty-four hours later he had managed to pull himself together sufficiently to report for duty. Priest listened with open mouth as John recounted some of what had happened.

They all wanted to know about it. Harry, Malcolm and Bill looked at each other in amazement as John related how Goody and Champs met their end. Even his driver Cliff was sympathetic. It was him that reminded John about Mrs Goody. 'Was Goody married?' He asked in that easy way he had of bringing up strange subjects. 'Where did he live?'

'I don't know,' John lied.

It reminded John that he was being headhunted by the anti-terrorist squad. He would have to clear the decks before he joined. He was safe: they were all dead except for Denise Ward-Riley who was pretending to be Mrs Goody. She knew too much and would have to go. He would have done the job a week ago if the Coventry bomber had not caused so much trouble. It was too risky but tomorrow morning before going to London he would see to it.

***

He got out of bed early on the Friday morning and drove along the M6 to Sutton Coldfield. He went to Goody's apartment and expected Denise to answer the door. After he shot her he would catch the train at Rugby, it was a perfect alibi. Just another unsolved murder, a statistic to remind the public that they needed the police.

Detective Chief Inspector John Bayliss, New Scotland Yard Anti-terrorist Department at your service ma'am, John said to himself as he pressed Denise's doorbell. Jane it's you!' John exclaimed, 'What are you doing here?'

As he fumbled in his pocket for his gun he saw the flash behind Jane and felt a burning sting in his chest. It's only piss he thought when he felt the blood running down his chest. I must catch the train from Rugby.

Jane was saying something, 'Come on sir you'll make it. Come on sir you'll make it. Come on sir you'll make it…'

***

The ambulance taking John to hospital rushed through the early traffic. Its sirens echoed and its blue lights flashed as the paramedic watched John go deep into a coma. It took over half an hour to reach Solihull hospital. The driver jumped out of the ambulance and ran to the back door. When he opened it his colleague said calmly. 'No need to rush Fred, he's DOA.'

'I thought we'd lose him,' the driver said. 'Did he say anything?'

'He was mumbling something until the end, but I couldn't make out what.'

***

'You were lucky darling', James said to Jane. 'If you hadn't acted on the spur of the moment he would have killed you.'

'Are you sure? I never saw a gun.'

'A Browning semi-automatic pistol was found on the ground beside his body.'

'Who found it?'

'Mr Ballivor.'

'That was very fortunate,' Jane said raising an eyebrow. 'Otherwise it would have been difficult to explain why he shot him.'

'I know what you're thinking darling, but they found Bayliss' fingerprints on the magazine.' James said. 'Can you explain that?'

'Well, it proves that John touched the magazine. And once you've done that who cares about dates and times.'

'Are you always going to be this cynical?'

'I'm not cynical darling. Just logical.'

'Will you miss all the excitement of deep undercover work?' James asked. 'You and that Seamus Ballivor just loved it. Where did he get that name from?'

'Who? I've never heard of a Seamus Ballivor or Chris the Hat, or Mr Knight with his mannequins for that matter.'

'Knight, that's the fellow with the dolls. They look so life-like I thought they were really his wife and children.'

'Your not the first to be fooled and I don't suppose you'll be the last. I think it's the old shoes she wears.'

***

Patrick and Denise were amused listening to the banter between James and Jane. They were in the queue to book their flights to Australia. 'Well Mrs Goody, how does it feel to be a merry widow?' Patrick asked.

'It has its advantages, young man,' Denise said squeezing his hand. 'I think the solicitor said three million pounds after death duty. My late husband was very well off, you know.'

'Do you think you'll ever marry again?'

'Is that a proposal of marriage kind sir?'

XXIX

✹

Mr Heart

SIR EDWARD HAD RETURNED the files on Operation Nettle Grabbers after ensuring that they were in order. A month had passed since the Birmingham Bombings and reports from the West Midlands Police indicated that they had the perpetrators in custody. It was not the role of MI5 to second-guess the police. Inspector Bayliss had been buried with full police ceremony.

Sir Edward felt he had underestimated the Detective Chief Superintendent. Harry the Chat was a crafty policeman. The meeting with the Chief Constable of West Midlands had not turned out as expected. The Chief explained that Harry wanted to charge Ballivor with being a member of the IRA and conspiracy.

The problem was that there was enough evidence to justify a prima faci case. It would have been highly embarrassing to have a member of MI5 charged with such a thing, not to mention appearing in court. The Chief Constable was a little too easy on Harry, in Sir Edwards' opinion. But there was a sort of perverse logic in his reasoning.

It would undermine the case against the Birmingham bombers if the Detective Chief Superintendent did not get his way. The Chief was kind enough not to mention the harm it would do to MI5. On that premise it was agreed that Harry would be promoted to Assistant Chief Constable and his replacement would be an officer not connected with the Serious Crime Squad.

It was a good solution made more palatable by the fact that Harry would take early retirement once the dust settled.

***

Now Sir Edward had to decide whether the person offering to exchange "certain diaries in Mr Champs' handwriting" for the release of one Dolores Flynn could be trusted. Michael Lynch could be arrested, but one would not have thought that by looking at his posture as he sat relaxed in the big leather armchair. 'Have we a deal?' He asked after explaining what he wanted in exchange for the diary.

'It's not that easy Mr Lynch,' Sir Edward said frostily. 'The person you want released has been convicted in a court of law and is serving a long prison sentence.'

'Please spare me the Sermon on the Mount,' Lynch interrupted. 'If we go back to who did what to whom we're not going to get very far, are we?'

'Yes, I take your point,' Sir Edward said. 'The short answer to your question is, maybe.'

'You have a week to decide and it might help you make the right decision after you read this sample of my merchandise,' Lynch said passing Sir Edward a photostat of a diary entry. 'I'm sure defence counsel for the men awaiting trial for the Birmingham Bombings would be as excited to receive a copy of this as would the News of the World.'

'And what guarantee have I that you won't send a copy, if we agree to your terms?'

'That's a fair question and I've thought about it,' Lynch said mulling it around in his head. 'We both know that it is not healthy to double-cross British Intelligence, so if you know where we are would that help?'

'Please continue, Mr Lynch.'

'Dolores and I are prepared to place ourselves under your protection, you know leave Ireland and live abroad?'

'Are you saying you want us to give you protection?'

'You can put it that way if it suits you. In fact I suppose I am because I know that you won't agree to my returning to my former occupation.'

'And who is going to take over from you, Mr Lynch?'

'Have we a deal?'

***

On 1st May 1975 Michael Lynch and Dolores Flynn landed in the Cayman Islands. The warm spring sun greeted them as they were escorted to a waiting car. After their luggage was placed in the car the MI5 agent who had accompanied them looked at Lynch. 'That's it then, it's goodbye Mr Lynch and hello Mr Hart.'

'It's a name I've always liked,' Lynch said, looking at his new passport. 'Mr and Mrs Jack Hart, it suits us.'

'MI6 will look out for you from here on Mr and Mrs Hart.'

'Thanks for everything, Mr Ballivor, I don't expect we'll meet again.'

I wouldn't bet on that, Ballivor said to himself as he walked away.

XXX

※

Post Trial Party

ON THE NIGHT OF 16th August 1975 a celebration was taking place in the inner sanctum of Lloyd House, the headquarters of West Midlands Police. It was to celebrate the conviction of nine men at Lancaster Crown Court the previous day. Six of the nine had been sentenced to life imprisonment for the murders arising out of the Birmingham Bombings and the other three received smaller sentences for lesser crimes.

Harry the Chat was the new Assistant Chief Constable (Crime) for the West Midlands Police and the toast of the party. William Guest called for order,' Ladies and Gentlemen,' he began. 'Your attention please.'

The assembly came to order as Bill took on the stance of a town crier reading a proclamation: 'Yesterday, his Lordship, Mr Justice Bridge, put into words what many of us have known for a long time. The judge singled out our Assistant Chief Constable, Mr Harry Robinson, for the highest commendation. It was for all the work that has been done to secure the convictions we are now celebrating. I quote the judge's exact words.

"I have no doubt in justice being done in one of the gravest criminal trials in this country in this century. I am entirely satisfied, and the jury by their verdict have shown, that these investigations both at Morecambe and Birmingham were carried out with scrupulous proprietary by all your officers."

Now my friends and colleagues, raise your glasses to our beloved leader'. Harry bowed in modest acknowledgement. It was not seemly for an assistant chief constable to wallow in his own glory.

Later he took Bill aside, 'Now William I don't want anything coming back to haunt us on this,' he said seriously. 'Big Tom McDermott is the one I'm worried about.'

'He decided his own fate sir,' Bill said reassuringly. 'He wanted to play the role of the IRA commander. We offered him the same deal as Kevin Kelly, but he was afraid that Dublin would kill his family.'

'He'll keep his mouth shut then?'

'He never spoke during the trial and the judge commented on it. I think Tom felt good when the judge said he was impressed with the way he conducted himself.'

'Kelly, is he happy with the way things went?'

'Yes sir, Kevin got a slap on the wrist from the judge and we are arranging to give him a new identity.'

'Whose looking after him?'

'MI5 have asked for the job. Something about sending him to the Cayman Islands.'

'A strange choice of location. Do we know who the agent is that's dealing with him?'

'No sir, but his voice did sound familiar.'

'That leaves the six,' Harry said. 'Has George Reid made sure that everything's in order? You remember I asked you to make sure that he got everything right.'

'George is sound sir, you heard what the judge said.'

'Yes, I think we can safely say that there won't be any flack from the Birmingham Six.

ISBN 1412089654